MARY HIGGINS CLARK

Two Little Girls in Blue

DOUBLEDAY LARGE PRINT HOME LIBRARY EDITION

SIMON & SCHUSTER

New York   London   Toronto   Sydney

This Large Print Edition, prepared especially for
Doubleday Large Print Home Library, contains
the complete, unabridged text of the original
Publisher's Edition.

SIMON & SCHUSTER
Rockefeller Center
1230 Avenue of the Americas
New York, NY 10020

SIMON & SCHUSTER and colophon are registered trademarks of
Simon & Schuster, Inc.

Manufactured in the United States of America

ISBN-13: 978-0-7394-6674-2
ISBN-10: 0-7394-6674-7

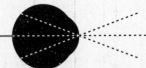

This Large Print Book carries the
Seal of Approval of N.A.V.H.

Acknowledgments

The telepathy that exists between some people has always fascinated me. From early childhood I can remember my mother, a worried frown on her face, saying, "I have a feeling about . . ." And as sure as day follows night, that person was experiencing or about to experience a problem.

I have used telepathy to a degree in some of my books, but the bond that exists between twins, particularly identical twins, is nothing short of fascinating. That subject has been growing in my mind as the plot of a novel for a long time.

My gratitude to the authors of books on this subject, particularly Guy Lyon Playfair for his *Twin Telepathy: the Psychic Connection;* Nancy L. Segal, Ph.D., for *Entwined Lives;* Donna M. Jackson for *Twin Tales: The*

Magic and Mystery of Multiple Births; Shannon Baker for her article, "On Being a Twin"; and to Jill Neimark for her cover story "Nature's Clones" in *Psychology Today.* The examples they offer of the psychic connection between twins were most helpful to me in the telling of this tale.

Others, as always, made the journey with me. My continuing gratitude to my forever editor, Michael V. Korda, and senior editor Chuck Adams for their gifted guidance.

Lisl Cade, my dear friend and publicist, is always in my corner. My circle of readers-in-progress remains constant. My thanks to them and to our children and granchildren, who cheer me along the way and keep my life lively and fun.

I wanted this book to be a tribute to the dedicated commitment of the Federal Bureau of Investigation following a kidnapping. I especially want to honor the memory of the late Leo McGillicuddy, a legend among his fellow agents.

Retired Agent Joseph Conley has been of tremendous help in the step-by-step unfolding of the behind-the-scenes activity of the Bureau. I have telescoped some of the procedures for the sake of the storytelling, but I hope I retain the sense of fierce commitment and compassion that is typical of the agents.

And now as another story begins to take root in my mind, it is time to let go of this one, sit by the fire with Himself, the ever-perfect John Conheeney, and wish all of you who begin these pages an enjoyable reading experience. Cheers!

For Michael V. Korda

Editor and Friend

With Love

1

"Hold on a minute, Rob, I think one of the twins is crying. Let me call you back."

Nineteen-year-old Trish Logan put down her cell phone, got up from the couch, and hurried across the living room. It was her first time babysitting for the Frawleys, the nice people who had moved into town a few months earlier. Trish had liked them immediately. Mrs. Frawley had told her that when she was a little girl, her family often visited friends who lived in Connecticut, and she liked it so much she always wanted to live there, too. "Last year when we started looking for a house and happened to drive through Ridgefield, I knew it was where I wanted to be," she told Trish.

The Frawleys had bought the old Cunningham farmhouse, a "fixer-upper" that

Trish's father thought should have been a "burner-upper." Today, Thursday, March 24th, was the third birthday of the Frawleys' identical twin girls, and Trish had been hired for the day to help with the party, then to stay for the evening while the parents attended a black-tie dinner in New York.

After the excitement of the party, I'd have sworn the kids were dead to the world, Trish thought as she started up the stairs, headed to the twins' room. The Frawleys had ripped out the worn carpet that had been in the house, and the nineteenth-century steps creaked under her feet.

Near the top step, she paused. The light she had left on in the hall was off. Probably another fuse had blown. The wiring in the old house was a mess. That had happened in the kitchen this afternoon.

The twins' bedroom was at the end of the hall. There was no sound coming from it now. Probably one of the twins had cried out in her sleep, Trish thought as she began to inch her way through the darkness. Suddenly she stopped. It's not just the hall light. I left the door to their room open so I could hear them if they woke up. The night-light in the room should be showing. The door's closed. But I couldn't have heard one of them crying if it was closed a minute ago.

Suddenly frightened, she listened intently. What was that sound? In an instant of sickening awareness, she identified it: soft footsteps. A hint of equally soft breathing. The acrid smell of perspiration. *Someone was behind her.*

Trish tried to scream, but only a moan escaped her lips. She tried to run, but her legs would not move. She felt a hand grab her hair and yank her head back. The last thing she remembered was a feeling of pressure on her neck.

The intruder released his grip on Trish and let her sink to the floor. Congratulating himself on how effectively and painlessly he had rendered her unconscious, he turned on his flashlight, tied her up, blindfolded and gagged her. Then directing the beam onto the floor, he stepped around her, swiftly covered the length of the hall, and opened the door to the twins' bedroom.

Three-year-olds Kathy and Kelly were lying in the double bed they shared, their eyes both sleepy and terrified. Kathy's right hand and Kelly's left hand were entwined. With their other hands they were trying to pull off cloths that covered their mouths.

The man who had planned the details of the kidnapping was standing beside the bed. "You're sure she didn't see you, *Harry?*" he snapped.

"I'm sure. I mean, I'm sure, *Bert,*" the other responded. They each carefully used the names they had assumed for this job: "Bert" and "Harry," after the cartoon characters in a sixties beer commercial.

Bert picked up Kathy and snapped. "Get the other one. Wrap a blanket around her. It's cold out."

Their footsteps nervously rapid, the two men raced down the back stairs, rushed through the kitchen and out to the driveway, not bothering to close the door behind them. Once in the van, Harry sat on the floor of the backseat, the twins wrapped in his beefy arms. Bert drove the van as it moved forward from the shadows of the porch.

Twenty minutes later they arrived at the cottage where Angie Ames was waiting. "They're adorable," she cooed as the men carried the children in and laid them in the hospital-style crib that had been prepared for them. With a quick, deft movement of her hands she untied the gags that had kept the little girls silent.

The children grabbed for each other and began to wail. "Mommy . . . Mommy," they screamed in unison.

"Sshhhh, sshhhh, don't be scared," Angie said soothingly as she pulled up the side of the crib. It was too high for her to reach over it, so she slipped her arms through the rails and began to pat their dark blond ringlets. "It's all right," she singsonged, "go to sleep. Kathy, Kelly, go back to sleep. Mona will take care of you. Mona loves you."

"Mona" was the name she had been ordered to use around the twins. "I don't like that name," she'd complained when she first heard it. "Why does it have to be Mona?"

"Because it sounds close to 'Momma.' Because when we get the money and they pick up the kids, we don't want them to say, 'A lady named Angie took care of us,' and one more good reason for that name is because you're always moaning," the man called Bert had snapped.

"Quiet them down," he ordered now. "They're making too much noise."

"Relax, Bert. No one can hear them," Harry reassured him.

He's right, thought Lucas Wohl, the real name of the one called "Bert." One of the reasons, after careful deliberation, that he had invited Clint Downes—"Harry's" actual name—to join him on the job was because nine months of the year Clint lived as caretaker in the cottage on the grounds of the Danbury Country Club. From Labor Day to May 31st the club was closed and the gates locked. The cottage was not even visible from the service road by which Clint entered and exited the grounds, and he had to use a code to open the service gate.

It was an ideal spot to hide the twins, and the fact that Clint's girlfriend, Angie, often worked as a babysitter completed the picture.

"They'll stop crying," Angie said. "I know babies. They'll go back to sleep." She began to rub their backs and sing off-key, "Two little girls in blue, lad, two little girls in blue . . ."

Lucas cursed under his breath, made his way through the narrow space between the crib and the double bed, and walked out of the bedroom, through the sitting room, and into the kitchen of the cottage. Only then did he and Clint pull off their hooded jackets and gloves. The full bottle of scotch and the two empty glasses they had left out as a reward for success in their mission were in front of them.

The men sat at opposite ends of the table, silently eyeing each other. Staring with disdain at his fellow kidnapper, Lucas was reminded once more that they could not have been more different in both appearance and temperament. Unsentimental about his appearance, he sometimes played eyewitness and described himself to himself: about fifty years old, scrawny build, average height, receding hairline, narrow face, close-set eyes. A self-employed limousine driver, he knew he had perfected the outward appearance of a servile and anxious-to-please employee, a persona he inhabited whenever he dressed in his black chauffeur's uniform.

He had met Clint when they were in prison together and over the years had worked with him on a series of burglaries. They had never been caught because Lucas was careful. They had never committed a crime in Connecticut because Lucas did not believe in soiling his own nest. This job, though terribly risky, had been too big to pass up, and he had broken that rule.

Now he watched as Clint opened the scotch and filled their glasses to the brim. "To next week on a boat in St. Kitts with our pockets bulging," he said, his eyes searching Lucas's face with a hopeful smile.

Lucas stared back, once again assessing his partner in crime. In his early forties, Clint was desperately out of shape. Fifty extra pounds on his already short frame made him perspire easily, even on a March night like this, that had suddenly turned cold. His barrel chest and thick arms looked incongruous with his cherubic face and long ponytail, which he had grown because Angie, his longtime girlfriend, had one.

Angie. Skinny as a twig on a dead branch, Lucas thought contemptuously. Terrible complexion. Like Clint, she always looked slovenly, dressed in a tired T-shirt and ragged jeans. Her only virtue in Lucas's eyes was that she was an experienced babysitter. Nothing must happen to either one of those kids before the ransom was paid and they could be dropped off. Now Lucas reminded himself that Angie had something else going for her. She's greedy.

She wants the money. She wants to live on a boat in the Caribbean.

Lucas lifted the glass to his lips. The Chivas Regal felt smooth on his tongue, and its warmth was soothing as it slid down his throat. "So far, so good," he said flatly. "I'm going home. You got the cell phone I gave you handy?"

"Yeah."

"If you hear from the boss, tell him I have a five A.M. pickup. I'm turning off my cell phone. I need some sleep."

"When do I get to meet him, Lucas?"

"You don't." Lucas downed the rest of the scotch in his glass and pushed back his chair. From the bedroom they could hear Angie continue to sing.

"They were sisters, we were brothers, and learned to love the two . . ."

2

The screeching of brakes on the road in front of the house told Ridgefield Police Captain Robert "Marty" Martinson that the parents of the missing twins had arrived home.

They had phoned the police station only minutes after the 911 call came in. "I'm Margaret Frawley," the woman had said, her voice shaking with fear. "We live at 10 Old Woods Road. We can't reach our babysitter. She doesn't answer the house phone or her cell phone. She's minding our three-year-old twins. Something may be wrong. We're on our way home from the city."

"We'll get right over there and check," Marty had promised. Because the parents were on the highway and no doubt already upset, he'd seen little use in telling them that he already knew something was terribly wrong. The babysitter's father had just phoned from 10 Old Woods Road: "My daughter is tied up and gagged. The twins she was minding are gone. There's a ransom note in their bedroom."

Now, an hour later, the property around the house and the driveway had already been taped off, awaiting the arrival of the forensic team. Marty would have liked to keep the media from getting wind of the kidnapping, but he knew that was hopeless. He had already learned that the babysitter's parents had told everyone in the hospital emergency room where Trish Logan was being treated that the twins were missing. Reporters would be showing up anytime. The FBI had been notified, and agents were on the way.

Marty braced himself as the kitchen door opened and the parents rushed in. Beginning with his first day as a twenty-one-year-old rookie cop, he had trained himself to retain his first impression of people connected with a crime, whether they were victims, perpetrators, or witnesses. Later he would jot those impressions down. In police circles he was known as "The Observer."

In their early thirties, he thought as Margaret and Steve Frawley moved hurriedly toward him. A handsome couple, both in evening clothes. The mother's brown hair hung loose around her shoulders. She was slender, but her clenched hands looked strong. Her fingernails were short, the polish colorless. Probably a good athlete, Marty thought. Her intense eyes were a shade of dark blue that seemed almost black as they stared at him.

Steve Frawley, the father, was tall, about six foot three, with dark blond hair and light blue eyes. His broad shoulders and powerful arms caused his too-small tuxedo jacket to strain at the seams. He could use a new one, Marty thought.

"Has anything happened to our daughters?" Frawley demanded.

Marty watched as Frawley put his hands on his wife's arms as though to brace her against possibly devastating news.

There was no gentle way to tell parents that their children had been kidnapped and a ransom note demanding eight million dollars left on their bed. The absolute incredulity on the faces of the young couple looked to be genuine, Marty thought, a reaction he would note in his case book, but appended with a question mark.

"Eight *million* dollars! *Eight million dollars!* Why not *eighty* million?" Steve Frawley demanded, his face ashen. "We brought every dime we had to the closing on this house. We've got about fifteen hundred dollars in the checking account right now, and that's it."

"Are there any wealthy relatives in either of your families?" Marty asked.

The Frawleys began to laugh, the high-pitched laugh of hys-teria. Then as Marty watched, Steve spun his wife around. They hugged each other as the laughter broke and the harsh sound of his dry sobs mingled with her wail. "I want my babies. I want my babies."

3

At eleven o'clock the special cell phone rang. Clint picked it up. "Hello, sir," he said.

"The Pied Piper here."

This guy, whoever he is, is trying to disguise his voice, Clint thought as he moved across the small living room to get as far away as possible from the sound of Angie crooning songs to the twins. For God's sake, the kids are asleep, he thought irritably. Shut up.

"What's the noise in the background?" the Pied Piper asked sharply.

"My girlfriend's singing to the kids she's babysitting." Clint knew he was furnishing the information the Pied Piper wanted. He and Lucas had been successful.

"I can't reach Bert."

"He told me to tell you he has a five A.M.

pickup to go to Kennedy Airport. He went home to sleep, so he turned off his phone. I hope that . . ."

"Harry, turn on the television," the Pied Piper interrupted. "There's a breaking story about a kidnapping. I'll get back to you in the morning."

Clint grabbed the remote button and snapped on the TV, then watched as the house on Old Woods Road came into view. Even though the night was overcast, the porch light revealed the house's peeling paint and sagging shutters. The yellow crime-scene tape used to keep the press and onlookers back extended to the road.

"The new owners, Stephen and Margaret Frawley, moved to this address only a few months ago," the reporter was saying. "Neighbors say they expected the house to be torn down but instead learned that the Frawleys intend to gradually renovate the existing structure. This afternoon some of the neighbors' children attended a third-birthday party for the missing twins. We have a picture that was taken at the party only hours ago."

The television screen was suddenly filled with the faces of the identical twins, their eyes wide in excitement as they looked at their birthday cake. Three candles were on each side of the festive confection. In the center was one larger candle. "The neighbor tells us that the center candle is the one to grow on. The twins are so identical in every way that their mother joked it would be a waste to put a second candle to grow on there."

Clint switched channels. A different picture of the twins in their blue velvet party dresses was being shown. They were holding hands.

"Clint, look how sweet they are. They're just beautiful," Angie said, startling him. "Even asleep they're still holding hands. Isn't that precious?"

He had not heard her come up behind him. Now she put her arms around his neck. "I always wanted to have a baby, but I was told I couldn't," she said, as she nuzzled his cheek.

"I know, Angie, honey," he said patiently. This was a story he had heard before.

"Then for a long time I wasn't with you."

"You had to be in that special hospital, honey. You hurt someone real bad."

"But now we're going to have a lot of

money and we'll live on a boat in the Caribbean."

"We've always talked about that. Very soon we'll be able to do it."

"I've got a good idea. Let's bring the little girls with us."

Clint snapped off the television and jumped up. He turned and grabbed her wrists. "Angie, why do we have those children?"

She looked at him and swallowed nervously. "We kidnapped them."

"Why?"

"So we'd have lots of money and could live on a boat."

"Instead of living like damn gypsies, and getting kicked out of this place every summer while the golf pro lives here. What happens to us if the police catch us?"

"We go to prison for a long, long time."

"What did you promise to do?"

"Take care of the kids, play with them, feed them, dress them."

"And isn't that what you're going to do?"

"Yes. Yes. I'm sorry, Clint. I love you. You can call me Mona. I don't like that name, but it's all right if you want me to use it."

"We must never use our real names in

front of the twins. In a couple of days we'll give them back and get our money."

"Clint, maybe we could . . ." Angie stopped. She knew he would be angry if she suggested they keep one of the twins. But we *will,* she promised herself slyly. I know how to make it happen. Lucas thinks he's so smart. But he's not as smart as I am.

4

Margaret Frawley folded her hands around the steaming cup of tea. She was so cold. Steve had pulled an afghan from the couch in the living room and wrapped it around her, but it did nothing to stop the trembling that shook her entire body.

The twins were missing. Kathy and Kelly were missing. Someone had taken them and left a ransom note. It didn't make sense. Like a litany, the words beat a cadence in her head: *The twins are missing. Kathy and Kelly are missing.*

The police had not allowed them to go into the girls' bedroom. "Our job is to get them back," Captain Martinson told them. "We can't risk losing any fingerprints or DNA samples by contaminating the area."

The restricted area also included the hall upstairs where someone had attacked the babysitter. Trish was going to be all right. She was in the hospital and had told the police everything she remembered. She said she'd been on her cell phone talking to her boyfriend when she thought she heard one of the twins crying. She'd gone up the stairs and knew instantly something was wrong because she couldn't see the light in the twins' room, and that was when she realized someone was behind her. She remembered nothing after that.

Had there been someone else, Margaret wondered, someone in the room with the girls? Kelly's the lighter sleeper, but Kathy might have been restless. She may be getting a cold.

If one of the girls started to cry, did someone make her stop?

Margaret dropped the cup she was holding and winced as hot tea splattered over the blouse and skirt she had bought at a discount house for tonight's black-tie company dinner at the Waldorf.

Even though the price was one-third of what it would have been on Fifth Avenue, it had been too pricey for their budget.

Steve urged me to buy it, she thought dully. It was an important company dinner. Anyhow, I wanted to get dressed up tonight. We haven't gone to a black-tie affair in at least a year.

Steve was trying to dry her clothes with a towel. "Marg, are you okay? Did the tea burn you?"

I have to go upstairs, Margaret thought. Maybe the twins are hiding in the closet. I remember they did that once. I pretended to keep looking for them. I could hear them giggling when I called their names.

"Kathy . . . Kelly . . . Kathy . . . Kelly . . . where are you? . . ."

Steve came home just then. I called down to him. "Steve . . . Steve . . . our twins are missing."

More giggles from the closet.

Steve could tell I was joking. He came up to their room. I pointed to the closet. He walked over to it and yelled, "Maybe Kathy and Kelly ran away. Maybe they don't like us any more. Well, there's no use looking for them. Let's turn out the lights and go out for dinner."

An instant later the closet door flew open.

"We like you, we like you," they'd wailed in unison.

Margaret remembered how scared they'd looked. They must have been terrified when somebody grabbed them, she thought. Somebody is hiding them now.

This isn't happening. It's a nightmare and I'm going to wake up. *I want my babies.* Why does my arm hurt? Why is Steve putting something cold on it?

Margaret closed her eyes. She was vaguely aware that Captain Martinson was talking to someone.

"Mrs. Frawley."

She looked up. Another man had come into the room.

"Mrs. Frawley, I'm FBI Agent Walter Carlson. I have three kids of my own and I know how you must be feeling. I'm here to help you get your children back, but we need your help. Can you answer some questions?"

Walter Carlson's eyes were kind. He didn't look to be more than his mid-forties, so his children were probably not much older than teenagers. "Why would someone take my babies?" Margaret asked him.

"That's what we're going to find out, Mrs. Frawley."

Carlson moved swiftly to catch Margaret as she began to slide from the chair.

5

Franklin Bailey, the chief financial officer of a family-owned grocery chain, was Lucas's five A.M. pickup. A frequent overnight traveler up and down the East Coast, he was a regular customer. Some days, like today, Lucas would drive him into Manhattan for a meeting, and then wait for him and drive him home.

It never even occurred to Lucas to say he wasn't available this morning. He knew that one of the first things the cops would check out would be any workmen who had been anywhere around the Frawleys' house. Chances were he'd made their list because Bailey lived on High Ridge, which was only two blocks from Old Woods.

Of course the cops have no reason to give me a second look, he assured himself.

I've been picking up people in and around this town for twenty years, and I've always kept below the radar screen. He knew that his neighbors in nearby Danbury, where he lived, looked at him as a quiet, solitary guy whose hobby was to fly a small plane out of Danbury Airport. It also amused him to tell people how much he liked to hike, an explanation he used to cover the occasional times when he'd have a backup driver cover a job for him. The place where he was hiking, of course, was usually a house he had chosen to burglarize.

On the way to pick up Bailey this morning, he resisted the temptation to drive past the Frawley home. That would have been crazy. He could picture the activity inside now. He wondered if the FBI was in on it yet. What were they figuring out? he asked himself with some amusement. That the backdoor lock could be slipped with a credit card? That, hidden by the overgrown foundation shrubs, it would have been easy to see the babysitter sprawled on the couch yakking on her phone? That it was obvious from looking in the kitchen window that the back stairs would get an intruder to the second floor without the babysitter having a

clue? That there had to be at least two people in on the job, one to get rid of the
babysitter, one to keep the kids quiet?

He pulled into Franklin Bailey's driveway
at five minutes of five, kept the car idling to
be sure it stayed nice and warm for the big-
shot accountant, and contented himself
with envisioning the money he would get as
his share of the ransom payment.

The front door of the handsome Tudor-
style home opened. Lucas sprang out of the
car and opened the rear door for his client.
It was one of his little courtesies that the
front passenger seat was always pulled up
as far as possible to allow maximum leg
room in the back.

Bailey, a silver-haired man in his late sixties, murmured a greeting, his tone dis-
tracted. But when the car began to move,
he said, "Lucas, turn onto Old Woods Road.
I want to see if the cops are still there."

Lucas felt his throat tighten. What would
make Bailey decide to go by there? he wondered. He wasn't a gawker. He had to have
a reason. Of course, Bailey was a big shot
in town, Lucas reminded himself. He'd been
mayor at one time. The fact that he showed
up there wouldn't draw attention to the limo

he was in. On the other hand, Lucas always trusted the cold prickly feeling he experienced when he felt himself nearing the law-enforcement radar range, and he was feeling it now.

"Anything you say, Mr. Bailey. But why would there be cops on Old Woods Road?"

"Obviously you haven't been watching the news, Lucas. The three-year-old twins of the couple who recently moved into the old Cunningham house were kidnapped last night."

"Kidnapped! You've got to be kidding, sir."

"I wish I were," Franklin Bailey said grimly. "Nothing like this has ever happened in Ridgefield. I've met the Frawleys a number of times and am very fond of them."

Lucas drove two blocks, then turned the car onto Old Woods Road. Police barricades were in front of the house where eight hours ago he had broken in and grabbed the kids. In spite of his unease and his sense that it would be a lot safer not to be there now, he couldn't help thinking smugly, If you dopes only knew.

There were media trucks parked across the street from the Frawley home. Two po-

licemen were standing in front of the barricades to prevent anyone from turning into
the driveway. Lucas could see that they
were carrying notebooks.

Franklin Bailey opened the back window
and was recognized immediately by the sergeant in charge, who began to apologize
that he could not allow him to park.

Bailey cut him short. "Ned, I don't intend
to park. But maybe I can be of service. I've
got a seven o'clock breakfast meeting in
New York and will be back by eleven
o'clock. Who's inside, Marty Martinson?"

"Yes, sir. And the FBI."

"I know how these things work. Give
Marty my card. I've been listening to the reports half the night. The Frawleys are new in
town and don't seem to have close relatives
to rely on. Tell Marty that if I can be any help
as contact person for the kidnappers, I'm
available. Tell him I remember that during
the Lindbergh kidnapping, a professor who
offered to be a contact person was the one
who heard from the kidnappers."

"I'll tell him, sir." Sergeant Ned Barker
took the card and made a note in his book.
Then with a somewhat apologetic tone, he

said, "I have to identify anyone who drives past, sir. I'm sure you understand."

"Of course."

Barker looked at Lucas. "May I see your license, sir?"

Lucas smiled, his eager, anxious-to-please smile. "Of course, officer, of course."

"I can vouch for Lucas," Franklin Bailey said. "He's been my driver for years."

"Strictly following orders, Mr. Bailey. I'm sure you understand."

The sergeant examined the driver's license. His eyes flickered over Lucas. Without comment he returned it and wrote something in his notebook.

Franklin Bailey closed the window and leaned back. "All right, Lucas. Let's step on it. That was probably a wasted gesture, but somehow I felt I had to do it."

"I think it was a wonderful gesture, sir. I never had kids, but it doesn't take a lot of imagination to figure out what those poor parents are feeling now." I just hope they're feeling bad enough to come up with eight million dollars, he thought with an inner smile.

6

Clint was pulled from a heavy Chivas Regal–assisted sleep by the persistent voices of two children calling "Mommy." When there was no response, they had begun to try to climb over the high sides of the crib in which they had been sleeping.

Angie lay next to him, snoring, oblivious to the children's voices or the sound of the crib rattling. He wondered how much she had had to drink after he went to bed. Angie loved to sit up half the night and watch old movies, a bottle of wine by her side. Charlie Chaplin, Greer Garson, Marilyn Monroe, Clark Gable—she loved them all. "They were *actors*," she would tell him, her voice slurred. "Today they all look alike. Blond. Gorgeous. Botox. Face-lifts. Liposuction. But can they act? No."

It was only lately, after all these years of being around her that Clint had realized Angie was jealous. She wanted to be beautiful. He'd used it as another way to get her to agree to mind the kids. "We'll have so much money that if you want to go to a spa or change the color of your hair or have some great plastic surgeon make you more gorgeous, you can do it. All you have to do is take good care of them, maybe for a few days or a week."

Now he dug an elbow into her side. "Get up."

She burrowed deeper into the pillow.

He shook her shoulder. "I said, get up," he snarled.

Reluctantly she lifted her head and looked over at the crib.

"Lie down! Get back to sleep, you two!" she snapped.

Kathy and Kelly saw the anger on her face and began to cry. "Mommy . . . Daddy."

"Shut up, I said! Shut up!"

Whimpering, the twins lay down again, clinging to each other. The soft sound of their muted sobs escaped from the crib.

"I said shut up!"

The sobs became hiccups.

Angie poked Clint. "At nine o'clock, Mona will start to love them. Not one minute sooner."

7

Margaret and Steve sat up all night with Marty Martinson and Agent Carlson. After her fainting spell, Margaret had adamantly refused to go to the hospital. "You said yourself that you need my help," she insisted.

Together she and Steve answered Carlson's questions. Once again they emphatically denied they had any access to any meaningful sum of money, let alone millions of dollars.

"My father died when I was fifteen," Margaret told Carlson. "My mother lives in Florida with her sister. She's a secretary in a doctor's office. I have college and law school loans I'll be paying off for another ten years."

"My father is a retired New York City fire

captain," Steve said. "He and my mother live in a condo in North Carolina. They bought it before prices went crazy."

When they were questioned about other relatives, Steve admitted that he was on bad terms with his half-brother, Richie. "He's thirty-six, five years older than I am. My mother was a young widow when she met my father. Richie always had a kind of wild streak in him. We were never close. Then, to cap it off, he met Margaret before I did."

"We didn't date," Margaret said quickly. "We happened to be at the same wedding and danced a few times. He did leave a message for me, but I didn't return the call. It was a coincidence that I met Steve in law school about a month later."

"Where is Richie now?" Carlson asked Steve.

"He's a baggage handler at Newark Airport. He's been divorced twice. He dropped out of school, and resents me for finishing college and getting a law degree." He hesitated. "I might as well tell you. He had a juvenile record and spent five years in prison for his part in a money-laundering scam. But he'd never do anything like this."

"Maybe not, but we'll check him out," Carlson said. "Now let's go over anyone else who might have a grudge against you or who might have come in contact with the twins and decided to kidnap them. Have you had any workmen in the house since you moved in?"

"No. My dad could fix anything and he was a good teacher," Steve explained, his tone hollow with fatigue. "I've been spending nights and weekends doing basic repairs. I'm probably Home Depot's best customer."

"What about the moving company you used?" Carlson asked next.

"They're off-duty cops," Steve answered, and for an instant almost smiled. "They've all got kids. They even showed me their pictures. A couple of them are about the age of our twins."

"What about the people you work with?"

"I've been with my company only three months. C.F.G.&Y. is an investment firm specializing in pension funds."

Carlson seized on the fact that until the twins were born, Margaret had worked as a public defender in Manhattan. "Mrs. Frawley, is it possible that one of the people you defended might hold a grudge against you?"

"I don't think so." Then she hesitated. "There was one guy who ended up with a life sentence. I begged him to accept a plea bargain but he refused, and when he was found guilty, the judge threw the book at him. His family was screaming obscenities at me when they took him away."

It's odd, she thought as she watched Carlson write down the name of the convicted defendant. Right now, I just feel numb. Nothing else, just numb.

At seven o'clock, as light began to show through the drawn shades, Carlson stood up. "I urge you two to get some sleep. The clearer your heads are, the more helpful you'll be to us. I'll be right here. I promise we'll let you know the minute the kidnappers make contact with us, and we may be wanting you to make a statement to the media later in the day. You can go up to your own room, but do *not* go near the girls' bedroom. The forensic team is still going over it."

Steve and Margaret nodded mutely. Their bodies sagged with fatigue as they got up and walked through the living room headed to the staircase.

"They're on the level," Carlson said flatly to Martinson. "I'd stake my life on it. They don't have any money. Which makes me wonder if this ransom demand isn't a hoax. Somebody who just wanted the kids may be trying to throw us off."

"I've been thinking that," Martinson agreed. "Isn't it a fact that most ransom notes would warn the parents not to call the police?"

"Exactly. I only pray to God that those kids aren't on a plane to South America right now."

8

On Friday morning, the kidnapping of the Frawley twins was headline news all along the East Coast and by early afternoon had become a national media event. The birthday picture of the beautiful three-year-olds, with their angelic faces and long blond hair and dressed in their blue velvet birthday party dresses, was shown on television news channels and printed in newspapers all over the country.

A command center was set up in the dining room of 10 Old Woods Road. At five o'clock in the afternoon Steve and Margaret appeared on television in front of their home, begging the captors to take good care of the girls and return them unharmed. "We don't have money," Margaret said imploringly. "But our friends have been calling all day. They're taking up a collection. It's up to nearly two hundred thousand dollars. Please, you must have mistaken us for people who could raise eight million dollars. We can't. But please don't hurt our girls. Give them back. I can promise you we will have two hundred thousand dollars in cash."

Steve, his arm around Margaret, said, "Please get in touch with us. We need to know that our girls are alive."

Captain Martinson followed them in the interview. "We are posting the phone and fax number of Franklin Bailey, who at one time was mayor of this town. If you are afraid to contact the Frawleys directly, please contact him."

But Friday evening, Saturday, and then Sunday all passed without word from the kidnappers.

On Monday morning, Katie Couric was interrupted on the *Today* show as she was interviewing a retired FBI agent about the kidnapping. She suddenly paused in the middle of asking a question, pressed her hand against her earphone, listened intently, then said, "This may be a hoax, but it also may be terribly important. Someone claiming to be the kidnapper of the Frawley twins is on the phone. At his request our engineers are putting the call on the air now."

A husky, obviously disguised voice, its tone angry, said, "Tell the Frawleys time is running out. We said eight million and we mean eight million. Listen to the kids."

Young voices said in unison, "Mommy, I love you. Daddy, I love you." Then one of the girls cried, "We want to go home."

The segment was replayed five minutes later with Steve and Margaret listening. Martinson and Carlson did not need to ask the Frawleys if the call was legitimate. The look on their faces was enough to convince them that at last contact had been made with the kidnappers.

9

An increasingly nervous Lucas had stopped in at the caretaker cottage on both Saturday and Sunday evenings. The last thing he wanted was to spend any time around the twins, so he timed his arrival for nine o'clock, when he thought they would be asleep.

On Saturday evening he tried to feel reassured by Clint's boast that Angie was great with the kids. "They ate real good. She played games with them. She put them down for naps all afternoon. She really loves them. She always wanted to have kids. But I tell you, it's almost spooky to watch them. It's like they're two parts of the same person."

"Did you get them on tape?" Lucas snapped.

"Oh, sure. We got them both to say, 'Mommy, I love you. Daddy, I love you.' They sound real good. Then one of them started yelling, 'We want to go home,' and Angie got sore at her. She raised her hand like she was going to hit her, and they both started crying. We got all of that on the tape, too."

That's the first smart thing you've done, Lucas thought as he pocketed the tape. By pre-arrangement with the boss, he drove to Clancy's Pub on Route 7, arriving there at ten thirty. As instructed, he left the limo in the crowded parking lot with the door unlocked, and the tape on the seat and then went in for a beer. When he returned to the limo, the tape was gone.

That was Saturday night. On Sunday night it had been clear that Angie's patience was wearing thin. "Damn dryer is broken, and of course we can't call anyone to fix it. You don't think 'Harry' knows how, do you?" As she spat out the words, she was taking two sets of identical long-sleeved T-shirts and overalls from the washing machine and draping them on wire hangers. "You said it would be a couple of days. How long am I supposed to keep this up? It's been three days already."

"The Pied Piper will tell us when and where to drop the kids off," Lucas reminded her, biting back the desire to tell her to go to hell.

"How do we know he won't just get scared and disappear, and leave us stuck with them?"

Lucas had not intended to tell Angie and Clint about the Pied Piper's plan, but he felt it was necessary to appease her. "We know because he's going to make a ransom demand sometime between eight and nine o'clock tomorrow morning on the *Today* show."

That had shut her up. You got to hand it to the boss, Lucas thought the next morning, as he watched the show and witnessed the dramatic response to the Pied Piper's phone call. The whole world will be wanting to send money to get those kids back.

But we're the ones taking all the risk, he thought hours later, after listening to the commentators on every station jabbering about the kidnapping. We grabbed the kids. We're hiding them. We're the ones who will pick up the money when they raise it. I know who the boss is, but there's nothing to tie him to me. If we get caught, he could say I was nuts if I say he's behind it.

Lucas had no jobs scheduled until the next morning, Tuesday, and at two o'clock decided there was no way he could sit in his apartment and stew. The Pied Piper had told him to be sure to watch the CBS evening news, that another contact would be made then.

He decided he had time to go for a plane ride. He drove to Danbury Airport where he was a member of a flying club. There, he rented one of the single-engine prop planes and went for a spin. His favorite trip was to fly up the Connecticut coast to Rhode Island, then go out over the Atlantic for a while. Flying two thousand feet above the earth gave him a sense of complete control, something he badly needed to experience now.

It was a cold day with only a slight breeze and some clouds to the west: fine flying weather. But as he tried to relax in the cockpit and enjoy the freedom of being airborne, Lucas could not shake off the persistent worry that was plaguing him.

He felt certain he had missed something,

but figuring out just what—that was the problem. Grabbing the kids had been easy. The babysitter only remembered that whoever had come up behind her smelled of perspiration.

She got that one right, Lucas thought with a brief grin, as he flew over Newport. Angie should stick Clint's shirts in that washing machine of hers every time he peels one off.

The washing machine.

That was it! Those clothes she was washing. Two sets each of identical shirts and overalls. Where did she get them? The kids had been wearing pajamas when they grabbed them. Had that stupid airhead gone shopping for twin outfits that would fit three-year-olds?

She had. He was sure of it. And soon some clerk out there would start putting two and two together.

Icy with rage, Lucas involuntarily yanked back on the yoke, forcing the nose of the plane to rise nearly perpendicular to the earth below. His anger increased when he realized what he had done, and he quickly tried to level off. His action was too late, however, and the plane entered a stall. His heart beating faster, he pushed the nose down, recovered his air speed, and averted the stall. Next thing, that stupid broad will probably take the kids to McDonald's for a hamburger, he thought frantically.

10

There was no way to put a good face on delivering the latest communication from the kidnapper. On Monday evening, Walter Carlson received a phone call and went into the living room where Margaret and Steve Frawley were sitting side by side on the couch. "Fifteen minutes ago, the kidnapper called the network during the *CBS Evening News*," he said, grimly. "They're replaying that segment now. It has the same tape of the twins' voices they played this morning on Katie Couric, with an addition."

It's like watching people being thrown into a cauldron of boiling oil, he thought, as he saw the agony on their faces at the sound of a childish voice protesting, "We want to go home . . ."

"Kelly," Margaret whispered.

A pause . . .

Then the wailing of the twins began.

Margaret buried her face in her hands. "I cannot . . . cannot . . . cannot . . ."

Then a harsh, obviously disguised voice snarled, "I said *eight million. I want it now. This is your last chance.*"

"Margaret," Walter Carlson interrupted, his tone urgent, "there *is* a bright spot here. The kidnapper is communicating with us. You have proof that the girls are alive. We are going to find them."

"And are you going to come up with an eight-million-dollar ransom?" Steve asked bitterly.

Carlson did not know whether to raise their hopes yet. Agent Dom Picella, heading a team of agents, had spent the day at C.F.G.&Y., the global investment firm at which Steve was a new employee, interviewing Steve's co-workers to learn if any of them knew of someone who resented Steve, or who perhaps had wanted the job Steve had been hired to fill. The firm had recently suffered bad publicity because of insider trading accusations, and Picella had learned that a board of directors meeting had been hastily scheduled with conference call links to directors all over the world. The rumor was that the company might offer to put up the ransom money for the Frawley twins.

"One of the secretaries is a world-class gossip," Picella told Carlson late that afternoon. "She says the firm has egg on its face for some of the fast stuff it pulled. It just paid a whopping five-hundred-million-dollar fine imposed by the Securities and Exchange Commission and has gotten tons of bad press. Her guess is that paying the eight-million ransom gives C.F.G.&Y. better publicity than if they hired a slew of PR agencies to whitewash their image. The board meeting is scheduled for eight o'clock tonight."

Carlson studied the Frawleys, who, in the three days since the twins went missing, seemed to have aged ten years. Both were pale, their eyes heavy with fatigue, their shoulders slumping. He knew that neither one of them had touched a morsel of food all day. He knew from experience that this was a time when relatives usually rallied around, but he'd overheard Margaret begging her mother to stay in Florida. "Mom, you can do me more good by praying round the clock," Margaret had said, her voice breaking during the phone call. "We'll keep you posted, but if you were here crying with me, I don't think I could handle it."

Steve's mother had recently had knee replacements and could neither travel nor be left alone. Friends had flooded the house with calls but had been asked to get off the line quickly in case the kidnapper called the Frawleys directly.

Not at all sure that he was doing the right thing, Walter Carlson hesitated, then spoke. "Margaret, Steve, I don't want to raise your hopes only to have them dashed, but, Steve, the CEO of your company has called an emergency board of directors meeting. From what I understand, there's a chance that they'll vote to pay the ransom."

Don't let it go the other way, he prayed, as he saw hope come alive in their faces. "Now I don't know about you two," he said, "but I'm hungry. Your next door neighbor gave a note to one of the cops. She has dinner cooked for you and will send it over anytime you want."

"We will eat something," Steve said firmly. He looked at Carlson. "I know it sounds crazy. I'm a new employee at

C.F.G.&Y., but in the back of my mind it did occur to me that maybe, just maybe, they'd offer to put up the money. Eight million dollars is peanuts to them."

Oh, my God, Carlson thought. The half-brother may not be the only bad egg in this family. Could Steve Frawley be behind all this?

11

Kathy and Kelly looked up from the couch. They had been watching Barney tapes, but Mona had switched to the television and listened to the news. They were both scared of Mona. A little while ago Harry had started yelling at her after he got a phone call. He was mad at her for buying the clothes for them.

Mona had yelled back, "I suppose they should have been running around in pajamas for three days? Of *course* I bought some clothes, and some toys, and some Barney tapes, and in case you forgot, I bought the crib from a medical supply company. By the way, I also bought cereal and orange juice and fruit. And now shut up and go out and get some hamburgers for all of us. I'm sick of cooking. Got it?"

Then, just when Harry came back with the hamburgers, they heard the man on television say, "We may be receiving a call from the kidnapper of the Frawley twins."

"They're talking about us," Kathy whispered.

They listened, as over the television they could hear Kelly's voice, saying, "We want to go home."

Kathy tried to squeeze back tears. "I *do* want to go home," she said, "I want Mommy. I feel sick."

"I can't understand a word of what the kid is saying," Harry complained.

"Sometimes when they talk to each other, I can't understand it, either," Angie snapped. "They have twin talk. I read about it." She dismissed the subject. "Why didn't the Pied Piper tell them where to leave the money? What's he waiting for? Why did he just say, 'You'll hear from me again'?"

"Bert says it's his way of wearing them down. He's going to make another contact tomorrow."

Clint/Harry was still holding the McDonald's bag. "Let's eat these while they're hot. Come over to the table, kids."

Kelly jumped up from the couch, but

Kathy lay down and curled up into a ball. "I don't want to eat. I feel sick."

Angie hurried over to the couch and felt Kathy's forehead. "This kid is getting a fever." She looked at Clint. "Finish that hamburger fast and go out and get some baby aspirin. That's all we need for one of them to get pneumonia."

She bent over Kathy. "Oh, sweetie, don't cry. Mona will take good care of you. Mona loves you." She looked angrily at the table where Kelly had started to eat the hamburger, then kissed Kathy's cheek. "Mona loves you best, Kathy. You're nicer than your sister. You're Mona's little girl, aren't you?"

12

In the Park Avenue boardroom of C.F.G.&Y., Robinson Alan Geisler, the chairman and chief executive officer, waited impatiently while the out-of-town directors confirmed their presence at the meeting. His job already in jeopardy as a result of the fallout from the fine imposed by the SEC, Geisler knew that the position he was going to take in the agonizing Frawley situation might be a fatal mistake. Twenty years with the company but only eleven months in the top job, he knew he was still considered tainted by his close association with the former CEO.

The question was simple. If C.F.G.&Y. offered to pay the eight-million-dollar ransom, would the result be a superb public relations gesture, or would it be, as he knew some of the directors believed, an invitation for other kidnappers to have a field day?

Gregg Stanford, the chief financial officer, took the latter position. "It's a tragedy, but if we pay to get the Frawley kids back, what do we do when another employee's wife or child is taken? We're a global company, and a dozen of the places where we have offices are already potential hot spots for this kind of thing."

Geisler knew that at least a third of the fifteen directors shared that same viewpoint. On the other hand, he told himself, how would it look for a company that had just paid a five-hundred-million-dollar fine to refuse to pay a fraction of that amount to save the lives of two little girls? It was the question he planned to throw on the table. And if I'm wrong and we pay the money and next week another employee's child is kidnapped, I'll be the one who gets burned at the stake, he thought grimly.

At age fifty-six, Rob Geisler had finally achieved the job he wanted. A small, thin man, he had to overcome the inevitable prejudice the business world held for people of short stature. He had made it to the top because he was acknowledged to be a financial genius and had shown he knew how to consolidate and control power. But on the way up he had made countless enemies, and at least three of them were sitting at the table with him now.

The final off-site director reported in, and all eyes turned to Geisler. "We all know why we're here," he said brusquely, "and I'm very much aware of the feeling some of you hold that we're caving in to kidnappers if we offer to pay the ransom that has been demanded."

"That's *exactly* the way some of us feel, Rob," Gregg Stanford said quietly. "This company has already had enough bad publicity. Cooperating with criminals shouldn't even be a consideration."

Geisler looked disdainfully at his colleague, not bothering to hide his intense dislike for the man. In appearance, Stanford was the television version of a corporate executive. He was forty-six years old, six feet four inches in height, uncommonly handsome with sun-streaked sandy hair, and had perfect teeth that gleamed in his ready smile. Stanford was always impeccably dressed, his manner unfailingly charming even when he was stabbing a friend in the

back. He had married his way into the corporate world—his third and current wife
was an heiress whose family owned 10 percent of the shares of the company.

Geisler knew that Stanford coveted his
job, and that if he prevailed today in his "no
ransom" position, Geisler would be the one
the media would turn on when the company
publicly declined to offer the bribe money.

He nodded to the secretary who was taking minutes of the meeting, and she got up
and turned on the television. "I want all of
you to watch this," Geisler snapped. "Then
put yourself in the position of the Frawleys."

At his order, the media department had
put together a videotape covering the sequence of events of the kidnapping: the exterior of the Frawley house, the desperate
pleas of the parents on television, the call to
Katie Couric, and the later call to CBS. The
tape ended with a small voice saying, "We
want to go home," then the terrified crying
of the twins followed by the ominous demands of the kidnappers.

"Most of you at this table are parents," he
said. "We can at least try to save those children. We may not succeed. We may recover
the money, or we may not. But I don't see

how any one of you could sit here and refuse to vote to pay the ransom."

He watched as heads turned to get Gregg
Stanford's reaction. "You lie down with
dogs, you get up with fleas. I say we should
never cooperate with criminals," Stanford
said, as he looked down at the conference
table and twirled a pen in his hands.

Norman Bond was the next director to offer an opinion. "I was responsible for hiring
Steve Frawley, and I made a very good
choice. It isn't relevant to this discussion,
but he's going to go places with us. I vote
for offering to put up the ransom money,
and I urge that it be a unanimous vote from
this board. And I'd like to remind Gregg that
years ago J. Paul Getty refused to pay ransom for one of his grand-children, but
changed his mind when his grandson's ear
was sent to him in the mail. These children
are in jeopardy, and the faster we move to
save them, the better the chances that the
kidnappers won't panic and harm them."

This support came from an unexpected
source. Geisler and Bond often went head
to head at board meetings. Bond had hired
Frawley when three others in the company
had been panting for the job. For the right

man, it was a shortcut to upper management. Geisler had cautioned Bond against going outside the company, but Bond had been adamant about wanting Frawley. "He's got an MBA and a law degree," he had said. "He's smart and he's solid."

Geisler had half-expected Bond, in his late forties, divorced with no children, to vote against paying the ransom, thinking that if he hadn't hired Frawley, the company wouldn't be in this position.

"Thank you, Norman," he said. "And for anyone else who still wants to discuss the advisability of this company responding to the desperate need of one of its employees, I suggest we watch the tape one more time and then take a vote."

At eight forty-five the vote was fourteen to one to pay the ransom. Geisler turned to Stanford. "I want a unanimous vote," he said, his tone icy. "Then, as usual, you can feel free to have an anonymous source let the media know that you felt making the payment might jeopardize the children rather than save them. But as long as I sit in this chair and you don't, I want a unanimous vote."

Gregg Stanford's smile was close to a

sneer. He nodded. "The vote will be unanimous," he said. "And tomorrow morning
when you do a photo op for the media in
front of that rundown dump that is the Frawley home, I'm sure whoever on the board is
available will be in the picture with you."

"Including you, of course?" Geisler asked
sarcastically.

"Excluding me," Stanford said, standing.
"I shall save my appearance before the media for another day."

13

Margaret managed to swallow a few bites of the roast chicken dinner that Rena Chapman, her next-door neighbor, had sent over. Then, while Steve waited with FBI Agent Carlson to learn the outcome of the C.F.G.&Y. board meeting, she slipped upstairs to the twins' bedroom.

It was the one room they had fully decorated before they moved in. Steve had painted the walls pale blue and tacked down a final-sale remnant of white carpet over the shabby floorboards. Then they had splurged on an antique white four-poster double bed and a matching dresser.

We knew it was silly to buy two single beds, Margaret thought as she sat on the slipper chair that had been in her own bedroom as a child. They would have ended up in the same bed anyhow, and it was one more way to save money.

The FBI agents had taken the sheets, blanket, quilt, and pillowcases to test for DNA evidence. They had dusted the furniture for fingerprints and taken the clothing the twins had worn after the party to be sniffed by the dogs that for the past three days had been led by Connecticut State Police handlers through the nearby parks. Margaret knew what that kind of search meant: There was always the chance that whoever took the twins had killed them immediately and buried them nearby. But I don't believe that, she told herself. *They are not dead;* I would know it if they were dead.

On Saturday, after the forensic team was finished and she and Steve made their plea to the media, it had been an emotional outlet to come upstairs and clean their room and remake the bed with the other set of Cinderella sheets. They'll be tired and frightened when they come home, Margaret had reasoned. After they come back, I'll lie down with them until they're settled.

She shivered. I can't get warm, she thought, even with a sweater under a running suit, I still can't get warm. This is the way Anne Morrow Lindbergh must have felt when her baby was kidnapped. She wrote about it in a book that I read when I was in high school. It was called *Hour of Gold, Hour of Lead.*

Lead. I am leaden. I want my babies back.

Margaret got up and walked across the room to the window seat. She bent down and picked up first one and then the other of the shabby teddy bears that were the twins' favorite stuffed animals, hugging them fiercely against her.

She looked out the window and was surprised to see that it was beginning to rain. It had been sunny all day—cold, but sunny. Kathy had been starting with a cold. Margaret could feel sobs beginning to choke her throat. She forced them back and tried to remind herself of what FBI Agent Carlson had told her.

There are FBI agents searching for the twins—dozens of them. Others are going through the files at the FBI headquarters at Quantico and investigating anyone who has any kind of record for extortion or child abuse. They are questioning sex offenders who live in this area.

Dear God, not that, she thought with a shudder. Don't let anyone molest them.

Captain Martinson is sending policemen to every house in town to ask if anyone saw anybody who might have seemed suspicious in any way. They've even talked to the Realtor who sold us the house to find out who else may have been looking at it and would be familiar with the layout. Captain Martinson and Agent Carlson both say there will be a break. Somebody must have seen something. They're putting the girls' pictures on flyers and sending them out all over the country. Their pictures are on the Internet. They're on the front page of newspapers.

Holding the teddy bears, Margaret walked over to the closet and opened it. She ran her hand over the velvet dresses the twins had worn on their birthday, then stared at them. The twins had been wearing their pajamas when they were kidnapped. Were they still wearing them?

The bedroom door opened. Margaret turned, looked at Steve's face, and knew from the vast relief she saw in his eyes that his company had volunteered to pay the ransom money. "They're making the announcement immediately," he told her, the words tumbling from his lips. "Then in the morning, the chairman and some of the directors will come here and go on camera with us. We'll ask for instructions on how to deliver the money, and we'll demand proof that the girls are still alive."

He hesitated. "Margaret, the FBI wants both of us to take lie detector tests."

14

At nine fifteen on Monday night, sitting in his apartment over a shabby hardware store near Main Street in Danbury, Lucas was watching television when a news bulletin interrupted the routine programming. C.F.G.&Y. had agreed to pay the ransom for the Frawley twins. An instant later his special cell phone rang. Lucas turned on the recording device he had purchased on his way home from the airport.

"It's beginning to happen," the hoarse voice whispered.

Deep Throat, Lucas thought sarcastically. The police have sophisticated voice-imaging stuff. Just in case anything goes wrong, I do have something that will help to cut a deal with them. I deliver you.

"I was watching for the announcement," he said.

"I called Harry an hour ago," the Pied Piper told him. "I could hear one of the kids crying. Have you checked on them?"

"I saw them last night. I'd say they were okay."

"Mona is taking good care of them? I don't want any slip-ups."

This opening was too much for Lucas to resist. "That dumb broad is taking such good care of them that she's been buying matching outfits for them."

This time the voice was not disguised. "Where?"

"I don't know."

"Does she plan to have them all dressed up when we dump them? Does she plan to have the cops tracing the clothes, and then some clerk saying, 'Sure, I remember the woman who bought matching outfits for three-year-olds'?"

Lucas liked the way the Pied Piper was getting agitated. It took some of the gnawing fear off him. Anything could go wrong. He knew that. He needed to share that worry. "I told Harry not to let her out of the house again," he said.

"In forty-eight hours this will be over, and we'll be home free," the Pied Piper said. "Tomorrow I make contact and give instructions about the money. Wednesday you pick up the cash. Wednesday night I tell you where to leave the kids. Make sure they're wearing exactly what they were wearing when you grabbed them."

The connection ended.

Lucas pushed the stop button on the recording device. Seven million for you; half a million each for me and Clint, he thought. I don't think so, Mr. Pied Piper.

15

The time for Robinson Geisler to stand with Margaret and Steve Frawley and address the media was set for ten A.M. on Tuesday morning. None of the other directors elected to be present at the event. As one of them told Geisler, "I voted to pay the ransom, but I've got three young kids myself. I don't want to give anyone any ideas about kidnapping them."

Unable to sleep most of the night, at six A.M. Margaret got up. She showered for long minutes, raising her face under the streaming water, feeling it hot against her skin, willing it to dispel the icy chill of her body. Then, wrapped in Steve's heavy robe, she got back into bed. Steve was up and headed out for a run, slipping through backyards to avoid the media. Suddenly exhausted from the sleepless night, Margaret felt her eyes begin to close.

It was nine o'clock when Steve awakened her and set a tray with coffee and toast and juice on the night table. "Mr. Geisler just got here," he said. "You'd better start getting dressed, honey. I'm so glad you got some sleep. When it's time to go outside, I'll come up and get you."

Margaret forced herself to drink the orange juice and nibble at the toast. Then, sipping the coffee, she got out of bed and began to dress. But as she was pulling on black jeans, she stopped. A week ago this evening I went shopping for birthday dresses for the twins at the outlet mall on Route 7, she thought. While I was there I dashed into the sports store and picked up a new running suit, a red one, because the twins loved my old red sweats. Maybe whoever has them is letting them watch television. Maybe in less than half an hour they'll be seeing us.

"I like red because it's a happy color," Kelly had told her, her tone solemn.

I'll wear red for them today, Margaret decided, as she yanked the new jacket and pants from the hanger. She dressed quickly as her mind began to focus on what Steve had told her. After the broadcast, they were going to take the lie detector tests. How could they even imagine that Steve and I had anything to do with this? she wondered.

After she tied her sneakers, she made the bed, then sat on the edge of it, her hands folded, her head bent. *Dear God, let them come home safely. Please. Please.*

She did not realize Steve was in the room until he asked, "Are you ready, sweetheart?" He came over to her, took her face in his hands, and kissed her. Then he let his fingers run over her shoulders, entwining them in her hair.

Margaret knew that he had been on the verge of collapse before they learned that the ransom would be paid. She had thought he was asleep during the night, but at some point he had said quietly, "Marg, the only reason the FBI wants us to take a lie detector test is because of that brother of mine. I know what the agents are thinking. Richie leaving Friday to drive to North Carolina to see Mom looks to them as though he was creating an alibi for himself. He hasn't visited her in a year. Then the minute I told

Carlson I had been wondering if the company would volunteer the ransom, I realized I became a suspect. But that's Carlson's job. I *want* him to be suspicious of everyone."

It's Carlson's job to find my children, Margaret thought, as she and Steve walked down the stairs. In the foyer she approached Robinson Geisler. "I am so grateful to you and your company," she said. Steve opened the door and took her hand as cameras began to flash. Joined by Geisler, they walked to the table and chairs that had been set up for the interview. She was glad to see that Franklin Bailey, who had offered to be the intermediary, was also present. She had met him for the first time in the post office when she was buying stamps. Kelly had darted out the door, and he had grabbed her at the curb before she could run into the busy street.

The overnight rain had stopped. The late March morning hinted of spring. Margaret looked blankly at the gathered media, at the police officers holding back the onlookers, at the row of media trucks parked along the road. She had heard that people who are dying sometimes have a sense of hovering above the scene, of being observers rather than participants of the event that was centered around them. She listened to Robinson Geisler offer to pay the ransom, and to Steve's insistence that they must have proof the girls were still alive, and to Franklin Bailey as he offered his services as contact person and slowly gave his phone number.

"Mrs. Frawley, now that you know the kidnapper's demands are being met, what is your greatest fear?" someone asked.

A stupid question, Margaret thought before answering. "Of course my greatest fear is that somehow something will go wrong between the payment of the ransom and the return of our children. The longer the delay, the greater the chance something might happen. I believe Kathy was beginning to get a cold. She goes into bronchitis easily. We almost lost her when she was an infant." She stared into the camera. "Please, I beg of you, if she is sick, get her to a doctor, or at least get some medicine for her. The girls were just wearing pajamas when you took them."

Her voice trailed off. I didn't know I was going to say that, she thought. Why did I say that? There had been a reason for everything, but she couldn't remember it. It was something about the pajamas.

Mr. Geisler and Steve and Franklin Bailey were answering questions. So many questions. Suppose the girls were watching them. I must talk to them, Margaret thought. Interrupting a reporter, she said abruptly, "I love you, Kelly. I love you, Kathy. Very soon, I promise, we'll find a way to bring you home."

As the cameras focused on her, Margaret became silent, forcing back the words that had almost escaped her: *There's a connection I've got to make! There's something I've got to remember!*

16

At five o'clock that afternoon, Franklin Bailey's neighbor, retired Judge Benedict Sylvan, pounded on his door. When Bailey yanked it open, a breathless Sylvan blurted out, "Franklin, I just received a phone call. I think it's from the kidnapper. He's going to call you back at my house in exactly three minutes. He said he has instructions for you."

"He has to know my phone is monitored," Bailey said. "That's why he's calling you."

The two men rushed across the wide lawns that separated their houses. They had barely reached the open door of the judge's home when the phone in his study rang. The judge raced ahead to grab it. Gasping for breath, he managed to say,

"Franklin Bailey is with me," and handed the phone to Bailey.

The caller identified himself as "The Pied Piper." His instructions were brief and explicit: by ten A.M. tomorrow morning, C.F.G.&Y. was to be prepared to wire seven million dollars to an overseas account. The remaining million dollars in ransom was to be ready for delivery. It must be in used fifty- and twenty-dollar bills, and their serial numbers must be nonsequential. "When the wire transfer goes through, further instructions will be issued for delivery of the cash."

Bailey had been scribbling on a pad on the judge's desk. "We must have proof that the girls are alive," he said, his voice tense and unsteady.

"Hang up now. In one minute you will hear the voices of the Two Little Girls in Blue."

Franklin Bailey and Judge Sylvan stared at each other as Bailey returned the phone to the cradle. Moments later it rang. When he picked it up, Bailey heard a child's voice saying, "Hello, Mr. Bailey. We saw you on television this morning with Mommy and Daddy."

A second voice whispered, "Hello, Mr. . . ."
But her words were interrupted as she began
to cough, a deep racking cough that echoed
in Bailey's head as the line went dead.

17

As the Pied Piper was giving instructions to Franklin Bailey, Angie was pushing a cart through the aisles of the CVS drugstore, shopping for anything she thought might keep Kathy from getting any sicker. She'd already tossed baby aspirin, nose drops, rubbing alcohol, and a vaporizer into the cart.

Grandma used to put Vick's in the vaporizer when I was a kid, she thought. I wonder if you're still supposed to do that. Maybe I'd better ask Julio. He's a good pharmacist. When Clint sprained his shoulder, whatever he gave me for him did the trick.

She knew that Lucas would have a fit if he thought she was buying any baby products. But what does he want me to do, let the kid die, she asked herself.

She and Clint had watched the interview on TV this morning when the guy who was head of Steve Frawley's company promised to pay the ransom money. They had kept the kids in the bedroom while the program was on because they didn't want them getting all upset by seeing their mother and father on television.

That turned out to be a mistake, because after the program, the Pied Piper had phoned and insisted they get a recording of the kids talking to that Bailey guy as though they'd seen the program. But when they tried to get the kids to talk into the cell phone, Kelly, the bratty one, put up a squawk.

"We didn't see him and we didn't see Mommy and Daddy on TV and we want to go home," she'd insisted. Then Kathy started coughing every time she tried to say, "Hello, Mr. Bailey."

We finally got Kelly to say what the Pied Piper wanted by promising to take her home, Angie thought. When Clint played it back for him, the Pied Piper said it was okay that Kathy only said a few words. He liked that deep cough of hers. He recorded it on his own phone.

She pushed the cart into the pharmacy section, then felt her mouth go dry. A life-sized picture of the twins was displayed next to the counter. In bold letters, the headline read, MISSING. REWARD FOR ANY IN-FORMATION AS TO THEIR WHEREABOUTS.

There was no one waiting, and Julio beckoned to her. "Hi, Angie," he said, then pointed to the picture. "Pretty awful, that kidnapping. You have to wonder who could do anything like that."

"Yeah, it's awful," Angie agreed.

"Makes me glad that Connecticut still has the death penalty on the books. If anything happens to those kids, I'll volunteer to per-sonally prepare the lethal injection for the rats who took them." He shook his head. "Guess we can only pray they'll get home safe. Angie, what can I do for you?"

Aware of the nervous perspiration gather-ing on her forehead, Angie made a show of fishing through her pocketbook, then shrugged her shoulders. "Can't do much. I guess I forgot my prescription." Even to her ears, the explanation sounded lame.

"I can call your doctor."

"Oh thanks, but he's in New York. I know he won't be there now. I'll come back later."

She thought back to the time she'd gotten the liniment for Clint's shoulder. She had talked with Julio for a couple of minutes and had happened to mention that she lived with Clint in the caretaker cottage of the country club. That had been at least six months ago, yet Julio had remembered her name the minute he saw her. Would he remember where she lived as well? Sure he would!

Julio was a tall Latin type, about her age. He wore glasses with really sexy frames that enhanced his eyes. She watched as his gaze flickered over the contents of her cart.

It was all out there for him to see. Baby aspirin. Children's nose drops. Rubbing alcohol. The vaporizer.

Will he get to wondering why I was buying stuff for a sick kid? Angie wondered as she struggled to push back the frightening possibility. She didn't want to think about it. She was there on a mission. I'll buy a jar of Vick's and stick some of it in the vaporizer, she decided. It worked good enough when I was a kid.

She hurried back to aisle 3, grabbed the jar of Vick's, and rushed to the checkout. One register was closed, the other one already had six people on line. Three of them were taken care of fairly quickly, but then the clerk called out, "I'm off duty. It will be just a minute."

Stupid dope, Angie thought, as the new clerk proceeded to take forever to set up at the register.

Hurry up, Angie thought, giving the shopping cart an impatient push.

The guy in front of her, a heavyset man with a loaded cart, turned around. His look of annoyance changed to a broad grin. "Hi, Angie, what are you trying to do, cut my feet off?"

"Hi, Gus," Angie said, attempting a smile. Gus Svenson was a pesky guy they sometimes ran into when she and Clint ate at the Danbury Pub, the kind of jerk who was always trying to start a conversation with other people at the bar. A plumber with his own business, he often did work at the golf club during the season. So the fact that she and Clint lived in the caretaker cottage when the club was closed made Gus act as if they had something big in common. Blood brothers because they both did the grub work for people with money, she thought with contempt.

"How's my boy Clint?" Gus asked.

Gus was born with a loudspeaker on his vocal cords, Angie thought, as people turned to look at them.

"Never better, Gus. Hey, I think the dynamo behind the counter is about ready for you."

"Sure, sure." Gus unloaded his purchases on the counter and turned back to peer in Angie's basket. "Baby aspirin. Baby nose drops. Hey, you two got news for me?"

Angie's worry about the pharmacist now deepened into outright fear. Lucas was right, she thought. I shouldn't be shopping for anything for the kids, or at least I shouldn't be shopping where they know me. "Don't be silly, Gus," she snapped. "I'm babysitting for a friend, and the kid's getting a cold."

"That will be $122.18," the clerk told Gus.

He opened his wallet and pulled out his credit card. "Cheap at half the price." He turned back to Angie. "Listen, if you're stuck babysitting, maybe my old friend Clint would like to meet me for a few beers. I'll pick him up. That way you don't have to worry if he ties one on. You know me. I know when to quit gulping the suds. I'll give him a call."

Before she could respond, he had scrawled his signature on the credit slip, grabbed his purchases, and was on his way to the exit. Angie slammed the contents of her cart on the counter. The bill came to forty-three dollars. She knew she didn't have more than twenty-five dollars in her pocketbook, which meant she had to use her credit card. She hadn't thought about that when she took the vaporizer off the shelf.

Lucas had given them cash to buy the crib. "That way there won't be a paper trail," he'd said. But there would be a paper trail. She'd had to use the card to pay for the outfits she bought the twins at the children's outlet store, and she had to use it now.

It'll be over soon, she promised herself as she headed for the exit. A guard was standing by the door. She abandoned the cart and picked up the packages. Now all I need is for the alarm to go off, she thought as she passed the guard. That happens when the dopey clerks don't scan the stuff.

Two days at the most and we'll have the money and be out of here, she reminded herself as she crossed the parking lot and got into Clint's twelve-year-old Chevy van. A Mercedes-Benz parked next to her was just pulling out. Her headlights caught the model of the car, an SL500.

Probably cost way over a hundred thou, Angie thought. Maybe we should buy one. In two days we'll have five times that much money, and all of it in cash.

On the short ride home, she reviewed the timetable. According to Lucas, tomorrow the Pied Piper would get the wire transfer. Tomorrow evening they'd get the million dollars cash. When they were sure it was all there, early Thursday morning they'd drop the kids somewhere and tip the parents off where to find them.

That was the timetable according to Lucas, Angie thought. But not according to me.

18

On Wednesday morning, the unpredictable March weather had once again turned bitterly cold. A biting wind rattled the windows of the dining room where Steve and Margaret sat with Walter Carlson and his colleague, Agent Tony Realto. A second pot of coffee sat untouched on the table.

Carlson had not thought it was his right to soft-pedal what Franklin Bailey had told him, that one of the twins had been coughing, a deep bronchial-sounding cough. "Steve and Margaret, I know it's frightening to think that Kathy is sick," he told them. "On the other hand it proves that Bailey really was listening to them. You've been worried that Kathy was getting a cold."

"Don't you think that the Pied Piper will know better than to call Bailey's neighbor again?" Steve asked. "He has to be smart enough to guess that you've got that line tapped by now."

"Steve, criminals make mistakes. They think they've thought of everything, but they *do* make mistakes."

"I wonder if whoever has them is giving Kathy anything to keep her from going into pneumonia," Margaret said, her voice breaking.

Carlson looked across the table. Margaret Frawley's skin was paper white. Her dark blue eyes were heavily circled. Every time she said anything, she would then press her lips tightly together, as though afraid of what she might say next.

"My guess is that whoever has the children wants to return them safely."

It was quarter of ten. The Pied Piper had said he would be in touch at ten o'clock. The three fell into silence. They could only wait.

At ten o'clock, Rena Chapman, the neighbor who had cooked dinner for the Frawleys, raced over from her house. "Somebody on my phone says he has important information about the twins for the FBI," she said breathlessly to the police officer on guard outside the house.

Steve and Margaret at their heels, Realto and Carlson ran to the Chapman home. Carlson grabbed the phone and identified himself.

"Have you pen and paper?" the caller asked.

Carlson pulled his notebook and pen from his breast pocket.

"I want seven million dollars transferred to Account 507964 in the Nemidonam Bank in Hong Kong," the Pied Piper told him. "You have three minutes to make it happen. When I know the transfer is completed, I'll call back."

"It will be completed immediately," Carlson snapped. Before he could finish the sentence he heard the click of the phone.

"Is it the kidnapper?" Margaret demanded. "Were the girls with him?"

"It was the kidnapper. He didn't refer to the girls. It was only about the ransom." Carlson dialed Robinson Geisler's private number at the executive office of C.F.G.&Y. Geisler had promised to be waiting there for instructions about the money transfer. In his precise, clipped voice, he repeated the name of the bank in Hong Kong and the account number. "The transfer will be made within sixty seconds, and we have the suitcases with the cash waiting to be delivered," he assured the FBI agent.

Margaret listened as Carlson next barked instructions to the FBI communications unit to try to triangulate the Chapmans' phone line in the hope that they might pinpoint the Pied Piper's location when he called back.

He's too smart for that, Margaret thought. Now he has the seven million dollars. Will we hear from him again?

Carlson had explained to her and Steve that, for a commission, some overseas banks will accept wire transfers, then allow them to be moved again immediately. Suppose that satisfies him, she agonized. Suppose we never hear from him again. But yesterday Franklin Bailey heard the girls' voices. They talked about seeing us with him on television. They were alive yesterday morning.

"Mr. Carlson. Right away. Another call. Three houses down." A Ridgefield policeman on duty outside the Frawley house had rushed to Rena Chapman's kitchen door and opened it without knocking.

The wind blew Margaret's hair into her eyes as she and Steve, their hands joined, ran behind Carlson and Realto to the house where a neighbor she had never met was frantically waving them in.

The Pied Piper had disconnected, but called back less than a minute later. "You have been very wise," he told Carlson. "Thank you for the wire transfer. Now get this straight. Your helpful friend, Franklin Bailey, must be standing in Manhattan in front of the Time Warner building at Columbus Circle at eight o'clock tonight. Tell him to wear a blue tie, and to have a red tie in his pocket. He must have the suitcases with the money and be carrying a cell phone. What is the number of your cell phone, Mr. FBI agent?"

"It's 917-555-3291," Carlson said.

"I'll repeat that: 917-555-3291. Give your cell phone to Franklin Bailey. Remember we will be watching him. Any attempt to follow him or to apprehend the messenger who accepts the suitcases will mean that the twins will disappear forever. The alternative is that once we have validated the amount and authenticity of the cash, sometime after midnight, someone will receive a phone call telling you where to pick up the twins. They're very homesick and one of them has a fever. I suggest you make sure there are no slip-ups."

19

Walking back from their neighbor's house, clutching Steve's arm, Margaret tried to believe that within twenty-four hours the twins really would be home. I *have* to believe it, she told herself. Kathy, I love you. Kelly, I love you.

In her rush to get first to Rena Chapman's house, and then to their other neighbor for the second call, she had not even been conscious of the media vans parked on the street. But now the reporters were outside the house clamoring for a statement.

"Have the kidnappers contacted you?"

"Has the ransom been paid?"

"Have you confirmation that the twins are alive?"

"There will be no statement at this time," Carlson said brusquely.

Ignoring the questions that were shouted to them, Margaret and Steve darted up the walk. Captain Martinson was waiting for them on the porch. Ever since Friday night, he had been in and out of the house, sometimes conferring privately with the FBI agents, other times simply a reassuring presence. Margaret knew that his officers at the Ridgefield Police Department and the Connecticut State Police had distributed hundreds of posters with the picture of the girls standing by their birthday cake. One of the posters she had seen had a question printed on it: DO YOU KNOW ANYONE WHO OWNS, OR OWNED, A ROYAL MANUAL TYPEWRITER?

That was the typewriter on which the ransom note for the twins had been written.

Yesterday, Martinson told them that people in town had pledged a ten-thousand-dollar reward for any information that would lead to the safe return of the twins. Could someone have responded to that? Had someone come forward with information? He looks upset, but surely it *can't* be bad news, Margaret promised herself, as they stepped into the foyer. He doesn't know yet that a ransom drop has already been arranged.

As though afraid that they would somehow be overheard by the media, Martinson waited until they were in the living room before he spoke. "We've got a problem," he said. "Franklin Bailey had a fainting spell early this morning. His housekeeper called 911 and he was rushed to the hospital. His cardiogram was okay. His doctor thinks he had an anxiety attack brought on by stress."

"We've just been told by the kidnapper that Bailey is to be in front of the Time Warner building at eight o'clock tonight," Carlson snapped. "If he doesn't show up, whoever has the children will suspect a double cross."

"But he's *got* to be there!" Margaret heard the hint of hysteria in her voice, and bit her lip so hard she tasted blood. "He's *got* to be there," she repeated, this time in a whisper. She looked across the room at the pictures of the twins that were on top of the piano. My two little girls in blue, she thought. Oh, God, please bring them home to me.

"He's planning to be there," Martinson said. "He wouldn't stay at the hospital." He and the agents looked at each other.

But it was Steve who voiced what they all were thinking: "Suppose he has another weak spell and becomes confused or passes out while he's getting the instructions on delivering the cash? What happens then? If Bailey doesn't make contact, the Pied Piper said we'd never see our children again."

Agent Tony Realto did not reveal the concern that had been growing in his mind to a virtual certainty. We never should have let Bailey get involved. And why did he insist on "helping"?

20

At twenty minutes past ten on Wednesday morning, Lucas was staring out the front window of his apartment, puffing nervously on his fifth cigarette of the day. Suppose the Pied Piper gets the seven million dollar wire transfer and decides to dump us? I have the voice recording of him, but maybe that isn't enough, he thought. If he pulls out, what do we do with the kids?

Even if the Pied Piper plays it straight and arranges delivery of the million in cash, it will take both me and Clint to try to make the pickup and get away without being caught. Something would go wrong. Lucas knew it in his bones, and he respected this kind of warning. It had proved accurate when he was a juvenile and was caught by the cops. Ignoring it as an adult had sent him to prison for six years. That time, when he broke into the house, he had sensed that he shouldn't set foot in it even though he had successfully bypassed the alarm.

And he'd been right. Cameras on a separate system had recorded his every move. Tonight, if he and Clint got caught, he'd be facing life.

And how sick was the one kid? If she died, it could be a lot worse.

His phone rang. It was the Pied Piper. Lucas turned on his recorder.

"Things are going smoothly, Bert" the Pied Piper said. "The wire transfer went through. It's very clear to me that the FBI won't jeopar-dize getting the children back by following you too closely."

He was using the phony growl that he thought passed for a disguised voice. Lucas ground out the rest of his cigarette on the window sill. Keep talking, pal, he thought.

"It's your ball game now," the Pied Piper continued. "If you want to be counting money tonight, listen very carefully to my plan. As you know, you will need a stolen vehicle. You have assured me that Harry is capable of securing one easily."

"Yeah. It's the one thing he's good at."

"We will begin making contact with Franklin Bailey at eight o'clock this evening in front of the Time Warner building on Columbus Circle. At that time, you and Harry must be parked on West Fifty-sixth Street, at the passageway to Fifty-seventh Street that is just east of Sixth Avenue. You will be in the stolen vehicle. You will have replaced the license plates of that car or van with plates from another vehicle."

"No problem."

"Here is the way we're going to work it."

As Lucas listened, he grudgingly admitted that the plan had a good chance of succeeding. Finally, after unnecessarily assuring the Pied Piper that he would be carrying his special cell phone, he heard the click that meant the connection was broken.

Okay, he thought. I know what we're doing. Maybe it'll work. As he lit a fresh cigarette, his own cell phone rang.

The phone was on the dresser in his bedroom, and he hurried to answer it. "Lucas," a weak and strained voice began, "this is

Franklin Bailey. I need you this evening. If you are already engaged, please use your replacement driver for that engagement. I have a most important errand in Manhattan and must be in Columbus Circle at eight o'clock."

His brain racing, Lucas jammed the phone against his ear, at the same time grabbing the half-empty pack of cigarettes from his pocket. "I do have a booking, but maybe we can work it out. How long do you expect to be, Mr. Bailey?"

"I don't know."

Lucas thought of the funny way the cop had eyed him on Friday when Bailey had driven over to the Frawleys' house to offer to be the go-between. If the feds decided that it was a good idea for Bailey to have his own driver, and then found out he was un-available, they might start asking what was so important that he couldn't accommodate a longtime client.

I can't refuse, Lucas thought. "Mr. Bailey," he said, trying to make his voice strike its usual eager-to-please timbre, "I'll get some-one for my other job. What time do you want me, sir?"

"At six o'clock. We'll probably be quite

early, but I cannot take any chance of being late."

"Six on the button, sir."

Lucas threw his cell phone on the bed, went back the short distance to his dingy living room and picked up the special cell phone. When the Pied Piper answered, Lucas brushed nervously at the sweat on his forehead and told him what had happened. "I couldn't refuse, so now we can't go ahead with the plan."

Even though the Pied Piper was still trying to disguise his voice, the note of amusement in it crept through. "You're both right and wrong, Bert. You couldn't refuse, but we *are* going ahead with our plan. In fact, this little development may work beautifully for us. You're planning to go for a plane ride, aren't you?"

"Yeah, after I get the stuff from Harry."

"Make sure that the typewriter that was used for the ransom note goes with you, as well as the clothing and toys that were bought for the children. There should be no trace of children having been present in Harry's cottage."

"I know. I know." They'd already gone over this part of the plan.

"Have Harry phone me when he has secured the car. You phone me as soon as you drop Bailey off at the Time Warner building. I'll tell you what to do next."

21

At ten thirty, Angie was at the breakfast table with the twins. Now on her third cup of black coffee, her head was beginning to clear. She'd had a lousy night's sleep. She looked at Kathy. She could tell the vaporizer and aspirin had done some good. Though the bedroom reeked of Vick's, at least the steam had loosened her cough a bit. She was still a pretty sick kid, though, and had been awake a lot during the night, crying for her mother. I'm tired, Angie thought, really tired. At least the other one slept pretty well, even though sometimes when Kathy was coughing hard, Kelly would start coughing, too.

"Is she getting sick, too?" Clint had asked a half-dozen times.

"No, she isn't. Get back to sleep," Angie

had ordered. "I don't want you to be half-dead tonight."

She looked at Kelly, who stared back at her. It was all she could do not to slap that fresh kid. "We want to go home," she kept saying every other minute. "Kathy and I want to go home. You promised you would take us home."

I can't *wait* for you to go home, Angie thought.

It was obvious Clint was a nervous wreck. He'd taken his coffee over to the sofa in front of the television set and kept drumming his fingers on the piece of junk that passed for a coffee table. He'd been watching the news to see if there was anything more about the kidnapping, but he knew enough to keep the remote on the mute setting. The kids' backs were to the TV.

Kelly had eaten some of the cereal Angie had fixed them, and Kathy had at least a few bites. They both looked pale, Angie admitted to herself, and their hair was kind of messy. Maybe she'd better try brushing it, but on the other hand, she didn't need them yelling if there were knots to untangle. Forget it, she decided.

She pushed back her chair. "Okay, kids. Time for a little nap."

They had gotten used to being shoved back into the crib after breakfast. Kathy even raised her arms to be picked up. She knows I love her, Angie thought, then cursed under her breath as Kathy's elbow hit the dish of cereal, which then spilled down the front of her pajamas.

Kathy began to cry, a sick wail that ended in a cough.

"It's okay. It's okay," Angie snapped. Now what do I do? she wondered. That jerk Lucas is getting here soon, and I was told to leave the kids in their pajamas all day. Maybe if I just pin a towel under the wet part, it'll dry.

"Shush," she said impatiently as she picked up Kathy. The sopping pajama top dampened her own shirt as she carried her into the bedroom. Kelly got down from the chair and walked beside them, her hand reaching up to pat her sister's foot.

Angie put Kathy in the crib and grabbed a towel from the top of the dresser. By the time she pinned it under the pajama top, Kathy had folded herself into a ball and was sucking her thumb. That was something new, Angie thought as she picked up Kelly and dropped her into the crib.

Kelly immediately struggled to her feet and put her hands tightly around the railing. "We want to go home now," she said. "You promised."

"You're going home tonight," Angie said. "So shut up."

The shades were pulled all the way down in the bedroom. Angie started to raise one of them but then changed her mind. If I keep it dark, the kids might fall asleep, she decided. She went back to the kitchen, slamming the door behind her as a warning to Kelly not to cause trouble. Last night when the kid had started to rock the crib, a good pinch on her arm had taught her it wasn't a good idea.

Clint was still watching the television. Angie began to clear the table. "Pick up those Barney tapes," she ordered him as she dumped dishes in the sink. "Put them in the box with the typewriter."

The Pied Piper, whoever he was, had ordered Lucas to dump in the ocean anything they had that could be connected to the kidnapping. "He means the typewriter that we used for the ransom note, any clothes or toys or sheets or blankets that might have their DNA on them," Lucas had told Clint.

None of them know how well that fits in with *my* plans, Angie thought.

"Angie, this box is too big," Clint protested. "It'll be hard for Lucas to dump it."

"It's not too big," she snapped. "I'm putting the vaporizer in it. Okay? Okay?"

"Too bad we can't put the crib in it."

"When we drop off the kids, you can come back here and take it apart. Tomorrow you get rid of it."

Two hours later, she was prepared for Lucas's explosive reaction when he caught sight of the box. "Couldn't you have found a smaller one?" he barked.

"Sure, I could have. I could even have gone to the grocery store and explain why I wanted one and what I'd put in it. This one was in the cellar. It will do the job, okay?"

"Angie, I think we have smaller boxes downstairs," Clint volunteered.

"I sealed and tied this box," Angie shouted. "This is it."

A minute later, she watched with intense satisfaction as Lucas carried the heavy, bulky box to his car.

22

Lila Jackson, a sales clerk at Abby's Quality Discount on Route 7, had become something of a celebrity to her family and friends. She had been the one to sell the twins' blue velvet dresses to Margaret Frawley two days before the kidnapping.

Thirty-four years old, small of stature, and bustling with energy, Lila had recently quit her well-paid secretarial job in Manhattan, moved in with her widowed mother, and taken the job at Abby's. As she explained to her astonished friends, "I realized that I hated sitting at a desk, and the most fun I'd ever had working was when I did part-time at Bloomingdale's. I love clothes. I love selling them. As soon as I can do it, I'm going to open my own place." To that end, she was taking business courses at the community college.

The day the news of the kidnapping broke, Lila had recognized both Margaret and the dresses the kidnapped twins were wearing in the picture she saw on television.

"She was the nicest person," Lila breathlessly told a widening group of people who were fascinated by the fact that only a couple of days before the twins were stolen, she had been in contact with their mother. "Mrs. Frawley is real class, in a quiet, nice way. And she really knows quality. I told her that the same dresses cost four hundred dollars each in Bergdorf's all season, and that at forty-two dollars, they were a steal. She said that was still more than she wanted to spend, and I showed her a lot of other stuff, but she kept coming back to those. Finally she bought them. She kind of laughed when she was paying and said she only hoped she'd get a good picture of her twins in the dresses before something got spilled on them.

"We had a nice chat," Lila reminisced, dragging out every detail of the encounter. "I told Mrs. Frawley that another lady had just been in, buying matching outfits for twins. They couldn't have been hers, though, because she wasn't sure what size to get. She asked my opinion. She said they were average-sized three-year-olds."

Lila caught the noon news on Wednesday morning as she was getting ready to leave for work. Shaking her head in sympathy, she stared at the video of Margaret and Steve Frawley racing down the street to a neighbor's home, and then a few minutes later, running to another house farther down the block.

"Although neither the family nor the FBI will confirm it, it is believed that this morning the Pied Piper, as the kidnapper calls himself, has communicated his demands for paying the ransom by calling the Frawleys on their neighbors' phones," the CBS anchorman was saying.

Lila watched as a close-up of Margaret Frawley showed her anguished expression and the deep circles under her eyes.

"Robinson Geisler, chairman of C.F.G.&Y., is not available to answer questions as to whether or not a transfer of funds is in process," the reporter continued, "but if that is the case, it is clear that the next twenty-four hours will be crucial. It is the sixth day since Kathy and Kelly were taken from their bedroom. The kidnapping took place around nine P.M. last Thursday night."

They must have been in their pajamas when they were taken, Lila thought as she reached for her car key. It was a thought that teased her as she drove to work, and stayed with her as she hung up her coat and ran a comb through the mop of red hair that had been tousled in the windy parking lot. She pinned on her WELCOME TO ABBY'S—I'M LILA badge, then went to the cubicle where the accounting was handled.

"I just want to check my sales from last Wednesday, Jean," she explained to the accountant. I don't remember the name of that woman who bought clothing for twins, she thought, but I can tell by the receipt. She bought two sets of matching overalls and polo shirts, underwear, and socks. She didn't buy shoes because she didn't have any idea of size.

In five minutes of thumbing through receipts, she had found what she wanted. The receipt for the clothes had been signed by Mrs. Clint Downes, using a Visa credit card. Should I get Jean to phone Visa now and get her address? Lila wondered. Don't be a fool, she told herself, as she hurried onto the sales floor.

Later, still unable to shake the feeling that she should follow up on her uncomfortable hunch, Lila asked the accountant to try to get the address of the woman who had purchased the identical outfits for three-year-olds.

"Sure, Lila. If they give me any grief about releasing the address, I'll say that the woman may have left a package here."

"Thanks, Jean."

At Visa, Mrs. Clint Downes was recorded as living at 100 Orchard Avenue, in Danbury.

Now even more uncertain of what to do, Lila remembered that Jim Gilbert, a retired Danbury cop, was having dinner with her mother that night. She'd ask him about it.

When she arrived home, her mother had held dinner for her, and she and Jim were having a cocktail in the study. Lila poured a glass of wine for herself and sat on the raised hearth, her back to the fire. "Jim," she said, "I guess Mother told you I sold those blue velvet dresses to Margaret Frawley."

"I heard." His deep baritone voice always seemed incongruous to Lila, coming as it did from Jim's narrow frame. His amiable expression hardened as he spoke. "Mark my words. They're not going to get those kids back, alive *or* dead. My guess is they're out of the country by now, and all this talk of ransom was just meant to be a diversion."

"Jim, I know it's crazy, but just a few minutes before I sold the dresses to Margaret Frawley, I waited on a woman who was buying matching outfits for three-year-olds, and didn't even seem to know the right size to buy."

"So?"

Lila took the plunge. "I mean, wouldn't it be extraordinary if that woman was connected to the kidnapping and was buying clothes, anticipating they'd be needed? The Frawley twins were wearing their pajamas when they were taken. Kids that age spill things. They can't be in the same outfit five days."

"Lila, you're letting your imagination run away with you," Jim Gilbert said indulgently. "Do you know how many tips like that the Ridgefield cops and the FBI have been getting?"

"The woman's name is Mrs. Clint Downes, and she lives at 100 Orchard Street, right here in Danbury," Lila persisted. "I just feel like taking a ride over and ringing her bell and making up a story that one of the polo shirts was from an imperfect batch, just to satisfy my own curiosity."

"Lila, stick to fashion. I know Clint Downes. He's the caretaker who lives in the cottage at the club; 100 Orchard Street is the address of the club. Was the woman skinny with kind of a sloppy ponytail?"

"Yes."

"That's Clint's girlfriend, Angie. She may be signing herself as Mrs. Downes, but she's *not* Mrs. Downes. She does a fair amount of babysitting. Cross both of them off your list of suspects, Lila. In a million years, neither one of those two is bright enough to pull off a kidnapping like this."

23

Lucas knew that Charley Fox, a new mechanic at the airport, was watching him as he climbed into the plane, holding the bulky box in his arms. He's asking himself why I'm carrying something like this, and then he's going to figure out that I'm going to dump it, Lucas told himself. Then he's going to decide that it must be something I want to get rid of real bad, or maybe that I'm ferrying drugs somewhere. So the next time a cop comes around and asks about anyone who uses the airport and looks suspicious, he'll tell him about me.

Still, it was a good idea to clear the house of anything that could connect the twins to the cottage, he admitted as he plopped the box down on the co-pilot's seat in the cockpit. Tonight, after we drop the kids, I'll help

Clint take the crib apart and then we'll lose the parts somewhere. The kids' DNA would be all over the mattress.

As he performed his checkout before taking off, Lucas permitted himself a sour smile. He'd read somewhere that identical twins had the same DNA. So they can only prove we had *one* of them, he thought. Swell!

The wind was still brisk. It wasn't the best day to go flying in a light plane, but the cutting edge of danger was always soothing to Lucas. Today it would relieve his mushrooming anxiety about what was going to happen tonight. Forget the cash, an insistent voice kept repeating in his head. Tell the Pied Piper to pay us a million out of the wire transfer. Dump the kids where they'll be found. That way there's no chance of being followed and caught.

But the Pied Piper won't go along with that, Lucas thought bitterly as he felt the wheels of the plane begin to lift. Either we collect the cash tonight, or we're stuck with no money and a kidnapping rap if we get caught.

It was a short flight, just long enough to get out over the ocean a few miles, hold the yoke firm with his knees, reduce his speed, struggle to get his hands around the box, position it on his lap, carefully open the door, and give the box a shove. He watched its descent. The ocean was gray and choppy. The box disappeared into the waves, sending a spray of foam cascading through the air. Lucas pulled the door closed and put his hand on the yoke. Now for the real job, he thought.

When he landed at the airport, he did not see Charley Fox, which was fine with him. That way he won't know whether I brought the box back with me or not, he thought.

It was almost four o'clock. The wind was starting to die down, but the clouds over-head were threatening. Would rain be good for them, or would it be a problem? Lucas walked over to the parking lot and got into his car. He sat for a few minutes, trying to decide if it was better with rain or without rain. Only time will tell, he decided. For now, he should get the limo out of the garage and run it over to the car wash to have it sparkling for Mr. Bailey. In case the feds happened to be at Bailey's house, it would be one way of showing that he was a con-scientious limo driver, no more, no less.

Plus it was something to keep him busy. If he just sat in the apartment, he'd go nuts. The decision made, he turned the key.

Two hours later, freshly showered and shaved, neatly dressed in his chauffeur's uniform, Lucas drove his clean and polished limousine into the driveway of Franklin Bailey's home.

24

"Margaret, we are as certain as any human beings can be that you had nothing to do with the twins' disappearance," Agent Carlson said. "Your second lie detector test was inconclusive, even more so than the first one. Your emotional state can be the explanation for that. Contrary to everything you read in novels or see on television, lie detector tests are not always accurate, which is why they're not admissible as evidence in court."

"What are you telling me?" Margaret asked, her tone almost indifferent. What does it matter? she was thinking. When I took the tests, I could hardly understand the questions. They were just words. An hour ago Steve had insisted that she take a sedative that the doctor had prescribed. It was the first one she had

had all day, although she was supposed to take one every four hours. She didn't like the feeling of vagueness that it gave her. She was having trouble focusing on what the FBI agent was saying.

"On both tests, you were asked if you knew the person responsible for the kidnapping," Walter Carlson repeated quietly. "When you said that you did not, on the second test it registered as a lie." He raised his hand at the protest he saw forming on her lips. "Margaret, listen to me. You're not lying. We know that. But it is possible that subconsciously there is someone you suspect of being involved with the kidnapping, and it is affecting the test results even though you are not aware of it."

It's getting dark, Margaret thought. It's seven o'clock. In another hour, Franklin Bailey will be outside the Time Warner building waiting for someone to contact him. If he delivers the money, I may have my babies tonight.

"Margaret, listen," Steve urged.

Margaret could hear the sound of the kettle beginning to whistle. Rena Chapman had come over carrying a casserole of baked macaroni and cheese and slices of freshly baked Virginia ham. We have such good neighbors, she thought. I've hardly had a chance to get to know them. When we get the twins back, I'll invite all of them in to thank them.

"Margaret, I want you to look again at the files of some of the people you defended," Carlson was saying. "We've narrowed it down to three or four who, after their convictions, blamed you for the fact they lost their cases."

Margaret forced herself to focus on the names of the defendants. "I gave them the best defense that I could. The evidence against them was very strong," she said. "They were all guilty, and I'd worked out good plea bargains, but they wouldn't accept them. Then, when they were found guilty at trial, and got longer sentences than if they'd accepted the plea, it became my fault. That happens a lot to public defenders."

"After his conviction, Donny Mars hanged himself in his cell." Carlson persisted. "At his funeral, his mother screamed, 'Wait till Frawley finds out what it is to lose a child.' "

"That was four years ago, long before the girls were born. She was hysterical," Margaret said.

"She may have been hysterical, but she's dropped out of sight completely, and so has her other son. Do you think there is any chance that without realizing it you may be suspicious of her?"

"She was hysterical," Margaret repeated calmly, and wondered that she could sound so matter-of-fact. "Donny was bipolar. I begged the judge to send him to a hospital. He should have been under a doctor's care. His brother wrote a note apologizing to me for what his mother said. She didn't mean it." She closed her eyes, then opened them again slowly.

"That's the other thing I've been trying to remember," she said suddenly.

Carlson and Steve stared at her. She's withdrawing, Carlson thought. The sedative was beginning to relax her and make her sleepy. The timbre of her voice was dropping, and he had to lean forward to hear what she was saying. "I should call Dr. Harris," Margaret whispered. "Kathy is sick. When we get her and Kelly back, I want Dr. Harris to be the one to take care of Kathy."

Carlson looked at Steve. "Is Dr. Harris a pediatrician?"

"Yes. She's at New York-Presbyterian in

Manhattan and has written extensively about the behavior pattern of twins. When we knew we were expecting twins, Margaret called her. She's been taking care of the girls ever since."

"When we know where to find the girls, they'll be taken immediately to a nearby hospital for a check-up," Carlson told them. "Maybe Dr. Harris would meet us there."

We're talking as though it's an accomplished fact that we'll have them back, Steve thought. I wonder if they'll still be wearing their pajamas. He turned his head as rain began slapping at the windows, then he looked at Carlson. He thought he knew what Carlson was thinking. The rain would make the surveillance of the kidnappers that much more difficult.

But FBI Agent Walter Carlson was not thinking about the weather. He was concentrating on what Margaret had just said. "That's the *other* thing I'm trying to remember." Margaret, he thought, what else, what else? *You may have the key. Remember it before it's too late.*

25

The trip from Ridgefield to Manhattan took an hour and fifteen minutes. At a quarter past seven, Franklin Bailey was hunched in the backseat of the limo which Lucas had parked on Central Park South, half a block from the Time Warner building.

The rain had started falling in earnest. On the drive into the city, Bailey had nervously explained the reason he had insisted Lucas be available for him. "The FBI will tell me to get out of whatever car I'm in. They know the kidnappers will suspect that an agent is driving me. If somehow they were able to watch us at home, by my arriving with the driver and limousine I always use, the kidnappers may understand that all we want is to get the children back safely."

"I can understand that, Mr. Bailey," Lucas said.

"I know that there are agents swarming around the Time Warner building and driving cabs by it and in private cars, all ready to follow me when I get instructions," Bailey said, his voice a nervous quiver.

Lucas glanced into the rearview mirror. He looks as shaky as I feel, he thought bitterly. This is all a trap for me and Clint. The FBI is just waiting to spring it. For all I know, they're putting cuffs on Angie right now.

"Lucas, you have your cell phone?" Bailey asked for the tenth time.

"Yes, sir, I do."

"When the transfer of money is completed, I'll call you immediately. You'll be parked around here?"

"Yes, sir, and ready to pick you up wherever you are."

"I know one of the agents will ride with us. They told me they'd want to question me about any impressions I was able to make of the kidnapper's contact person. I understand the need for that, but I told them I wanted to be in my own car." Bailey attempted a faint chuckle. "I mean *your* own car, Lucas. Not mine."

"It's yours whenever you want it, Mr. Bailey." Lucas felt his hands grow clammy, and he rubbed them together. Let's get started, he thought. Enough of this waiting.

At two minutes of eight he pulled the car in front of the Time Warner building. He pushed the trunk button, sprang out of the limo, and opened the door for Bailey. His gaze lingered on the two suitcases as he hoisted them from the trunk.

The FBI agent who had been at Bailey's home had put the suitcases in the trunk and added a luggage cart. "When you drop off Mr. Bailey, be sure to load the suitcases on the cart," he'd told Lucas. "They're too heavy for him to carry."

With hands that itched to grab the suitcases and run, Lucas stacked them on the cart and secured them to the handle.

The rain was a steady downpour now, and Bailey turned up the collar of his coat. He had put on a cap, but not soon enough to prevent strands of damp white hair from falling onto his forehead. From his pocket he pulled out FBI agent Carlson's phone and held it anxiously to his ear.

"I'd better go, Mr. Bailey," Lucas said.

"Good luck, sir. I'll be waiting to hear from you."

"Thank you. Thank you, Lucas."

Lucas got into the limo and took a quick look around. Bailey was at the curb. Traffic was moving slowly around Columbus Circle. On every corner people were vainly signaling for cabs. Lucas pulled out and drove slowly back down Central Park South. As he had expected, there was no place to park. He made a right on Seventh Avenue and another right on Fifty-fifth Street. Between Eighth and Ninth Avenues, he parked in front of a fire hydrant and waited for a call from the Pied Piper.

26

The kids had been asleep for a good part of the afternoon. When they woke up, Angie noticed that Kathy was looking flushed and, sure enough, she was getting another fever. I shouldn't have left her in those wet pajamas, she told herself, feeling them. They're still damp. Still, she waited until Clint left at five o'clock to change Kathy into one of the sets of overalls and polo shirts that she hadn't thrown away.

"I want to get dressed, too," Kelly protested. Then acknowledging Angie's angry glare, she turned her attention to the TV and the Nickelodeon channel.

At seven o'clock, Clint phoned to say that he had purchased a new car, a black Toyota, and that he'd bought it in New Jersey, meaning he'd stolen a car and it now had

Jersey plates. He ended the call by saying, "Don't worry, Angie, we'll be celebrating tonight."

You *bet* we will, Angie told herself.

At eight o'clock, she put the twins back in the crib. Kathy's breathing was heavy and she was still warm. Angie gave her another aspirin, then watched as she curled up into a bundle, her thumb in her mouth. Right now, Clint and Lucas are hooking up with whoever has the money, she thought, her nerves tingling.

Kelly was sitting up, her arm around her sister. The blue teddy-bear pajamas she'd worn since last night were wrinkled and had become unbuttoned at the neck. The overalls Kathy was now wearing were dark blue, the polo shirt a blue and white check pattern.

"Two little girls in blue, lad," Angie began singing. "Two little girls in blue . . ."

Kelly looked up at her, her eyes solemn as Angie repeated the last line of the refrain twice, "But we have drifted apart."

Angie turned out the light, closed the bedroom door, and went into the living room. Apple-pie order, she thought, sarcastically. Better than it's looked in a long time. I should have kept the vaporizer though. Getting rid of it was Lucas's fault.

She looked at the clock. It was ten after eight. The only thing Clint knew about the ransom payment was that he had to be parked a couple of blocks from Columbus Circle in a stolen car at eight o'clock. By now the Pied Piper should have things rolling.

Clint hadn't been told to carry a gun, but with her encouragement, he had decided to do so anyway. "Look at it this way," she had told him. "Suppose you're getting away with the cash and somebody's following you. You're good with a gun. If you're really cornered, aim for the cop's leg or the tires of his car."

Now Clint's unregistered pistol was in his pocket.

Angie made a pot of coffee, sat on the couch, and turned on the television to the news channel. A cup of mouth-burning black coffee in one hand and a cigarette in the other, she watched intently as the anchorman speculated that the ransom payment transaction might be in progress between the kidnappers and the Frawley family. "Our Web site has been flooded with messages from our viewers who are praying that very, very soon the two little girls in blue will be back in the arms of their heartbroken parents."

Angie laughed. "Guess again, pal," she said, smirking at the solemn-faced anchorman.

27

A recent magazine article had described her as "sixty-three years old, with wise and compassionate hazel eyes, a full head of finger-waved gray hair, and a rounded body that offers a comfortable lap to babies and toddlers." Dr. Sylvia Harris was the director of pediatric services at the Children's Hospital of New York-Presbyterian in Manhattan. When the news of the kidnapping first broke, she had tried to get through to Steve and Margaret Frawley but had only been able to leave a message. Frustrated, she had phoned Steve's office and asked his secretary to tell him that she had everyone she knew praying for the safe return of the twins.

In the five days since the twins had been missing, she had kept her normal appointments and made her rounds with never a moment going by when the twins were not on her mind.

Like a videotape being constantly replayed, Dr. Harris remembered the late autumn day three and a half years ago when Margaret Frawley had called to make an appointment with her. "How old is the baby?" she had asked Margaret.

"They're due on March twenty-fourth," Margaret had said, her voice excited and happy. "I've just been told I'm expecting twin girls, and I've read some of your articles about twins. That's why I want *you* to take care of them when they're born."

The Frawleys came in for a preliminary appointment, and they liked each other immediately. Even before the twins arrived, their relationship with Dr. Harris had evolved into a warm friendship. She had given them a stack of books to read about the special bond between twins, and when she was lecturing on the subject, the Frawleys would often be in the audience. They had been fascinated by the examples she gave of identical twins experiencing each other's physical pain and receiving telepathic messages from each other, even when they were continents apart.

When Kathy and Kelly were born, healthy and beautiful, Steve and Margaret had been ecstatic. And so was I, on every level, professional and personal, Sylvia thought now as she locked her desk and prepared to go home. It gave me the chance to study identical twins from the minute they were born— and the girls bear out everything that has ever been written about the twin bond. She thought of the time when they rushed Kathy in to see her because her cold had gone into bronchitis. Steve was sitting in the waiting room with Kelly. The minute I gave Kathy the shot in the examining room, Sylvia remembered, Kelly began to wail like a banshee. And that was only one of many similar instances. For these past three years, Margaret has been keeping a log for me. How often have I mentioned to her and Steve that Josh would have loved to be involved in taking care of the girls and studying them?

She had told Steve and Margaret about her late husband, saying that they reminded her of the relationship between herself and Josh when they first married. The Frawleys had met in law school. She and Josh had been fellow medical students at Columbia. The difference was that the Frawleys had the twins, while she and Josh had never had the good fortune to have children. After completing their residencies, they had set up a pediatric practice together. Then when he was only forty-two, Josh had admitted that he'd been feeling terribly tired. Tests showed that he had terminal lung cancer, an irony that only Sylvia's great faith had enabled her to accept without bitterness.

"The only time I ever saw him cross with a patient was when a mother came in with the smell of smoke clinging to her clothes," she told Steve and Margaret. "Josh asked her in a steely voice, 'You smoke around this baby? Won't you please understand the danger you're putting her in? You must stop *at once.*' "

On television, Margaret had said that she was afraid Kathy was getting a cold. Then the kidnapper had played a tape of the twins' voices, and one of the twins was coughing. Kathy went into pneumonia easily, Sylvia thought. It wasn't likely a kidnapper would take her to a doctor. Maybe I should call the police station in Ridgefield and explain I'm the twins' pediatrician and see if they can have the television stations broadcast some precautions the kidnappers can take if Kathy is running a fever.

Her telephone rang. For a moment she was tempted to let the service pick it up, but then on impulse she reached for the receiver. It was Margaret, a Margaret whose voice was almost catatonic.

"Dr. Sylvia. The ransom is being paid right now, and we believe we are going to get the girls back sometime soon. Could you possibly come up here and be with us? I know it's asking a lot, but we don't know what may have happened to them. I do know that Kathy has a heavy cough."

"I'm on my way," Sylvia Harris said. "Put someone on to give me directions to your house."

28

The cell phone Franklin Bailey was holding began to ring. His fingers trembling, he snapped it open and pressed it to his ear. "Franklin Bailey," he said, as his mouth went dry.

"Mr. Bailey, you are admirably prompt. My congratulations." The voice was a husky whisper. "You must immediately begin walking down Eighth Avenue to Fifty-seventh Street. Turn right on Fifty-seventh and walk west to Ninth Avenue. Wait on the northwest corner. You are being watched every step of the way. I will call you back in precisely five minutes."

FBI Agent Angus Sommers, dressed in the tattered and soiled clothes of a homeless man, was curled on the sidewalk, leaning against the architectural curiosity that had once been the Huntington Hartford Museum. Beside him stood a shabby cart, covered with plastic and filled with old clothes and newspapers, providing him some protection from a potential observer. Like a score of other agents in the vicinity, his cell phone had been programmed to pick up the call that Franklin Bailey would receive from the Pied Piper. Now he watched Bailey begin to drag the luggage cart across the street. Even from a distance, Sommers could see that Bailey was straining with the weight of the suitcases and was quickly becoming soaked from the now heavy rain.

With narrowed eyes, Sommers scanned the circumference of Columbus Circle. Was the kidnapper and his gang somewhere in the crowd of people scurrying under umbrellas to their destinations? Or was it a single person who would send Bailey on a wild-goose chase all over New York in his attempt to identify and shake off anyone following him?

As Bailey moved out of sight, Sommers got up slowly, pushed his shopping cart to the corner, and waited for the light. He knew cameras hooked up at the Time Warner building and in the rotunda were filming every inch of the scene.

He crossed Fifty-eighth street and turned left. There a junior agent, also dressed in the shabby garb of the homeless, took over his cart. Sommers got into one of the waiting FBI cars, and two minutes later, changed into a Burberry raincoat and matching hat, was dropped off at the Holiday Inn on Fifty-seventh Street, half a block from Ninth Avenue.

"Bert, this is the Pied Piper. State your location."

"I'm parked at Fifty-fifth Street between Eighth and Ninth. I'm in front of a hydrant. I can't stay long. I warn you. According to Bailey, this place is swarming with the FBI."

"I would expect no less of them. I want you to drive to Tenth Avenue, then turn east on Fifty-sixth Street. Pull over to the curb as soon as you can and wait for further instructions."

A moment later, Clint's cell phone rang. He was parked on West Sixty-first Street in the car he had stolen. He was given the same instructions by the Pied Piper.

* * *

Franklin Bailey waited on the northwest corner of Ninth Avenue and Fifty-seventh Street. By now he was soaked to the skin and out of breath from pulling the heavy suitcases. Even the certainty that his every step had been tracked by FBI agents did nothing to relieve the stress of the cat-and-mouse game he was playing with the kidnappers. When the cell phone rang again, his hand shook so much that he dropped it. Praying that it was still functioning, he snapped it open and said, "I'm here."

"I can see that. You are now to walk to Fifty-ninth Street and Tenth Avenue. Go into the Duane Reade store on the northwest corner. Purchase a cell phone with prepaid hours and a box of trash bags. I will call you in ten minutes."

He's going to make him get rid of our phone, Agent Sommers thought as he stood in the driveway of the Holiday Inn and listened to the call. If he's able to observe Bailey's every move, he may be in one of those apartment buildings around here. He watched as a taxi pulled up across the street and a couple got out. He knew that a dozen agents were driving cabs with other agents in the backseat. The plan was to drop the supposed passengers off near where Bailey was waiting so that if he were told to hail a cab it would not seem unusual that one became immediately available. But now the Pied Piper was trying to make sure that anyone following Bailey would become obvious.

Four more blocks in this rain, dragging those suitcases, Sommers worried as he watched Bailey turn north, following the Pied Piper's instructions. I just hope he doesn't collapse before he gets to hand over the money.

A car with Taxi and Limousine Commission license plates pulled up at the curb. Sommers raced to get it. "We'll go around Columbus Circle," he said to the agent who was driving, "and park on Tenth around Sixtieth Street."

It took Franklin Bailey ten minutes to reach and enter the Duane Reade store. When he came back out, he was holding a small package in one hand and a phone in the other, but they could no longer hear what the Pied Piper was telling him. As Sommers watched, Bailey got into a car and was driven away.

Inside Duane Reade, Mike Benzara, a Fordham/Lincoln Center student and part-time stock clerk, was walking by a cash register. He stopped when he saw a cell phone lying amidst the gum and candy displayed on the counter. Pretty fancy phone, he thought as he handed it to the cashier. "Too bad it isn't finders, keepers," he joked.

"That's the second one today," the cashier said as she took it from him and dropped it into the drawer below the register. "Dollars to donuts this one belongs to that old guy who was dragging those suitcases. He no sooner paid for the garbage bags and phone he just bought than the phone in his pocket rang. He asked me to give the number of the new one to whoever was calling him. He said his glasses were too blurred for him to read it."

"Maybe he's got a girlfriend and doesn't want his wife to find her number when she's going over the bills."

"No. It was a guy he was talking to. Probably his bookie."

* * *

"There is a sedan outside waiting for you," the Pied Piper had instructed Bailey. "Your name is displayed on the window of the passenger side. You need not be afraid to get in. It is car 142 of the Excel Driving Service. It has been reserved in your name and prepaid. Be sure to take the suitcases from the carrier and have the driver place them in the backseat with you."

Excel driver Angel Rosario pulled up to the corner of Fifty-ninth Street and Tenth Avenue and double-parked. The old guy dragging a luggage cart and trying to look in the windows of the cars parked at the curb had to be his passenger. Angel jumped out. "Mr. Bailey?"

"Yes. Yes."

Angel reached for the handle of the cart. "I'll open the trunk, sir."

"No, I must get something out of the bags. Put them in the back seat."

"They're wet," Angel objected.

"Then put them on the floor," Bailey snapped. "Do it. Do it."

"Okay. Okay. Don't have a heart attack." In his twenty years of driving for Excel, Angel had had his share of kooky passengers, but this old guy was a definite worry. He looked like he was about to have a heart at- tack, and Angel didn't intend to contribute to it by arguing. Besides, there might be a good tip if he was helpful, he reasoned. Even though Bailey's clothes were soaked, Angel could tell they were expensive, and his voice had a classy tone, not like his last passenger, a woman who argued about be- ing billed for waiting time. She had sounded like a buzz saw in action.

Angel opened the rear door of the car, but Bailey wouldn't get in until the suitcases had been unsnapped from the cart and hoisted onto the floor. I ought to put the cart on his lap, Angel thought as he folded it and tossed it into the front passenger seat. He closed the door, ran around to the driver's side, and got in. "The Brooklyn Museum, right, sir?"

"That's what you've been told." It was both a question and an answer.

"Yeah. We're going to pick up your friend and bring him back with you to the Pierre Hotel. I warn you. It's gonna take a long time. There's a lot of traffic, and with the rain, the driving is lousy."

"I understand."

As the car started, Franklin Bailey's new cell phone began to ring. "You have met your driver?" the Pied Piper asked.

"Yes. I'm in the car."

"Begin to transfer the money from the suitcases into two trash bags. Secure the bags with the blue tie you are wearing and the red tie you were instructed to carry. I will call you again shortly."

It was twenty minutes of nine.

29

At nine fifteen, the phone in the cottage rang, a loud, startling jangle that made Angie almost jump out of her skin. She had just opened the bedroom door to look in on the kids. Hastily, she pulled the door closed and ran to answer the phone. She knew it couldn't be Clint—he always called her on her cell phone. She picked up the receiver. "Hello."

"Angie, I'm insulted, ree-al-ly insulted. I thought my old buddy Clint was going to call me about having a beer last night."

Oh, no, Angie thought. It was that stupid dope Gus, and she could tell from the sounds in the background that he was in the Danbury Pub. So much for your knowing how much suds to drink, Angie thought, noting his slurred voice. Still she knew she had to be careful, remembering that one time Gus had shown up uninvited at the door, looking for company.

"Hi, Gus," she said, trying to sound friendly. "Didn't Clint phone you? I told him to. He felt kind of lousy last night and went to bed early."

From inside the bedroom, she heard Kathy begin to cry, a loud, distressed wail, and she realized that in her hurry to answer the phone, she had not closed the bedroom door completely. She tried to cover the mouthpiece with her hand, but it was too late.

"Is that the kid you're minding? I can hear her crying."

"That's the kid I'm minding, and I got to go check on her. Clint went to look at a car some guy is selling in Yonkers. I'll tell him to meet you for a drink tomorrow night for sure."

"You could use a new car. That's some rattletrap you're running around in now."

"Agreed. Gus, you can hear the kid crying. Tomorrow night for sure with Clint, okay?"

Angie began to hang up, but before the

receiver was in its cradle a now-awakened Kelly began to scream, "Mommy, Mommy!"

Would Gus realize that he was hearing two kids, or was he already too drunk to know the difference? Angie wondered with concern. It would be just like him to call back. He wanted to talk to someone, that was for sure. She went into the bedroom. Both twins were standing now, grasping the rails of the crib and hollering for their mother. Well, I can fix one of you, Angie thought as she yanked a sock out of the dresser and began to tie it around Kelly's mouth.

30

Agent Angus Sommers held his cell phone to his ear as, along with Agent Ben Taglione, who was driving, he kept his eyes riveted to the car in front of them, the sedan containing Franklin Bailey. Immediately upon seeing the Excel Driving Service logo, Sommers had contacted the dispatcher at the company. Car 142 had been hired in the name of Bailey and charged to his American Express card. The car's destination was the Brooklyn Museum for a passenger pickup, and from there they were to go to the Pierre Hotel on Sixty-first Street and Fifth Avenue. It's too pat, Sommers thought, a feeling shared by the rest of the kidnap team. Even so, a dozen FBI agents were already on the way to the museum, and several were also staked out at the Pierre.

How did the Pied Piper get Bailey's American Express card number? he wondered. The feeling that the person behind the kidnapping was someone known to the family became more and more certain to Sommers. But that was not his concern now. First they had to get the girls back. Then they could focus on the perpetrators.

Five other vehicles with agents were following Bailey's car. On the West Side Drive the traffic was almost at a standstill. Whoever was planning to meet Bailey and take the money might easily get nervous waiting at the contact point, Sommers worried silently. He knew they all had the same concern. It was vital that the transfer of cash be made before the kidnapper or kidnappers panicked. If that happened, there was no predicting what they might do to the twins.

At what had been the exit from the West Side Highway to the World Trade Center, the cause of the delay became apparent. A fender bender had tied up two lanes. When they finally inched around the battered vehicles, the traffic began to move dramatically faster. Sommers leaned forward, squinting to be sure that the black sedan, one of many dark vehicles that looked alike in the rain, did not get away from them.

Keeping three cars between them and the Excel sedan, they followed it down around the tip of Manhattan and as it turned north on the FDR Drive. The Brooklyn Bridge, its lights dim in the wind-swept rain, became visible. Then at South Street the Excel car made an abrupt left turn and disappeared onto the exit. Agent Taglione muttered an expletive as he tried to shift to the left lane, but it was impossible to do without colliding with the SUV that was parallel to them.

As Sommers clenched his hands into fists, his cell phone rang. "We're still behind them," Agent Buddy Winters told him. "He's heading north again."

It was nine thirty P.M.

31

Dr. Sylvia Harris wrapped her arms around a sobbing Margaret Frawley. Words are not just inadequate at a time like this, she thought. In fact, they are useless. Over Margaret's shoulder, Steve met her gaze. Gaunt and pale, he looked vulnerable and younger than his thirty-one years. She could see that he was fighting to keep his own tears from welling up.

"They've *got* to come back tonight," Margaret whispered, her voice broken. "They're *going* to come back tonight. I *know* they are!"

"We need you, Dr. Sylvia." Steve's voice was choked with emotion. Then, with an obvious effort, he said, "Even if whoever has the girls has treated them decently, we know they're bound to be upset and frightened. And Kathy has a heavy cough."

"Margaret told me that when she called," Sylvia said quietly.

Walter Carlson saw the concern on her face and felt that he could read her mind. If Dr. Harris had already treated Kathy for pneumonia, she had to be thinking that an untreated heavy cough was particularly dangerous for her little patient.

"I made a fire in the study," Steve said. "Let's go in there. The trouble with old houses like this is that the forced air heating makes most of the rooms either too hot or too cool, depending on which way you try to adjust the thermostat."

Carlson knew that Steve was trying to steer Margaret's thoughts away from the escalating apprehension she had begun to exhibit. From the moment she had phoned Dr. Harris and begged her to come, Margaret had voiced her conviction that Kathy was very sick. Standing at the window, she had said, "If, after the money is paid, the kidnappers leave the girls out somewhere in the rain, Kathy might go into pneumonia."

Then Margaret had asked Steve to go to their room and get the journal she had been keeping since the twins were born. "I should have written in it this week," she explained to Carlson, speaking in an almost catatonic tone. "I mean, when we get them back, maybe I'll be so happy and relieved I'll try to blot it all out. I want to write what it's like to be waiting now." Then, almost rambling, she added, "My grandmother had an expression she used to repeat when I was a kid and impatient for my birthday or Christmas to come. The expression was, 'Waiting does not seem long once it is accomplished.' "

When Steve brought her the leather journal, Margaret read aloud a few excerpts. An early one told how, even in their sleep, Kathy and Kelly would open and close their hands at the same time. Another entry she read was about a day last year when Kathy tripped and banged her knee against the dresser in the bedroom. Kelly who was in the kitchen, grabbed her knee at the same moment, for no apparent reason. "Dr. Harris is the one who told me to keep the journal," she explained.

Carlson left them in the study and went back to the dining room where the monitored phone was on the table. Something in his gut told him that the Pied Piper might still decide to make direct contact with the Frawleys.

It was nine forty-five, almost two hours since Franklin Bailey had begun to follow the Pied Piper's orders to initiate the ransom drop.

32

"Bert, in the next two minutes you will receive a call from Franklin Bailey instructing
you to wait for him on Fifty-sixth Street, at
the passageway that runs between Fifty-
sixth and Fifty-seventh Streets just east of
Sixth Avenue," the Pied Piper told Lucas.
"Harry will already be parked there. When I
have confirmed that you are in place, I will
direct Bailey to drop the trash bags with the
money onto the curb in front of Cohen
Fashion Optical on Fifty-seventh Street. He
will place them on top of the trash bags already there waiting for the sanitation department to pick up. They will each be fastened with a necktie. You and Harry will run
up the passageway, grab the bags, run
them back through the passageway, place
them in the trunk of Harry's car, and he will

drive off. He should be gone before the agents are able to connect with him."

"You mean we have to run the length of a block carrying the trash bags? That doesn't make sense," Lucas protested.

"It makes a great deal of sense. Even if the FBI has managed to continue to follow Bailey's car, they will be far enough behind to give you the opportunity to grab the bags, and for Harry to drive away. You will stay there, and when Bailey and the FBI show up, you will truthfully state that you were directed by Mr. Bailey to pick him up where you are waiting. No agents would dare to follow you too closely down the passageway where you might spot them. When they do arrive, you will be their witness and say that you saw two men drop bags into a car parked near you. Then you will provide a partial and misleading description of that car." With that, he broke the phone connection.

It was six minutes of ten.

It had been necessary for Franklin Bailey to tell Angel Rosario why they were constantly changing directions. From his rearview mirror, Rosario had been able to see that cash was being transferred from the

suitcases to the trash bags and had threat-
ened to drive to the nearest police station.
Frantically, Bailey had explained that the
cash was the ransom money for the Frawley
twins and begged for the driver's cooperation. "And you'll be eligible for a reward," he
had added.

"I've got two kids myself," Angel had responded. "I'll drive anywhere that guy tells
us to go."

After veering off the South Street exit,
they had been instructed to drive up First
Avenue, turn west on Fifty-fifth Street, and
find a place to stand as near as possible to
Tenth Avenue. Fifteen minutes passed before the Pied Piper called again. "Mr. Bailey,
we are at the final phase of our association.
You are to phone your personal driver and
instruct him to wait for you on West Fifty-
sixth Street, at the passageway that con-
nects Fifty-seventh to Fifty-sixth. Tell him it
is just a quarter of a block east of Sixth Avenue. Make the phone call. I will be back in
touch."

Ten minutes later the Pied Piper phoned
Bailey again "Have you reached your
driver?"

"Yes. He was in the vicinity. He'll be there momentarily."

"It is a rainy night, Mr. Bailey. I want to be considerate of you. Instruct your driver to proceed to Fifty-seventh, turn right, and drive east, slowing down and keeping near the curb after you cross over Sixth Avenue."

"You're talking too fast," Bailey protested.

"Listen carefully if you want the Frawleys to see their children again. In front of Cohen Fashion Optical, you will see a pile of trash bags waiting to be picked up. Open the door of your sedan, take out the trash bags with the money, and place them on top of the other trash bags, making sure that your neckties are clearly visible. Then immediately get back in the car and instruct your driver to continue driving east. I will call you back."

It was 10:06.

"Bert, this is the Pied Piper. Proceed immediately through the passageway. The trash bags are being dropped now."

Lucas had taken off his chauffeur's cap and pulled on a hooded rain slicker and dark glasses that covered half his face. He leaped out of the car, opened his large umbrella, and followed Clint, who was similarly dressed and also carrying an umbrella, down the corridor. The rain was still so heavy that Lucas was certain that the few other people going back and forth nearby were oblivious to them.

From the protection of the umbrella shielding his face, he saw Franklin Bailey climbing into a car. He held back as Clint grabbed the trash bags with the ties and ran back across the sidewalk to the corridor. Lucas waited until Bailey's car pulled away and he was certain he could not be seen before joining Clint and grabbing one of the bags.

In seconds, they were back on Fifty-sixth Street. Clint pushed the trunk button of the stolen Toyota but it would not open. Swearing under his breath, he yanked at the back door nearest the curb, but it, too, was locked.

Lucas knew they had only seconds to spare. He flipped open the trunk of the limo. "Throw them in there," he snarled as he looked frantically at the corridor, then up and down the street. The people who had passed the corridor as they were running through it were already almost out of sight.

He was back behind the driver's seat, the rain slicker rolled under the front seat, his uniform cap on, when men he was sure must be FBI agents came running through the corridor and from both ends of the block. His nerves racing, but his demeanor calm, Lucas responded to the sharp rap on his window. "Is something wrong?" he asked.

"Did you see a man carrying or dragging trash bags coming out of this passageway not more than a minute ago?" Agent Sommers demanded.

"Yes. They were parked right here." Lucas pointed to the spot Clint had just vacated.

"They? You mean there were two of them?"

"Yes. One was stocky, the other a tall, thin guy. I didn't see their faces."

Sommers had been too far back to see the drop because their car had gotten boxed in at the light on Sixth Avenue. They arrived in time to glimpse the Excel car pulling away from the curb in front of the optical store. Seeing no sign of the suitcases on the piles of trash there, they had continued to follow the car to Fifth Avenue.

Alerted to their mistake by a call from another agent, they parked and ran back. A pedestrian who had stopped to answer his cell phone told them he had seen a stocky man drag two just-abandoned trash bags into the corridor. They'd arrived here to find Bailey's limo and driver waiting for him.

"Describe the car you saw," Sommers ordered Lucas.

"Dark blue or black. Late model, four-door Lexus."

"The two men got in it?"

"Yes, sir."

His hands clammy, Lucas managed to answer questions in the obsequious voice he used when he addressed Franklin Bailey. In the next minutes, still nervous but secretly amused, he watched as the street swarmed with agents. By now they probably have every cop in New York looking for the Lexus, he thought. The car Clint had stolen was an older, black Toyota.

A few more minutes passed, and the Excel car carrying Franklin Bailey pulled up behind him. Bailey, now on the verge of collapse, was helped into the limo. Accompanied by two agents, and followed by others, Lucas drove back to Ridgefield, listening as they queried Bailey on the instructions he had received from the Pied Piper. He was gratified to hear Bailey say, "I had asked Lucas to remain in the vicinity of Columbus Circle. At about ten o'clock, I was instructed to tell Lucas to wait for me at that spot on Fifty-sixth Street. My final order as we drove east after throwing out the trash bags was to meet him at that place. The Pied Piper said he didn't want me to get wet."

At quarter past twelve, Lucas pulled up in front of Bailey's home. One agent assisted Bailey inside. The other waited to thank Lucas and to tell him that he had been very helpful. With the ransom money still in the trunk, Lucas drove to his garage, switched the money from the limo to his old car, and drove to the cottage where a jubilant Clint and a strangely quiet Angie were waiting for him.

33

The ransom drop had been completed, but the agents had lost the people who picked up the money. Now they could only wait. Steve and Margaret and Dr. Harris sat quietly, silently praying that the phone would ring, that someone, maybe another neighbor, would say, "I just had a phone call telling me where the twins are." But there was only silence.

Where would they leave them? Margaret agonized. Maybe they'll find an empty house and put them in it. They couldn't walk into a public place like a bus station or a train station without being noticed. Everyone looks at the twins when I'm out with them. My two little girls in blue. That's what the papers call them.

The blue velvet dresses . . .

Suppose we don't hear from the kidnappers? They have the money. Suppose they got away.

Waiting does not seem long once it has been accomplished.

The blue velvet dresses . . .

34

"The king was in the counting house, counting up his money," Clint chortled. "I can't believe you drove the money home with the FBI guys in the car."

The piles of bills were on the floor of the living room in the cottage, mostly fifties, the remainder in twenties. As directed, the bills were not new. A hasty, random check showed that they were not in sequence.

"Believe it," Lucas snapped. "Start throwing your half in one of the bags. I'll take mine in the other one." Even though he was sitting here with the money in front of him, Lucas was still certain that something would go wrong. That airhead, Clint, had been too dumb to test the trunk of the car he'd stolen to make sure he could open it. If I hadn't been there with the limo, he'd have been caught redhanded, Lucas thought. Now they were waiting for a call from the Pied Piper to tell them where to drop the kids.

Wherever it was, it would be just like Angie to want to stop and buy them an ice cream. He took some comfort in knowing that they couldn't find a Dairy Queen open in the middle of the night. Lucas felt as though his guts were twisted into knots. *Why hadn't the Pied Piper called?*

At 3:05 A.M., the sharp crack of the cottage phone made them all jump. Angie scrambled up from the floor and ran to answer it, muttering, "It better not be that creepy Gus."

It was the Pied Piper. "Put Bert on," he ordered.

"It's him," Angie gasped nervously.

Lucas got up, taking his time to cross the room and take the receiver from her. "I was wondering when you'd get around to us," he snarled.

"You don't sound like a man who's staring at a million dollars. Listen to me carefully. You are to drive in the borrowed car to the parking lot of La Cantina, a restaurant on the northbound Saw Mill River Parkway in

Elmsford. The restaurant is near the entrance to the Great Hunger Memorial in V. E. Macy Park. It has been closed for many years."

"I know where it is."

"Then you must also know that the parking lot is behind the building, and out of sight of the parkway. Harry and Mona are to follow you in Harry's van, bringing the twins. They must transfer their charges to the borrowed car and lock them in it. The three of you will return to the cottage in the van. I will call by five A.M. to confirm that you have followed instructions. I will then take the final step. After that, none of you will hear from me again."

At three fifteen they began the trip. From behind the wheel of the stolen car, Lucas watched as Angie and Clint carried out the sleeping twins. If they get a flat tire in that old rattletrap; if we come across a road check; if some drunk slams into one of us . . . The range of possibilities for disaster leaped into his head as he started the engine, then noted with alarm that there was less than a quarter of a tank of gas in the car.

It's enough, he tried to reassure himself.

The rain was still falling but not with the same force as it had been earlier. Lucas tried to take that as a good sign. As he drove through Danbury heading west, he made himself think about La Cantina Restaurant. Years ago he had stopped there for dinner after having completed a spectacularly successful heist in Larchmont. The family had been outside at the pool, and he'd slipped in through the unlocked side door, then went straight up to the master bedroom. Talk about luck! The wife of the hotel big shot had left the door to the safe open—not just unlocked, but *open!* After I fenced the jewelry, I spent three weeks in Vegas, Lucas thought. Lost most of it, but had a good time.

With *this* half million, he was going to be more careful. No gambling it away. My luck is bound to run out, he thought. And I don't want to spend the rest of my life in a prison cell. That was another worry. He wouldn't put it past Angie to call attention to herself by going on another shopping spree.

He was turning onto the Saw Mill River Parkway. Another ten minutes and he'd be there. There was not much traffic on the road. His blood froze as he spotted a state

trooper's car. He glanced at the speedometer—he was going sixty in a fifty-five mile
zone. That was okay. He was in the right
hand lane, not darting back and forth. Clint
was far enough behind that no one would
even think he was following him.

The state trooper turned off at the next
exit. So far, so good, he thought. Lucas wet
his lips with the tip of his tongue. Less than
five minutes, he thought. Four minutes.
Three minutes. Two minutes.

The aging structure that had been La
Cantina Restaurant was coming up on the
right. There was no car in sight on either
side of the Saw Mill. With a quick flip of the
switch on the panel, Lucas turned off the
headlights, turned right onto the road that
passed the restaurant, and drove to the
parking lot behind it. There he turned off the
ignition and sat and waited until the sound
of an approaching car told him that the final
phase of the plan was about to be completed.

35

"It takes a long time to count one million dollars by hand," Walter Carlson said, hoping that he sounded reassuring.

"The money was transferred at a little after ten," Steve replied. "That was five hours ago." He glanced down, but Margaret did not open her eyes.

She was curled on the couch, her head in his lap. Occasionally, her even breathing told him that she had dozed off, but almost immediately afterward, there would be a quick gasp and her eyes would fly open.

Dr. Harris was sitting erect in the wing chair, her hands clasped in her lap. There was no sign of fatigue in either her posture or expression. It had occurred to Carlson that this must be the way she looked when she was sitting with a desperately sick patient. A calm and calming presence, he thought. Just what was needed.

Despite trying to sound encouraging, he knew that every passing minute suggested that they would not hear from the kidnappers. The Pied Piper told me that sometime after midnight we'd get a call about where to pick up the twins. Steve's right. They've had the money for hours. For all we know the twins are already dead.

Franklin Bailey heard their voices on Tuesday, he thought. That means we know that a day and a half ago the girls were alive, because they talked about seeing their parents on television. That is, if we believe Bailey's story.

As the hours wore on, a hunch had been taking shape in Carlson's mind, the kind of gut-level hunch that had served him well throughout his twenty years with the Bureau. The hunch was to check out Lucas Wohl, the ubiquitous chauffeur who so conveniently happened to be parked exactly where he could observe the kidnappers carrying the money, and then could give a description of the car they were supposedly driving.

Carlson conceded that maybe it was exactly as Bailey had claimed, that while he was being driven around in the Excel car, he had received instructions from the Pied Piper about where Lucas should meet him and that he had relayed those instructions to Lucas. But the now persistent thought that kept biting at him was that perhaps Bailey had made fools of them.

Angus Sommers, the FBI agent in charge of the New York group, had driven up with Bailey and was convinced he and the chauffeur were on the level. Even so, Carlson decided, he was going to put in a call to Connor Ryan, Special Agent in Charge in New Haven, and Carlson's immediate boss. Ryan was in his office now with his guys, ready to jump if the word came that the twins had been left in the northern part of Connecticut. He could start doing a rundown on Lucas immediately.

Margaret was slowly pulling herself up. She brushed back her hair with a gesture so weary that Carlson thought the effort to raise her arm was almost too much for her to make. "When you spoke to the Pied Piper, didn't he say that he would call around midnight?" she asked.

There was no answer to give her except the truth: "Yes, he did."

36

Clint knew they were nearing La Cantina Restaurant and was worried about over-shooting it. With narrowed eyes, he anxiously scanned the right side of the parkway. He had spotted the state trooper patrol car and dropped back to make sure the cop didn't get the idea he was following Lucas. Now Lucas was out of sight.

Angie was sitting beside him, rocking the sick kid in her arms. Since the minute they set foot in the van, she'd been singing the same "Two Little Girls in Blue" song over and over and over again. *" 'But . . . we . . . have . . . drifted . . . apart,' "* she crooned now, drawing out the last line.

Was that Lucas's car up ahead? Clint wondered. No it wasn't.

" *'Two little girls in blue, lad'* " Angie began again.

"Angie, I wish you'd quit that damn
singing," Clint snapped.

"Kathy likes me to sing to her," Angie re-
torted, her voice steely.

Clint glanced nervously at her. There was
something strange about Angie tonight. She
was in one of her crazy moods. When
they'd gone into the bedroom to get the
kids, he had seen that one of them was
sleeping with a sock tied around her mouth.
When he started to take it off, Angie had
grabbed his hand. "I don't need her hollering in the van." Then Angie insisted that he
put that kid on the floor of the backseat and
cover her with an open newspaper.

His protest that she might suffocate had
set Angie off. "She's not going to suffocate,
and if by any chance we hit some kind of
roadblock, we don't need to have the cops
looking at identical twins."

The other kid, the one Angie was holding,
was kind of restless and whimpering. It was
a good thing that she'd be back with the
parents soon. You didn't have to be a doctor to see that she was pretty sick.

That building had to be the restaurant,

Clint decided as he peered ahead. He edged the car into the right lane. He could feel perspiration begin to drip from all over his body. It was always like this at a crisis point in a job. He drove past the restaurant and turned right into the driveway beside it, then made another right into the parking lot behind. He could see that Lucas had stopped close to the building, so he pulled up directly behind him.

" 'They were sisters . . . ' " Angie sang, her voice suddenly louder.

In her arms, Kathy stirred and began to cry. From the floor of the backseat, Kelly's muffled whimper echoed her sister's tired protest at being awakened.

"Shut up!" Clint pleaded. "If Lucas opens the door and hears you making noise, there's no telling what he'll do to you."

Abruptly, she stopped singing. "I'm not afraid of him. Here, hold her." With a swift movement she thrust Kathy into his arms, opened the door, ran up to the driver's door of the stolen car, and rapped on the window.

As Clint watched, Lucas rolled down the window, and Angie leaned inside the car. An instant later, a loud bang that could only be caused by a gunshot echoed through the deserted parking lot.

Angie ran back to the van, opened the back door, and grabbed Kelly.

Still too numb to move or speak, Clint saw her deposit Kelly in the backseat of the stolen car and get in the front seat on the passenger side. When she came back she was holding both of Lucas's cell phones and a ring of keys. "When the Pied Piper calls, we have to be able to answer," she told him, her voice warm and bubbly.

"You killed Lucas!" Clint said numbly, his arms still around Kathy, whose crying had again dissolved into a coughing fit.

Angie took Kathy from him. "He left a note. It's typed on the same typewriter as the ransom note. It says that he didn't mean to kill Kathy. She was crying so much he put his hand over her mouth and when he realized she was dead he put her in a box and flew out over the ocean and dumped it. Wasn't that a good idea? I had to make it look like he committed suicide. Now we have the whole million dollars, and *I* have my baby. Come on. Let's get out of here."

Suddenly panicking, Clint turned on the engine and floored the gas.

"Slow up, you stupid jerk," Angie snapped, the bubbly tone vanishing from her tone. "Just drive your family home, nice and easy."

As he turned back onto the highway, Angie began to sing again, this time sotto voce: " *'They were sisters . . . but they have drifted apart.'* "

37

The lights had been burning all night in the executive offices of the C.F.G.&Y. building on Park Avenue. Some of the members of the board of directors had kept the vigil, wanting to be part of the triumphant return of the Frawley twins to the arms of their parents.

Everyone was keenly aware that the Pied Piper had promised that once the cash ransom had been successfully paid, he would make contact around midnight. As the hours after midnight wore on, the anticipation of generous press coverage and a huge public relations boost for the firm changed to worry and doubt.

Robinson Geisler knew that a number of newspapers had editorialized that paying a ransom was playing into the hands of kidnappers, thus making everyone vulnerable to becoming victims of copycat criminals.

Ransom, the Glenn Ford film in which the father sits in a television studio at a table piled with stacks of bills and warns the kidnappers that he will not pay the ransom, but instead will use that money to track them down, was being played on a number of TV channels. The happy ending in that movie was that the child was released unharmed. Would there be a happy ending to *this* story?

At five A.M. Geisler went into his private bathroom, showered and shaved, and changed his clothes. He remembered that the late Bennett Cerf, whom he had enjoyed watching on television, always looked as if he had stepped out of a bandbox. Cerf often wore a bow tie. Would it be too much to wear a bow tie when they film me with the twins? he wondered.

Of course it would. But a red tie always suggested optimism, even victory. He chose one from his closet.

He went back to his desk and rehearsed aloud the victory speech he would give to the media. "Paying the ransom may seem to some to be cooperating with criminals.

Talk to any FBI agent and they will tell you that their first concern is always to get the victims back. Only then can they relentlessly pursue the criminals. The example these criminals will set is not that they received ransom money, but that they never got a chance to spend it."

Let Gregg Stanford top *that,* he thought with a thin smile.

38

"The first thing we've gotta do is get rid of his car," Angie said matter-of-factly as they drove into Danbury. "First we get his share of the money out of the trunk of his car, then you drive it back and park it in front of his apartment. I'll be right behind you."

"We're not going to get away with this, Angie. You can't hide the kid forever."

"Yes, I can."

"Somebody might connect Lucas to us. Once they take his fingerprints, they'll figure out that the real Lucas Wohl's been dead for twenty years, and this guy's real name was Jimmy Nelson, and he was in prison. And I was his cell mate."

"So your real name isn't Clint Downes. But who else knows that? The only time you and Lucas were together was when you met for a job. The only times he came to the house were these past few weeks at night."

"He came yesterday afternoon when he picked up all that stuff."

"Even if somebody saw his car turn into the service road of the club, do you think they thought, 'Hey, there goes Lucas in his old brown Ford that looks like every other old brown Ford on the road'? It might be different if he came over in the limo. We know he never called you on the special phone, and now I've got it."

"I *still* think . . ."

"I still think we've got a million bucks, and I've got the baby I want, and that creep who always treated us like dirt is out of the way with his head on the steering wheel, so shut up."

At five after five, the special phone the Pied Piper had given Lucas began to ring. They had just pulled into the driveway at the cottage. Clint looked at the phone. "What are you going to tell him?"

"We're not going to answer," Angie said with a smirk. "Let him think we're still on the highway and maybe talking to a cop." She tossed him a set of keys. "These are his. Let's get rid of his car."

At five twenty, Clint parked Lucas's car in front of the hardware store. On the second floor a faint glow showed through the shaded window. Lucas had left a light on for himself.

Clint got out of the car and scrambled back to the van. His cherubic face dripping with perspiration, he got behind the wheel. The cell phone the Pied Piper had given to Lucas was ringing again. "He must be scared stiff," Angie chortled. "Okay, let's go home. My baby is waking up again."

"Mommy, Mommy . . ." Kathy was stirring and reaching out her hand.

"She's trying to touch her twin," Angie said. "Isn't that cute?" She tried to entwine her own fingers with Kathy's, but Kathy pulled away. "Kelly, I want my Kelly," she said, her voice hoarse but distinct. "I don't want Mona. I want Kelly."

As he turned on the ignition key, Clint looked nervously at Angie. She didn't like rejection, in fact, couldn't tolerate it. He knew she'd be sick of the kid before the week was up. What then? he wondered. She was off the deep end now. He had seen her vicious streak before. He had seen it again tonight. I've got to get out of here, he

thought, out of this town, out of Connecticut.

The street was quiet. Trying not to show
how panicked he was becoming, he drove
with the headlights off until they reached
Route 7. It wasn't until they had gone
through the service gate of the country club
that he was able to draw a deep breath.

"After you drop me off, put the van in the
garage," Angie told him. "Just in case that
drunk, Gus, gets a notion to drive by in the
morning, it makes it look like you're not
here."

"He never just drops over," Clint said,
knowing it was useless to protest.

"He called last night, didn't he? He's dying to get together with his old buddy."
Angie did not add that even though he had
been drunk when he called, Gus might have
heard both girls crying.

Kathy was crying again: "Kelly . . .
Kelly . . ." Clint stopped at the front door of
the cottage and hurried to open it. Kathy
in her arms, Angie went inside, walked
straight to the bedroom, and dropped the
little girl in the crib. "Get over it, baby doll,"
she said, as she turned and walked back
to the living room.

Clint was still standing at the front door. "I told you to put the van away," she ordered.

Before Clint could obey, the special phone rang. This time Angie picked it up. "Hello, Mr. Pied Piper," she said then listened. "We know Lucas hasn't been answering his cell phone. There was an accident on the parkway and it was teeming with cops. There's such a thing as a law against talking on a cell phone when you're driving, you know. Everything went fine. Lucas had a hunch that the feds might decide to talk with him again and he didn't want to be carrying this around. Yeah. Yeah. Everything went real smooth. Tell somebody where to pick up the Two Little Girls in Blue. I hope we never talk to you again. Good luck to you."

39

At five forty-five on Thursday morning the answering service for St. Mary's Catholic Church in Ridgefield received a phone call. "I'm desperate. I need to talk to a priest," a husky voice said.

Rita Schless, the telephone operator who took the call, was sure that whoever it was was trying to disguise his voice. Not *that* nonsense again, she thought. Last year some smart-aleck high school senior had phoned and begged to speak to a priest, claiming a terrible emergency was taking place in his home. She had awakened Monsignor Romney at four in the morning, and when he got on the phone, the kid, to the accompaniment of background laughter, had said, "We're dying, Father. We've run out of beer."

This call was not on the level either, Rita decided. "Are you injured or sick?" she asked crisply.

"Put me through to a priest immediately. This is a matter of life and death."

"Hold on, sir," Rita said. I don't believe him for one minute, she thought, but I can't take a chance. Reluctantly she rang seventy-five-year-old Monsignor Romney, who had told her to direct all middle-of-the night calls to him. "I'm an insomniac, Rita," he had explained. "Try me first."

"I don't think this guy's on the level," Rita explained now. "I swear he's trying to disguise his voice."

"We'll find out soon enough," The Reverend Monsignor Joseph Romney said wryly, as he sat up and swung his legs over the bed. Unconsciously he rubbed the right knee that always ached when he changed position. As he reached for his glasses, he heard the click of the call being transferred. "Monsignor Romney," he said. "How can I help you?"

"Monsignor, you heard about the twins who were kidnapped?"

"Yes, of course. The Frawleys are new members of our parish. We've been offering a daily Mass for their safe return." Rita is right, he acknowledged. Whoever this is, he's trying to disguise his voice.

"Kathy and Kelly are safe. They can be found in a locked car behind the old La Cantina Restaurant on the north side of the Saw Mill River Parkway near Elmsford."

Joseph Romney felt his heart begin to pound. "Is this a joke?" he demanded.

"It is not a joke, Monsignor Romney. I am the Pied Piper. The ransom has been paid, and I have chosen you to bring a message of joy to the Frawleys. The north side of the Saw Mill, behind the old La Cantina Restaurant near Elmsford. Have you got that straight?"

"Yes. Yes."

"Then I suggest you hurry to notify the authorities. It is an inclement night. The girls have been there for several hours, and Kathy has a heavy cold."

40

At dawn, unable any longer to watch the deepening misery on the faces of Margaret and Steve Frawley, Walter Carlson sat at the dining room table beside the phone. When it rang at five minutes of six, he steeled himself for bad news as he grabbed the receiver.

It was Marty Martinson calling from the police station. "Walt, Monsignor Romney of St. Mary's got a call from someone claiming to be the Pied Piper. He told the Monsignor that the twins are in a locked car behind an old restaurant on the Saw Mill River Parkway. We called the State Police. They'll be there in less than five minutes."

Carlson heard the sound of the Frawleys and Dr. Harris as they rushed into the dining room. Obviously they had heard the phone ring. He turned and looked up at them. The look of hope on their faces was almost as upsetting to see as the earlier misery. "Hold on, Marty," he told Captain Martinson. There was nothing he could offer the parents and Dr. Harris other than the simple truth. "We will know in a few minutes if a call Monsignor Romney received at the rectory is a hoax," he told them quietly.

"Was it from the Pied Piper?" Margaret gasped.

"Did he say where they are?" Steve demanded.

Carlson did not answer. "Marty," he said, speaking into the phone, "are the state troopers getting back to you?"

"Yes. I'll call you as soon as I hear from them."

"If it's for real, our guys need to do the forensics on the car."

"The troopers know that," Martinson said. "They're calling your Westchester office."

Carlson hung up the phone.

"Tell us what's going on," Steve insisted. "We have a right to know."

"We will ascertain in a few minutes whether or not the call Monsignor Romney received is real. If it is, the twins have been

left, unharmed, in a locked car just off the
Saw Mill River Parkway near Elmsford,"
Carlson told them. "The state troopers are
on the way there now."

"The Pied Piper kept his word," Margaret
cried. "My babies are coming home. My
babies are coming home!" She threw her
arms around Steve. "Steve, they're coming
home!"

"Margaret, it may be a hoax," Dr. Harris
cautioned, as her exterior calm broke, and
she began to clasp and unclasp her hands.

"God wouldn't do that to us," Margaret
said emphatically, as Steve, unable to
speak, buried his face in her hair.

When fifteen minutes went by without another call, Carlson was sure something was
terribly wrong. If it had been some nut
phoning, we'd have been told by now, he
thought. Then, when the doorbell rang, he
knew it had to be bad news. Even if the
twins were safe, it would have taken at least
forty minutes to drive them home from
Elmsford.

He was sure that the same thought was in
the minds of Steve and Margaret and the
doctor as they followed him to the foyer.
Carlson opened the door. Monsignor Rom-

ney and Marty Martinson were standing on the porch.

The priest went to Margaret and Steve and, in a voice trembling with compassion, said, "God has sent you back one of your little girls. Kelly is safe. Kathy has been taken to Him."

41

The news that one of the twins was dead triggered an avalanche of national sympathy. The few pictures the media were able to get of Kelly as her distraught parents carried her from the hospital in Elmsford where she had been taken to be examined were distinct enough to show the difference from the way she had appeared in her birthday picture of only a week ago. Her eyes were wide and frightened now, and there seemed to be a bruise on her face. In all the pictures, her one arm was around her mother's neck, while the other was stretched out, the fingers moving as though to grasp another hand.

The state trooper who was first to arrive at La Cantina Restaurant described the scene: "The car was locked. I could see the man slumped over the wheel. There was only one little girl there. She was curled up on the floor of the backseat. The car was cold. She was wearing only pajamas, and she was shivering. Then I saw that she had a gag on. It was so tight, it's a wonder she didn't choke. When I untied it, she started whimpering like a hurt puppy. I took my coat off and wrapped it around her, then carried her back to the squad car to warm her up. Right after that the other troopers and the FBI arrived, and found the suicide note on the front seat."

The Frawleys had declined to be interviewed. Their statement was read to the press by Monsignor Romney: "Margaret and Steve wish to express their undying gratitude for all the messages of compassion they have received. At this time they need privacy to comfort Kelly, who misses her twin, and to deal with their own grief in the loss of Kathy."

Walter Carlson went on camera with a different message. "The man known as Lucas Wohl is dead, but his associate or associates are alive. We will hunt them down, and we will find them. They will be brought to justice."

At C.F.G.&Y, Robinson Geisler did not get to deliver the triumphant message he had hoped to give. Instead, his voice halting, he expressed his tremendous sorrow at the loss of one of the twins, but said that he believed that the cooperation of his firm in paying the ransom had led to the safe return of the other one.

In a separate interview, board member Gregg Stanford broke ranks with his chairman and chief executive officer. "You may have heard that the vote to pay the ransom was unanimous," he said. "But it was a decision fiercely fought by a minority faction which I spearheaded. There is a crude but also accurate saying, 'If you lie down with dogs, you get up with fleas.' I firmly believe that if the ransom demand had been rejected out of hand, the kidnappers would have had a tough decision to make. If they harmed the children, they would only add to their terrible culpability. The death sentence in Connecticut is still on the books. On the other hand, if they released Kathy and Kelly, even if they were eventually caught, they could expect leniency. At C.F.G.&Y., we made a decision that I believe was wrong in every aspect, morally and logically. Now, as a member of the board of directors, I want to assure anyone who might believe that our firm will ever deal with criminals again—listen very carefully: *It is not going to happen.*"

42

"Mr. Pied Piper, Lucas is dead. Maybe he killed himself. Maybe he didn't. What difference is it to you? In fact, you should be grateful. He knew who you are. We don't. Just for the record, he was taping you on his phone. He had the cassettes in the glove compartment of his Ford. He probably was going to put the arm on you for more money."

"Is the other twin dead?"

"She is not dead. She's only sleeping," Angie said. "As a matter of fact, I'm holding her right now. Don't call again. You'll wake her up." She put down the phone and kissed Kathy's cheek. "Wouldn't you think that seven million dollars would satisfy him?" she asked Clint.

It was eleven o'clock. Clint was watching

television. Every station was carrying stories about the end of the Frawley kidnapping. One child, Kelly, had been found alive, a tight gag around her mouth. It was believed that the other twin, Kathy, had probably been unable to breathe if she was gagged in the same manner. It had been confirmed that Lucas Wohl had flown his plane out of Danbury Airport on Wednesday afternoon, carrying a heavy box, and had returned shortly after without the box. "That box is believed to have held the body of little Kathy Frawley," the announcer speculated. "According to the suicide note, Lucas Wohl buried Kathy at sea."

"What are we going to do with her?" Clint asked. The exhaustion of the sleepless night and the shock of watching Angie shoot Lucas was taking its toll. His heavy body was slumped in the chair. His eyes, always sunken in his full face, were now red-rimmed slits.

"We're going to take her to Florida and buy a boat and sail through the Caribbean on it, that's what we're going to do. But for now, I've got to go to the drugstore. I shouldn't have put the vaporizer in that box

I gave Lucas. I'll have to buy another one. She's having trouble breathing again."

"Angie, she's sick. She needs medicine, she needs to see a doctor. If she dies on us, and we get caught. . . ."

"She's not going to die, and stop worrying that anyone will connect us with Lucas," Angie interrupted. "We did everything right. Now, while I'm gone, I want you to take Kathy into the bathroom and let the shower run till it gets all steamed up. I'll be back soon. You kept some of the money out, like I told you, I hope?"

Clint had pulled down the ladder in the bedroom closet that led to the attic and dragged the bags of money up there. He had taken five hundred dollars in used twenty-dollar bills for ready cash. "Angie, if you start paying with a wad of twenty- or fifty-dollar bills, somebody will start asking questions."

"Every ATM machine in the country dishes out nothing but twenty-dollar bills." Angie spat out the words. "It's unusual to carry anything else." She thrust the drowsy Kathy at Clint. "Do as I tell you. Turn on that shower and keep the blanket around her. If the phone rings, don't answer it! I told your drinking buddy Gus that you'd meet him at the bar tonight. You can call him later, but I don't want him to get curious about what baby I'm minding."

Angie's eyes were glittering with anger, and Clint knew better than to try to reason with her. This kid's face has been on the front page of every newspaper in the country, he thought. She no more looks like me or Angie than I look like Elvis Presley. The minute we're with her anywhere in public, somebody will spot us. By now the cops must have figured out that Lucas is really Jimmy Nelson and that he did a stretch in Attica. Next they'll start asking questions about who might have been his pal there. And they'll come up with the name Ralphie Hudson, and sooner or later they'll trace him to this door, and after that nobody will call me Clint anymore.

I was crazy to take Angie back after she did that stretch in the psycho hospital, he thought as he carried Kathy to the bathroom and turned on the shower. She had almost killed the mother who tried to pick up the baby Angie was minding. I should have known better than to get her involved with kids again.

He put the lid of the toilet seat down and sat on it. With clumsy fingers he opened the top button of the polo shirt Kathy was still wearing. He turned her body so that she would breathe in the steam that was rapidly filling the small bathroom.

The kid was starting to babble. Nothing she was saying was making sense. Was that the twin talk stuff Angie had been talking about? he wondered. "I'm the only one listening, kid," he told her. "So if you have anything to say, say it straight."

43

Dr. Sylvia Harris knew that confronting the awful grief of losing Kathy was to some extent being postponed by Margaret and Steve. For now, their attention was riveted on Kelly. She had not spoken a single word since they had been reunited with her in the Elmsford hospital. The physical examination showed that she had not been molested, but the tight gag on her mouth had left bruises on the side of her face. The black and blue marks on her arms and legs suggested that she had been pinched viciously.

When she saw her parents come into the hospital room, Kelly stared at them and turned away. "She's angry at you now," Dr. Harris explained gently. "By tomorrow, she won't let you out of her sight."

They got back home at eleven o'clock,

rushing into the house as photographers scrambled to get pictures of Kelly. Margaret carried Kelly upstairs to the twins' bedroom and changed her into her Cinderella pajamas, while she tried not to think of the matching pair still neatly folded in the drawer. Troubled by Kelly's absolute lack of reaction, Dr. Harris gave her a mild sedative. "She needs to sleep," she whispered to Steve and Margaret.

Steve laid her in bed, put her teddy bear on her chest, and placed the other one on the empty pillow next to her. Kelly's eyes flew open. In a spontaneous gesture, she reached out, grabbed Kathy's teddy bear, and silently rocking back and forth, began to hug both of them. Only then, sitting on either side of her bed, did Steve and Margaret begin to weep, silent tears that broke Sylvia's heart.

She went downstairs to find that Agent Carlson was preparing to leave. Seeing how drawn and weary he looked, she said, "I hope you're going to get some rest now."

"Yes. I'm going to go home and crash for about eight hours. Otherwise, I won't be any use to anyone. But then I'm going to be back on this case, and I promise you, Doctor, that I'm not going to rest until the Pied Piper and whoever else was working with him are behind bars."

"May I make an observation?"

"Of course."

"Besides the potential danger of the gag, the only physical injury Kelly suffered were bruises that were probably caused by being pinched. As you can understand, in my volunteer work, I sometimes see abused children. Pinching is a woman's trick, not a man's."

"I would agree with you. We know from an eyewitness that two men grabbed the trash bags with the ransom money. It would make sense that a woman was involved in taking care of the twins while the men were picking up the cash."

"Was Lucas Wohl the Pied Piper?"

"Somehow I doubt it, but that's only a gut feeling." Carlson did not add that, pending the autopsy report, there was still a serious question about the angle of the bullet that had killed Lucas. Most people who kill themselves do not hold the gun up in the air and point the barrel down. They hold it directly to their forehead or against their skull, or put the muzzle in their mouths and then they pull the trigger. "Dr. Harris, how long will you be staying here?"

"For at least a few days. I was supposed to give a talk in Rhode Island this weekend, but I've cancelled it. After the kidnapping, the harsh treatment she received, and now the loss of her twin, Kelly is very fragile emotionally. I think I can help by being around for her as well as for Steve and Margaret."

"What about the Frawleys' families?"

"Margaret's mother and aunt are coming up next week, I believe. Margaret asked them to wait. Her mother is crying so much that she can hardly speak. Steve's mother cannot travel and his father can't leave her. Frankly, I think it's better that they are alone as much as possible with Kelly. She is going to be grieving intensely for her sister."

Carlson nodded. "The ironic part is that I believe Lucas didn't mean to kill her. There was a faint smell of Vick's on Kelly's pajamas. She isn't sick, so it probably means that whoever was taking care of the girls was trying to treat Kathy's cold. But you can't put a gag on a child whose nostrils are clogged and expect her to breathe. Of course, we checked immediately. Lucas

Wohl did go out on a plane Wednesday afternoon. He was carrying a heavy box when he took off and returned without it."

"Have you ever had a case like that before?"

Carlson picked up his briefcase. "One. The kidnapper had buried the girl alive, but there was enough air for her to last until we got him to tell us where he put her. The problem was that she hyperventilated and died. He's been rotting in prison for twenty years and will stay there until they carry him out to a cemetery, but that doesn't help the family of that girl." He shook his head in weary frustration. "Doctor, from what I understand, Kelly is a very bright three-year-old."

"Yes, she is."

"At some point we're going to want to talk to her or have a child psychiatrist question her. But for now, if she starts to speak, will you jot down anything she says that might possibly relate to her experiences?"

"Of course." The genuine grief on the agent's face moved Sylvia Harris to say, "I know Margaret and Steve believe you and your fellow agents did everything you could to save the girls."

"We did the best we could, but it wasn't good enough."

They both turned as they heard footsteps hurrying down the stairs. It was Steve. "Kelly began to talk in her sleep," he told them. "She said two names, 'Mona' and 'Harry.' "

"Do you or Margaret know anyone named either 'Mona' or 'Harry'?" Carlson demanded, his exhaustion forgotten.

"No. Definitely not. Do you think she was referring to the kidnappers?"

"Yes, I do. Is that all Kelly said?"

Steve's eyes welled with tears. "She's lapsed into twin talk. She's trying to talk to Kathy."

44

The elaborate plan to follow Franklin Bailey's limousine at a safe distance had not worked. Even though a host of agents had been scattered through the city to follow whatever vehicle the kidnapper used after the ransom drop, they had been outwitted. Angus Sommers, in charge of the New York City phase of the operation, realized now that while he had been riding in the limo back to Connecticut with Franklin Bailey, the ransom money may well have been only a few feet away from him in the trunk.

Lucas Wohl was the guy who told us that two men had driven away in a new Lexus, he thought grimly. They knew now that only one man either drove away or took off on foot. Lucas was the second man. Recent dirt and water stains on the floor of the otherwise immaculately clean trunk of the limo suggested that several wet and soiled objects had been in it. Objects like trash bags filled with money, Angus thought bitterly.

Was Lucas the Pied Piper? Angus didn't think so. If he had been, he would already have known that Kathy was dead. According to the suicide note, Lucas had flown her body over the ocean and tossed it from the plane. If he had intended to commit suicide, why would he have bothered to pick up the ransom money? It didn't make sense.

Was it possible that the Pied Piper, whoever he was, was unaware that Kathy was dead when he phoned Monsignor Romney and told him where the children could be found? According to the Monsignor, the Pied Piper had told him that he could deliver the joyful news to the parents that the girls were unharmed. Was that a macabre joke on the part of a sadistic mind, or was it possible that he had not been told of Kathy's death?

And had the Pied Piper really been giving directions to Franklin Bailey as Bailey claimed? These were the issues Sommers debated with Tony Realto as they drove to Bailey's home late Thursday afternoon.

Realto was having none of it. "Bailey is from an old Connecticut family. He's one of the people involved in this whole thing who I'd say is above reproach."

"Maybe," Sommers said as he rang Bailey's doorbell. Bailey's housekeeper, Sophie, a stocky woman of about sixty, examined their badges and admitted them with a worried frown. "Was Mr. Bailey expecting you?" she asked hesitantly.

"No," Realto said. "But we need to see him."

"I don't know if he's up to meeting you, sir. After he learned that Lucas Wohl had been connected with the kidnapping and had killed himself, he had terrible chest pains again. I begged him to go to the doctor, but he took a sedative and went to bed. I only heard him moving around a few minutes ago."

"We'll wait," Realto said firmly. "Tell Mr. Bailey that we absolutely must speak to him."

When Bailey came down to the library nearly twenty minutes later, Angus Sommers was shocked to see the marked change in his appearance. Last night he had seemed to be on the brink of exhaustion.

Now, his face was paper white, his eyes glazed.

Sophie was following him with a cup of tea. He sat down and took the cup from her, his hands visibly trembling. Only then did he address Sommers and Realto. "I simply cannot believe that Lucas was involved in this terrible affair," he began.

"Believe it, Mr. Bailey," Realto said crisply. "Naturally, that makes us re-examine the facts of the case. You told us that you injected yourself into the Frawley kidnapping, offering to act as a go-between with the Frawleys and the kidnappers, because you had formed a slight friendship with Margaret Frawley."

Franklin Bailey sat straighter in the chair and put aside the cup of tea. "Agent Realto, to use the word 'inject' in this case would suggest that I forced myself in, or was acting inappropriately. Neither is the case."

Realto looked at him without answering.

"As I told Mr. Carlson, the first time I met Margaret she was on line at the post office. I noticed one of the twins, Kelly, making a beeline for the door while Margaret was speaking to the clerk. I stopped the little girl before she darted into traffic and brought her to Margaret, who was very grateful. She and Steve attend the ten o'clock Mass at St. Mary's, where I am a parishioner. That following Sunday she introduced me to Steve. Since then we have chatted several times after Mass. I knew that they did not have any family nearby. I was mayor of this town for twenty years, and am well known in the community. Oddly, I recently reread a history of the Lindbergh kidnapping, and it was fresh in my mind that a professor from Fordham University offered his services as a go-between in that case, and he was the one finally contacted by the kidnapper."

Realto's cell phone rang. He opened it, glanced at the number calling him, and stepped into the foyer. When he returned, there was a noticeable difference in his attitude toward Franklin Bailey.

"Mr. Bailey," he said, brusquely. "Isn't it a fact that you lost a considerable amount of money in a scam about ten years ago?"

"Yes, that's true."

"How much did you lose in that scam?"

"Seven million dollars."

"What was the name of the man who cheated you?"

"Richard Mason, as slippery a con artist as I have ever had the bad luck to meet."

"Did you know that Mason is Steve Frawley's half brother?"

Bailey stared at him. "No, I did not. How could I have known?"

"Mr. Bailey, Richard Mason left his mother's home on Tuesday morning. He was supposed to have been at work as a baggage handler on Wednesday but he never showed up, nor has he been at home. Are you *sure* you have not been in touch with him?"

45

"You'd never know it was the same kid. She looks like a little boy," Angie said cheerfully, as she surveyed the effects of her makeover on Kathy. The little girl's dark blond hair was now charcoal brown, the same shade as Angie's. And it was no longer shoulder-length; it barely covered her ears.

She does look different, Clint admitted to himself. At least if someone were to see her, they'd think Angie was babysitting a boy. "I've got a great name for her, too," Angie added. "We're gonna call her 'Stephen.' After her father, get it? Do you like your new name, Stevie? Huh?"

"Angie, this is crazy. We've got to pack up and get out of here."

"No we don't. That would be the worst thing we could do. You have to write a letter to the manager of the club, whoever the new guy is, and say you've been offered a year-round job in Florida, and that you're giving notice. If you just disappear, they'll wonder what happened."

"Angie, I *know* how the feds work. Right now they're trying to find anyone who ever had contact with Lucas. Maybe this number is in his address book."

"Don't give me that. He never called you or let you phone him when you were talking about doing one of your 'business' ventures unless you were both on prepaid cell phones."

"Angie, if either one of us left just one fin-gerprint in that car, it could come up in the feds' database."

"You wore gloves when you stole that car, gloves when you drove Lucas's car back to his place. Anyhow, even if they find some, we've both disappeared. You've been known as Clint Downes for a good fifteen years. So stop, stop, stop!"

Kathy had been almost asleep. As Angie's voice rose, she slid down from Angie's lap and stood looking up at both of them.

In an abrupt change of mood, Angie said, "I swear Stevie is getting to look just like me, Clint. You must have done a pretty good job with the steam. She doesn't seem so choked up. But I'll keep the vaporizer going all night. And she did eat some cereal, so I guess that'll keep her going."

"Angie, she needs real medicine."

"I can take care of that if I have to." Angie did not tell Clint that she had rummaged in the bathroom cabinet and found a couple of penicillin tablets and cough medicine from when Clint had that lousy bronchitis attack last year. She'd started Kathy on the cough medicine. If that doesn't do the trick, I'll open the pills and dilute them, she thought. Penicillin cures just about everything.

"Why did you have to go and say that I'd meet Gus tonight? I'm half-dead. I don't want to go out."

"You have to go because that pain-in-the-neck needs somebody to bore to death. This way you get rid of him. You can even tell him that you're going to take another job. Just don't have a couple of beers and start crying for your pal Lucas."

Kathy turned and was walking toward the bedroom. Angie got up to follow her and watched as Kathy pulled the blanket from the crib, wrapped herself in it, and lay down on the floor.

"Listen, baby, if you're tired, you have a crib to crash in," Angie snapped. She picked up the unresisting child and cradled her. "Does Stevie love Mommy, hmmmm?"

Kathy closed her eyes and turned her head away. Angie shook her. "Being I'm so nice to you, I'm getting sick and tired of the way you treat me, and don't you dare start that double-talk again."

The sudden piercing sound of the door-bell made Angie go rigid. Maybe Clint was right. Maybe the feds *did* trace him through Lucas, she thought, paralyzed with fear.

Through the partially open door, she heard Clint moving with slow, heavy steps across the living room, followed by the sound of the door opening. "Hello, Clint, old buddy. Thought I'd pick you up and save you the trouble of driving. You can tell Angie, I promise, it'll be a two-beer night for me." It was the booming voice of Gus the plumber.

He suspects something is fishy, Angie thought angrily. He *did* hear the two kids crying, and now he's checking us out. Making a quick decision, she tucked the blanket around Kathy, allowing only the back of her head with its short brown hair to show, and stepped into the living room.

"Hi, Gus," she said.

"Angie, hi. Is this the kid you're minding?"

"Yeah. This is Stevie. He's the one you heard crying last night. His folks are at a family funeral in Wisconsin. They'll be back tomorrow. I love the little guy, but I'm ready to get some sleep." With a firm hand under the blanket, she kept Kathy from turning her head and letting Gus see her face.

"See you later, Angie," Clint said, edging Gus toward the door.

Angie could see that Gus's pickup was in front of the cot-tage. Which means that he came through the back gate, using the code. Which means that anytime he gets the idea to drop in, he'll do it. "Bye, have a good time," she said as the door closed behind them.

She watched from the window until the truck disappeared down the lane. Then she smoothed Kathy's hair. "Baby doll, you and me and our money are making tracks right now," she said. "For once, Daddy Clint was right. It isn't safe to hang around here any longer."

46

At seven o'clock, Monsignor Romney rang the bell of the Frawley home. Steve and Margaret answered it together. "Thank you for coming, Monsignor," Margaret said.

"I'm glad you wanted me to come, Margaret." He followed them into the study. They sat on the couch, close to each other. He took the chair nearest to them. "How is Kelly?" he asked.

"Doctor Harris gave her a sedative, so she's been sleeping most of the day," Steve said. "She is with her now."

"When Kelly's awake, she tries to talk to Kathy," Margaret told him. "She can't accept that Kathy's not coming home anymore. Neither can I."

"There is no greater sorrow than losing a child," Monsignor Romney said quietly. "At a wedding ceremony we pray that you will live to see your children's children. No matter whether it is a new-born infant who barely draws a single breath, or a toddler or a young adult or, for elderly parents, an offspring who is a senior citizen herself or himself, there is no pain to compare with it."

"My problem," Margaret said slowly, "is that I cannot believe that Kathy is gone. I can't accept that she won't come in here any minute, a step behind Kelly. Of the two, Kelly's the leader, the boss. Kathy's a little more timid, a little shy."

She looked at Steve, then at Monsignor Romney. "I broke my ankle ice skating when I was fifteen. It was a really nasty break and needed major surgery. I remember when I woke up, I only felt a dull ache, and I thought that recovering from the operation was going to be a slam dunk. Then, hours later, the nerve block began to wear off, and I was in agony. I think that's the way it's going to be for me. For now the nerve block is still working."

Monsignor Romney waited, sensing that Margaret was about to make a request of him. She looks so young, so vulnerable, he thought. The confident, smiling mother who had told him that she had put her law career on hold to be able to enjoy her twins, was a pale shadow of herself now, her dark blue eyes haunted and pain-filled. Next to her, Steve, his hair tousled, his eyes red rimmed from exhaustion, was shaking his head, as though in denial of what had happened.

"I know we must plan some kind of service that people can attend," Margaret said. "My mother and sister are coming up next week. Steve's father is getting a nurse for his mother so that he can be here, too. So many, many friends have e-mailed us and want to be with us. But before we plan a Mass that people can attend, I was wondering if early tomorrow morning, you might offer a private Mass for Kathy, with just Steve and Kelly and Dr. Harris and me there. Is that possible?"

"Of course it's possible. I can offer it tomorrow morning, either before or after the regularly scheduled Masses. That would be before the seven, or after the nine."

"Don't you call it a Mass of the Angels when it's for a small child?" Margaret asked.

"That's a layman's term that has come into use when the Mass is being offered for a young person. I'll select some appropriate readings."

"Honey, make it after the nine," Steve suggested. "It wouldn't hurt if we both took a sleeping pill tonight."

"To sleep, but not to dream," Margaret said wearily.

Monsignor Romney stood up and walked over to her. Placing his hand on her head, he blessed her, then turned to Steve and blessed him. "Ten o'clock at the church," he said. Looking at their grief-stricken faces, words of De Profundis rushed into his mind. *Out of the depths I have cried to Thee, O Lord . . . hear my voice. Let Thy ears be attentive to the voice of my supplication.*

47

Norman Bond was not surprised when two FBI agents arrived at his office on Friday morning. He knew they had been told that he had bypassed three well-qualified C.F.G.&Y. employees to hire Steve Frawley. He also assumed they had figured out that it took someone with sophisticated financial know-how to realize that some overseas banks will, for a fee, collect and pass on illegally obtained money.

Before he told his secretary to send the agents in, he hurried to his private bathroom and studied himself in the full-length mirror hung on the back of the door. The first money he'd spent after getting a job at C.F.G.&Y. twenty-five years ago had been for expensive laser treatments to rid himself of the scars from the acne that had made his adolescence an endless torture. In his mind the scars were still there, and so were the owl-like glasses that had been necessary to cure a lazy-eye muscle. Now contact lenses gave improved vision to his light blue eyes. He was grateful for a good head of hair but wondered if he had made a mistake not to dye it. The premature gray that was in his mother's side of the family had been bequeathed to him, but at age forty-eight he was becoming pure white rather than salt-and-pepper.

Conservative suits from Paul Stuart had replaced the hand-me-downs of his childhood, but a glance in the mirror was necessary to ensure that somehow a stain had not materialized on his collar or tie. He could never forget the time early in his employment at C.F.G.&Y. when, in the presence of the chairman, he used a dinner fork to spear an oyster. As it fell from the tines, it had slithered across his jacket, dripping cocktail sauce. That night, burning with shame, he bought a book on etiquette and a complete set of dinnerware, and for days practiced setting a formal table and using the proper fork or knife or spoon.

Now the mirror assured him that he

looked just fine. Passably good features. Good haircut. Crisp white shirt. Blue tie. No jewelry. A flash memory of throwing his wedding ring on the tracks before an on-coming commuter train rushed briefly through his mind. After all these years, he still wasn't certain if it was anger or sadness that had triggered that reaction. He told himself that it didn't matter any more.

He went back to his desk and signaled his secretary to send the FBI agents in. The first one, Angus Sommers, he had met on Wednesday. The second, a slender woman of about thirty, was introduced by Sommers as Agent Ruthanne Scaturro. He knew that other agents were swarming through the building asking questions.

Norman Bond acknowledged his visitors with a nod of his head. As a courtesy, he made a slight gesture of rising, but quickly settled back, his face impassive.

"Mr. Bond," Sommers began, "that was a pretty strong statement your chief financial officer, Gregg Stanford, made to the media yesterday. Did you agree with it?"

Bond raised one eyebrow, a trick it had taken him a long time to perfect. "As you know, Agent Sommers, the board of directors voted unanimously to pay the ransom. Unlike my distinguished colleague, I very much believed in making the payment. It is a terrible tragedy that one twin is dead, but perhaps the fact that the other one was returned safely is a result of the payment we made. Doesn't the suicide note left by that limo driver indicate that he had not intended to kill the other child?"

"Yes, it did. Then you don't agree with Mr. Stanford's position at all?"

"I never agree with Gregg Stanford's position. Or let me put it another way: He is chief financial officer because his wife's family owns ten percent of the voting stock. He knows that we all consider him a lightweight. He has the ridiculous notion that by taking the opposite viewpoint from our chairman, Robinson Geisler, he will attract a following. He covets the chairman's seat. More than that, he is lusting for it. In the matter of the ransom payment, he has seized the opportunity to be a post-tragedy sage."

"Do you covet the chairman's seat, Mr. Bond?" Agent Scaturro asked.

"In due course, I would hope to be considered for it. For the present, after the unpleasant upheaval of last year and the heavy fine the company paid, I think it is far better for the present board to present a united front to our stockholders. I think Stanford has done the company a great disservice by his public attack on Mr. Geisler."

"Let's talk about something else, Mr. Bond," Angus Sommers suggested. "Why did you hire Steve Frawley?"

"It seems to me that we went over that subject two days ago, Mr. Sommers," Bond said, deliberately letting a note of annoyance creep into his voice.

"Let's talk about it again. There are three rather bitter men in the company who felt you had neither the need nor the right to go outside for the position you gave Steve Frawley. It's a quantum leap for him, in terms of job level, isn't it?"

"Let me explain something about corporate politics, Mr. Sommers. The three men you mention want *my* job. They were protégés of the former chairman. Their loyalty was and is to him. I'm a pretty good judge of people, and Steve Frawley is smart, very smart. A combination of an MBA and a law degree, together with brains and personality, goes a long way in the corporate world.

We had a long talk about this company, about the problems we experienced last year, and about the future, and I liked what I heard. He also appears to me to be a truly ethical man, a rarity these days. Finally, I know he would be loyal to me, and that is the bottom line for me."

Norman Bond leaned back in his chair and pressed his hands together, the fingers pointing upward. "And now, if you'll forgive me, I must get to a meeting upstairs."

Neither Sommers nor Scaturro made a move to stand up. "Just a few more questions, Mr. Bond," Sommers said. "You didn't tell us the other day that you lived in Ridgefield, Connecticut, at one time."

"I have lived in many places since I started with this company. Ridgefield was over twenty years ago, when I was married."

"Did your wife not give birth to twin boys who died at birth?"

"Yes, she did." Bond's eyes became expressionless.

"You were very much in love with your wife, but she left you shortly after that, didn't she?"

"She moved to California. She wanted to

start all over. Grief separates as many people as it brings closer, Agent Sommers."

"After she left, you had something of a breakdown, didn't you, Mr. Bond?"

"Grief also causes depression, Mr. Sommers. I knew I needed help, so I checked into a facility. Today bereavement groups are common. Twenty years ago, they were not."

"Did you keep in touch with your former wife?"

"She remarried fairly quickly. It was better for both of us to close that chapter in our lives."

"But unfortunately her chapter isn't closed, is it? Your former wife disappeared several years after she remarried."

"I know that."

"Were you questioned about her disappearance?"

"Like her parents and siblings and friends, I was asked if I had any knowledge of where she might have gone. Of course, I did not. In fact, I contributed to the reward that was offered for information leading to her return."

"That reward has never been collected, has it, Mr. Bond?"

"No, it has not."

"Mr. Bond, when you met Steve Frawley, did you see something of yourself in him: a young, smart, and ambitious man, with an attractive, smart wife, and beautiful children?"

"Mr. Sommers, this questioning has become irrational. If I understand you, and I believe I do, you are suggesting that I might have had something to do with my late wife's disappearance, as well as with the kidnapping of the Frawley twins. How dare you insult me like that. Get out of my office."

"Your *late* wife, Mr. Bond? How do you know she's dead?"

48

"I've always been a just-in-case person, baby doll," Angie said more to herself than to Kathy, who was lying on the bed in the motel, propped on pillows, and covered with a blanket. "I think ahead all the time. That's the difference between me and Clint."

It was ten o'clock on Friday morning, and Angie was feeling pleased with herself. The night before, an hour after Clint and Gus had left for the tavern, she had the van packed and was on the road with Kathy. She had put the ransom money into suitcases, then thrown together some hastily packed clothes and the prepaid cell phones the Pied Piper had sent to Lucas and Clint. In her final trip from the house to the van, she remembered to grab the tapes Lucas had made when the Pied Piper called him, and the driver's license she had stolen from a woman whose kid she had minded last year.

Then, as an afterthought, she'd scribbled a note for Clint: "Don't worry. I'll call you in the morning. Needed to do some extra baby-sitting."

She drove for three-and-a-half hours straight to Cape Cod and the Hyannis motel where she had stayed years ago when she and some guy came up for a weekend. She'd liked the Cape so much that she got a summer job at the Seagull Marina in Harwich.

"I always had an escape plan in mind, just in case Clint got caught on one of the jobs he did with Lucas," she told Kathy with a chuckle. But then, seeing that Kathy was falling back asleep, she frowned and went over to the bed and tapped the little girl's shoulder. "Listen to me when I'm talking to you. You might learn something."

Kathy's eyes remained closed.

"Maybe I gave you too much of that cough medicine," Angie speculated. "If it made Clint sleepy when he used to take it last year, I guess it could really knock you out."

She went to the counter where a little of the coffee she'd made earlier still remained in the pot. I'm hungry, she thought. I could use a decent breakfast, but I can't be lugging the kid around half-asleep and with no coat on her back. Maybe I'll just lock her in the room and get something for myself, then go to a store and pick up some clothes for her. I'll leave the suitcases under the bed and put a DO NOT DISTURB sign on the door. Maybe I'll give her a little more of the cough medicine—then she'll *really* sleep.

Angie could feel her good mood evaporating and recognized that when she was hungry, she always got kind of edgy and irritated. They'd checked into the motel a little after midnight. She'd hardly been able to keep her eyes open at the time and had put the kid into bed and collapsed beside her. She'd fallen asleep immedi-ately but woke up before dawn when the kid started coughing and crying.

I never did get back to sleep, Angie thought. I just dozed off a little, which is why I don't feel so sharp right now. But I was sharp enough to remember to bring that driver's license, so now I'll be officially known around here as "Linda Hagen."

Last year she had done some babysitting for Linda Hagen, and one day Linda had come home all upset because she thought she'd left her wallet in the restaurant. Then the next time she took care of Hagen's kid, she had to use the family car to take her to a birthday party. It was then that she spotted the wallet that had slipped down between the front seats. Retrieving it, she found two hundred dollars in cash and, more importantly, a driver's license. Of course, Mrs. Hagen had cancelled the credit cards, but the license was a find.

We both have thin faces and dark brown hair, Angie thought. Mrs. Hagen wore thick glasses in the picture, and if I ever get stopped, I'll put on dark glasses. Someone would really have to study the picture to know it was a phony. Anyhow, I'm checked in here as Linda Hagen, and except for the feds tracing the van if they happen to catch up with Clint, I'm okay for awhile. And if I do decide to fly someplace else, with Linda's photo ID, I can get on a plane.

Angie figured that if the feds *did* nail Clint, he would probably tell them that she was on her way to Florida, because that's what he would think. But she also knew she needed to get rid of the van and use some of the cash to buy a second-hand car.

Then I can drive anywhere I want with no one the wiser, she thought. I'll abandon the van in a dump somewhere. Without the plates, nobody could trace it.

I'll keep in touch with Clint, and after I make sure there's no heat on him, maybe I'll tell him where I am so he can join me. And maybe I won't. But for now he's not going to have a clue. But I did tell him I'd call him this morning, so I'd better do that.

She picked up one of the prepaid cell phones and dialed Clint. He answered on the first ring. "Where are you?" he demanded.

"Clint, baby, it was better I got out fast. I've got the money, don't worry. If by any chance the feds do look you up, what would have happened if I was there and the kid was there and the money was there? Now listen to me: Get rid of the crib! Did you tell Gus you were going to give notice at the club?"

"Yeah, yeah. I told him I was offered a job in Orlando."

"Good. Give your notice today. If nosy Gussy comes around again, tell him the mother of the kid I was minding asked me to take him to Wisconsin. Tell him her father died and she needs to stay there and help out her mother. Say I'm going to meet you in Florida."

"Don't mess with me, Angie."

"I'm not messing with you. The feds come to talk to you, you're clean. I told Gus you were looking for a new car in Yonkers Wednesday night. Tell him you sold the van, then go rent yourself a car for now."

"You didn't leave me a dime of the money," he said bitterly. "Not even the five hundred bucks I left on the dresser."

"Suppose they have some of the serial numbers. I was just protecting you. Run up charges on the credit card. It won't matter. In another two weeks or so, we're gonna disappear from the face of the earth. I'm hungry. I gotta go. Goodbye."

Angie snapped closed the cover of the cell phone, walked back over to the bed, and looked down at Kathy. Was she asleep or just pretending to be asleep? she wondered. She's getting to be as nasty as the other one, Angie thought. No matter how nice I am, she ignores me, too.

The cough medicine was by the bed. She unscrewed the top and poured out a spoonful. Bending down, she forced Kathy's lips apart and tipped the spoon until the liquid was in her mouth. "Now swallow it," she ordered.

In a sleepy, reflexive action, Kathy swallowed most of the cough syrup. A few drops went into her windpipe and she began to cough and cry. Angie pushed her back on the pillow. "Oh, for God's sake, shut up," she said through gritted teeth.

Kathy closed her eyes and pulled the blanket over her face as she turned away, trying not to cry. In her mind she could see Kelly sitting in church, next to Mommy and Daddy. She didn't dare talk out loud, but did move her lips silently as she felt Angie begin to tie her to the bed.

In the front row of St. Mary's Church in Ridgefield, Margaret and Steve held onto Kelly's hands as they knelt at Mass. Beside them, Dr. Sylvia Harris was blinking back tears as she listened to the opening prayer Monsignor Romney was reciting:

> Lord God, from whom human sadness
>   is never hidden
> You know the burden of grief
> That we feel at the loss of this child
> As we mourn her passing from this life
> Comfort us with the knowledge
> That Kathryn Ann lives now in your
>   loving embrace.

Kelly tugged at Margaret's hand. "Mommy," she said, her voice loud and clear for the first time since she had been returned to them. "Kathy is very scared of that lady. She's crying for you. She wants you to bring her home, too. Right now!"

49

Special Agent Chris Smith, head of the Bureau's North Carolina office, had phoned to request a brief meeting with the parents of Steve Frawley in Winston-Salem.

Frawley's father, Tom, a retired and highly decorated captain of the New York City Fire Department, had not been pleased to hear from him. "We learned yesterday that one of our two grandchildren is dead. If that wasn't devastating enough, my wife had knee replacements three weeks ago and is still in terrible pain. Why do you want to see us?"

"We need to talk to you about Mrs. Frawley's older son, your stepson, Richie Mason," Smith had said.

"Oh, for God's sake, I might have known. Come over around eleven o'clock."

Smith, a fifty-two-year-old African-American, brought along Carla Rogers, a twenty-six-year-old agent recently assigned to his staff.

At eleven, Tom Frawley answered the door and invited the agents in. The first sight that greeted Smith was a collage of pictures of the twins on the wall opposite the door. Beautiful kids, he thought. What a damn shame we couldn't get both of them back.

At Frawley's invitation they followed him into the cozy family room that was an extension of the kitchen. Grace Frawley was seated in a roomy leather chair with her feet on an ottoman.

Smith went over to her. "Mrs. Frawley, I am terribly sorry to intrude. I know you've just lost one of your granddaughters and that you recently had surgery. I promise I won't take much of your time. Our office in Connecticut sent us to ask you and Mr. Frawley some questions about your son, Richard Mason."

"Sit down, please." Tom Frawley pointed to the couch and then pulled up a chair next to his wife for himself. "What kind of trouble is Richie in now?" he demanded.

"Mr. Frawley, I didn't say Richie was in trouble. I don't know that he is. We wanted to talk to him, but he did not report for work at Newark Airport Wednesday evening, and according to his neighbors, he has not been seen around his apartment building since last week."

Grace Frawley's eyes were swollen. As the agents watched, she kept raising the small linen handkerchief she was holding to her face. Smith realized that she was trying to conceal the quivering of her lips.

"He told us he was going back to work," she said nervously. "I had surgery three weeks ago. That was why Richie came down to visit last weekend. Could anything have happened to him? If he didn't go back to work, he might have been in an accident on the way home."

"Grace, be real," Tom gently insisted. "Richie hated that job. He said he was much too smart to be shoving baggage around. I wouldn't be surprised if he just made up his mind on the spur of the mo-ment to drive to Vegas or some place like it. He's done that sort of thing at least a dozen times before. He's okay, dear. You've got enough on your plate without worrying about *him.*"

Tom Frawley's tone was reassuring, but Chris Smith caught the note of irritation under the comforting words he was trying to offer his wife and was sure that Carla Rogers was picking up on it, too. From the record he'd read on Richie Mason, it looked as if he had been a lifelong heartache for the mother. School dropout, sealed juvenile record, five years in the slammer for a scam that had cost a dozen investors a fortune—including Franklin Bailey, who had lost seven million dollars.

Grace Frawley had the drawn, exhausted look of someone who was in a lot of pain, both physical and emotional. She was about sixty years old, Smith judged, an attractive woman with gray hair and a slight build. Tom Frawley was a big, broad-shouldered guy, maybe a few years older than she.

"Mrs. Frawley, you had surgery three weeks ago. Why did Richie wait so long to visit you?"

"I went to a rehab center for two weeks."

"I see. When did Richie get down here and when did he leave?" Smith asked.

"He arrived around three o'clock last Saturday morning. He got off from work at the airport at three o'clock in the afternoon, and we'd expected him by midnight," Tom Frawley answered for his wife. "But then he called to say that there was a lot of traffic, and we should go to bed and leave the door unlocked for him. I'm a light sleeper, so I heard him when he came in. He left about ten o'clock Tuesday morning, right after we all watched Steve and Margaret on television."

"Did he get or receive many phone calls?" Smith asked.

"Not on our phone. He had his cell, though. He used it some. I don't know how much."

"Was Richie in the habit of visiting you, Mrs. Frawley?" Carmen Rogers asked.

"He stopped in to see us when we visited Steve and Margaret and the twins right after they moved to Ridgefield. Before that, we hadn't seen him for almost a year," Grace Frawley said, her voice tired and sad. "I call him regularly. He almost never answers, but I leave a message on his cell phone just saying that we're thinking of him and that we love him. I know he's been in trouble, but underneath he's really a good boy. Richie's father died when he was only two. I married Tom three years later, and no human being could have been a better father to a child than Tom has been to Richie. But when he was a teenager, he got in with the wrong crowd and never got back on track again."

"What is his relationship with Steve?"

"Not the best," Tom Frawley admitted. "He's always been jealous of Steve. Richie could have gone to college. His grades were always up and down, but his SAT's were great. In fact, he started attending SUNY. He's smart, really smart, but he dropped out in his freshman year and took off for Las Vegas. That's how he got in with a crowd of gamblers and phonies. As you must know, he served time in prison for a scam he got involved in."

"Does the name Franklin Bailey mean anything to you, Mr. Frawley?"

"He's the man who my granddaughters' kidnapper contacted. We saw him on television, and then he's the one who passed the ransom money to the kidnappers."

"He was also one of the victims of the

scam that Richie helped run. That investment cost Mr. Bailey seven million dollars."

"Does Bailey know about Richie, I mean
that he's Steve's half brother?" Frawley
asked quickly, his tone at once astonished
and worried.

"He does now. Would you know if Richie
saw Mr. Bailey when he was in Ridgefield
visiting with you last month?"

"I wouldn't know that."

"Mr. Frawley, you say Richie left at about
ten o'clock on Tuesday morning?" Smith
asked.

"That's right. Within a half hour after Steve
and Margaret were on television with Bailey."

"Richie always claimed that he didn't
know the company he persuaded people
to invest in was a scam. Do you believe
that?"

"No, I do not," Frawley said. "When he
told us about the company, it sounded so
good that we offered to invest in it, but he
wouldn't let us. Does that tell you something?"

"Tom," Grace Frawley protested.

"Grace, Richie paid his debt to society for
being part of that scam. Pretending he was

an innocent fall guy is dishonest. The day Richie takes the blame for what he's done is the day he'll start to do something with the rest of his life."

"We've learned that before he realized he had been cheated, Franklin Bailey struck up a very warm friendship with Richie. Is it possible that Bailey believed Richie's story and has remained friends with him since Richie was released from prison?" Smith asked.

"Where are you going with these questions, Mr. Smith?" Frawley asked quietly.

"Mr. Frawley, your stepson Richie is extremely jealous of your son Steve. We know that he even tried to date your daughter-in-law before she met Steve. Richie is financially sophisticated, which is why he was able to deceive so many people with that phony investment. Franklin Bailey has become part of our overall investigation, and in the course of checking him out, we learned that a phone call was made from your phone in this condominium to Franklin Bailey at approximately ten minutes past ten on Tuesday morning."

The lines on Frawley's craggy face deepened. "I certainly did *not* contact Franklin

Bailey." He turned to his wife. "Grace, you didn't call him, did you?"

"But I did," Grace Frawley said firmly. "They gave his number on the television, and I called to thank him for helping Steve and Margaret. When he didn't answer, and the machine came on, I didn't leave a message." She looked at Agent Smith, anger replacing the suffering in her eyes. "Mr. Smith, I know that you and your agency are trying to bring to justice whoever kidnapped my granddaughters and caused Kathy's death, but listen to me and listen carefully. I don't care whether or not Richie showed up for work at Newark Airport. I think that you are insinuating there is something going on between him and Franklin Bailey, and that it may have to do with the kidnapping of our grandchildren. That is absolutely ridiculous, so don't waste *your* time or *our* time pursuing that line of investigation."

She pushed the ottoman back and stood up, grasping the arms of the chair for support. "My granddaughter is dead. I am in so much pain I almost can't bear it. My one son and my daughter-in-law are heartbroken. My other son is weak and foolish and even a thief, but he is not capable of anything so despicable as kidnapping his own nieces. Stop it, Mr. Smith. Tell your agency to stop it. Haven't I had enough? Haven't I had enough?"

In a gesture of utter despair, she threw up her hands, sank back into the chair, then leaned forward until her face touched her knees.

"Get out!" Tom Frawley pointed to the door, spitting out the words. "You couldn't save my granddaughter. Now at least go out and find her kidnapper. You're barking up the wrong tree if you're trying to tie Richie to this crime, so don't waste your time even thinking that he's involved."

Smith listened, his face impassive. "Mr. Frawley, if you hear from Richie, will you please tell him that we need to be in touch with him? I'll give you my card." With a nod to Grace Frawley, he turned and, followed by Agent Rogers, left the condo.

In the car, he put the key in the ignition before he asked, "What do you think of all that?"

Carla knew what he meant. "The phone call to Franklin Bailey—I think the mother may have been trying to cover for him."

"So do I. Richie didn't get here until early Saturday morning, which meant he could have had time to take part in the kidnapping. He was in the Ridgefield house a couple of months ago, so he knew the layout. He may have been setting up an alibi for himself by visiting his mother. He could have been one of the two men who picked up the ransom money."

"If he was one of the kidnappers, he would have to have been wearing a mask. Without one, even if the twins barely knew him, they still might have been able to identify him."

"Suppose one of them did? And suppose for that reason she couldn't be allowed to go home? And suppose Lucas Wohl's death wasn't a suicide?"

Rogers stared at her superior officer. "I didn't know the guys in New York and Connecticut were thinking that way."

"The guys in New York and Connecticut are thinking every way they can and following every single angle. They have the case, and a three-year-old child died on their watch. Somebody who calls himself the Pied Piper is still out there, and the blood of that child is on his hands and on the hands of anyone else who had a part in that kid-napping. As the Frawleys just told us, Richie Mason may be nothing more than a con artist, but I just can't help thinking that his mother is covering for him right now."

50

After her outburst in church, Kelly lapsed into silence. When they arrived back home, she went upstairs to her bedroom and brought down the two teddy bears clasped in her arms.

Rena Chapman, the kindly neighbor who had cooked dinner for them several times, and who had received one of the calls from the Pied Piper, was waiting for them to get home. "You have simply *got* to eat," she told them. She had set the round table in the breakfast alcove of the kitchen, and it was there that they settled, Margaret holding Kelly on her lap, Steve and Dr. Harris across from them. Rena placed the platters on the table and refused to stay. "You don't need me around now," she told them firmly.

Piping-hot scrambled eggs, thin sliced

ham on toast points, and strong, hot coffee warmed all of them. While they were having their second cup, Kelly slid off Margaret's lap. "Will you read me my book, Mommy?" she asked.

"I will, sweetheart," Steve said. "You bring it down to me."

Margaret waited until Kelly was out of the kitchen before speaking. She knew the reaction she would receive, but she had to tell them what she felt. "Kathy is alive. She and Kelly are in touch with each other."

"Margaret, Kelly is still trying to communicate with Kathy, and she's also beginning to tell you about her own experience. She was afraid of that woman, whoever it was who was minding them. She wanted to come home," Dr. Harris said gently.

"She was talking to Kathy," Margaret said firmly. "I know she was."

"Oh, honey," Steve protested. "Don't break your heart by even holding to a whisper of hope that Kathy is alive."

Margaret wrapped her fingers around the coffee cup, remembering how she had done exactly the same thing the night the twins had disappeared, trying to warm her hands with it. She realized that now the despair of the last twenty-four hours had been replaced by the desperate need to find Kathy—to find her before it was too late.

Be careful, she told herself. No one's going to believe me. If they think I'm going crazy with grief, they might want to sedate me. That sleeping pill last night knocked me out for hours. I can't let that happen again. *I've got to find her.*

Kelly came back with the Dr. Seuss book they had been reading to her before the kidnapping. Steve pushed back his chair and picked her up. "We'll go inside to my big chair in the study, okay?"

"Kathy likes this book, too," Kelly said.

"Well, we'll pretend that I'm reading to both of you." Steve managed to get the words out in a steady voice even as his eyes filled with tears.

"Oh, Daddy, that's silly. Kathy can't hear. She's asleep now, and she's all by herself, and that lady tied her to the bed."

"You mean the lady tied *you* to the bed, don't you, Kelly?" Steve asked quickly.

"No. Mona made us stay in the big crib, and we couldn't climb out of it. Kathy's in the bed now," Kelly insisted, then patted

Steve's cheek. "Daddy, why are you cry-ing?"

"Margaret, the sooner Kelly gets back to a normal routine, the easier it will be for her to become used to not being with Kathy," Dr. Harris said later, as she prepared to leave. "I think Steve is right. Taking her to nursery school was the best thing for her."

"As long as Steve doesn't let her out of his sight," Margaret said fearfully.

"Absolutely." Sylvia Harris put her arms around Margaret and gave her a brief hug. "I have to run down to the hospital to check on some of my patients, but I'll be back tonight, that is if you still feel I'm any help to you."

"Remember when Kathy had pneumonia, and that young nurse was about to give her penicillin. If you hadn't been there, God knows what might have happened," Margaret said. "You go down and check on your sick kids, and then come back. We need you."

"We certainly found out the first time Kathy had penicillin that she must never have it again," Dr. Harris said in agreement. She then added, "Margaret, grieve for her, but don't read hope into what Kelly may continue to say. Believe me, she is reliving her own experience."

Don't try to convince her! Margaret warned herself. She doesn't believe you. Steve doesn't believe you. I've got to talk to Agent Carlson, she decided. I've got to talk to him right away.

With a final squeeze of Margaret's hand, Sylvia Harris left. Alone in the house for the first time in a week, Margaret closed her eyes and drew in a deep breath, then hurried to the phone and dialed Walter Carlson's number.

He answered on the first ring. "Margaret, what can I do?"

"Kathy is alive," she told him, then before he could speak, she rushed on, "I know you won't believe me, but she is alive. Kelly is communicating with her. An hour ago, Kathy was asleep and tied to a bed. Kelly told me that."

"Margaret . . ."

"Don't try to placate me. *Trust* me. You have only the word of a dead man that Kathy is gone. You don't have her body. You know that Lucas got into his plane carrying a big box, and you're assuming that Kathy's body was in it. Stop assuming that and find her. Do you hear me? *Find her!*"

Before he could respond, Margaret slammed down the phone, then collapsed into a chair and held her head in both hands. There's something I have to remember. I know it has to do with the dresses I bought the twins for their birthday, she thought. I'll go up to their closet and hold the dresses and try to remember.

51

Early Friday afternoon, FBI Agents Angus Sommers and Ruthanne Scaturro rang the bell of 415 Walnut Street in Bronxville, New York, where Amy Lindcroft, Gregg Stanford's first wife, resided. In contrast to the large and elegant homes around her, she lived in a modest, white, Cape Cod house, with dark green shutters that glistened in the sunlight of the suddenly bright afternoon.

The house reminded Angus Sommers of the one in which he had grown up, on the other side of the Hudson River in Closter, New Jersey. A familiar regret passed through his mind: I should have bought the house when Mom and Dad moved to Florida; it's doubled in value over the past ten years.

This property is worth more than the house, was his next thought, as he heard the sound of footsteps approaching on the other side of the door.

It was Sommers's experience that even people with an untroubled conscience can experience a nervous reaction at a visit from the FBI. In this case, however, Amy Lindcroft had phoned and asked to see them, saying she wanted to discuss her former husband. She greeted them with a brief smile as she glanced at their credentials and then invited them in. A slightly plump woman in her mid-forties, with flashing brown eyes and salt-and-pepper hair that curled around her face, she was wearing a painter's smock over jeans.

The agents followed her into a living room tastefully furnished in Early American décor and dominated by an excellent watercolor painting of the Hudson River Palisades. Sommers walked over to study it. The signature in the corner was Amy Lindcroft.

"This is beautiful," he said sincerely.

"I make my living as a painter. I'd better be pretty good," Lindcroft said matter-of-factly. "Now, sit down, please. I won't keep you long, but what I say may be worth hearing."

In the car, Sommers had told Agent Scaturro to take the lead in the interview. Now she said, "Ms. Lindcroft, am I correct that you have something to tell us that you feel is relevant to the Frawley kidnapping?"

"*May* be relevant," Lindcroft emphasized. "I know this is going to sound like the woman scorned, and maybe it is, but Gregg has hurt so many people, and if what I'm going to tell you hurts him, so be it. I was the college roommate of Tina Olsen, the pharmaceutical heiress, and was always invited to visit the family's various homes. Looking back, I realize that Gregg married me so he could worm his way into Tina's world. He succeeded admirably. Gregg is smart, and he knows how to sell himself. When we were first married, he was working for a small investment firm. He kept ingratiating himself with Mr. Olsen, who finally asked him to join his staff. He managed to work his way up to becoming Olsen's right-hand man. The next thing I knew, he and Tina announced that they were in love. After ten years of marriage, I finally had become pregnant. The shock of my husband and my best friend cheating on me caused a miscarriage. To stop the hemorrhaging, I had to have a hysterectomy."

She's much more than a woman scorned, Angus Sommers thought as he observed the look of sadness that rushed into Amy Lindcroft's eyes.

"Then he married Tina Olsen," Scaturro prompted sympathetically.

"Yes. It lasted six years, until Tina found he was cheating with someone else and got rid of him. Needless to say, her father fired him as well. You must understand—Gregg is simply incapable of being faithful to any woman."

"What are you telling us, Ms. Lindcroft?" Angus Sommers asked.

"About six and a half years ago, after Gregg remarried, Tina phoned and apologized to me. She said she didn't expect me to accept the apology, but she had to extend it anyway. She said it wasn't only his womanizing that got to her; her father had learned that he'd been milking the company with phony expenses. Mr. Olsen covered the expenses himself to avoid a scandal. Tina said if it was any satisfaction to either one of us, Gregg may have bitten off more than he could chew with his new bride, Millicent Alwin Parker Huff. She's one tough lady, and Tina heard that she made him sign a prenup that says if the marriage doesn't last seven years, he gets zip, nothing, not a dollar."

Amy Lindcroft's smile had no mirth in it. "Tina called again yesterday, after she saw Gregg's interview with the press. She said he's trying desperately to impress Millicent. The prenup expires in a few weeks, and Millicent has been spending a lot of time in Europe, away from him. The last husband she booted out didn't know what was coming until he tried to get into their Fifth Avenue apartment and the doorman told him he wasn't allowed in the building."

"You're telling us that if Gregg is afraid that may happen to him, he might be behind the kidnapping because he'll need money? Isn't that a stretch, Ms. Lindcroft?"

"It might be if it weren't for one more fact."

Trained as he was to be impassive, the one more fact that Amy Lindcroft passed on with a certain amount of gleeful malice nonetheless elicited a startled expression from both FBI agents.

52

Margaret sat on the edge of the bed in the twins' bedroom, the blue velvet dresses she had bought for their birthday draped across her lap. She tried to push aside the memory of a week ago, when she'd dressed the twins for their party. Steve had come home from work early, because after the party they were going to the company dinner. The twins had been so excited that Steve finally had to hold Kelly on his lap while Margaret fastened the buttons on Kathy's dress.

They were giggling and talking twin talk, she remembered, and she was convinced they could read each other's minds. *That's why I know that Kathy really is alive: She has told Kelly that she wants to come home.*

The image of Kathy being scared and tied

to a bed made Margaret want to scream with rage and fear. Where can I look for her? she anguished. Where can I begin? What is it about the dresses? There's something about the dresses I need to remember. What is it? She ran her hands over the soft velvet fabric, remembering how, even though the price had been reduced, they still cost more than she wanted to pay. I kept looking through the racks, she thought, and I kept coming back to them. The sales-girl told me how much they'd cost at Bergdorf's. Then she said that it was funny I was there because she'd just finished wait-ing on another woman shopping for twins.

Margaret gasped. *That's* what I've been trying to remember! It's where I bought them. It's the clerk. She told me that she'd just sold clothes for three-year-old twins to a woman who didn't seem to know anything about what size to buy for them.

Margaret stood up and let the dresses slide to the floor. I'll know the clerk when I see her, she thought. It's probably just a crazy coincidence that someone else was buying clothes for three-year-old twins in that same store a few nights before the girls were kidnapped, but, on the other hand, if the kidnapping was being planned, it would be obvious that the twins would be in pajamas when they took them, and that they would need a change of clothes. I have to talk to that clerk.

When Margaret went downstairs, Steve was just returning with Kelly from the nursery school. "All her friends were so happy to see our little girl," he said, his voice heavy with false cheer. "Isn't that right, sweetheart?"

Without answering, Kelly dropped his hand and began to take off her jacket. Then she started to whisper under her breath.

Margaret looked at Steve. "She's talking to Kathy."

"She's *trying* to talk to Kathy," he corrected.

Margaret reached out her hand. "Steve, give me the keys to the car."

"Margaret . . ."

"Steve, I know what I'm doing. You stay with Kelly. Don't leave her for a minute. And make note of whatever she may be saying, *please.*"

"Where are you going?"

"Not far. Just to the store on Route 7

where I bought their party dresses. I have to talk to the clerk who waited on me."

"Why don't you call her?"

Margaret forced herself to draw a long, quiet breath. "Steve, just give me the keys. I'm all right. I won't be long."

"There's still a media van at the end of the street. They'll follow you."

"They won't get a chance. I'll be gone before they realize it's me. Steve, give me the keys."

In a sudden gesture, Kelly spun around and threw her arms around Steve's leg. "I'm sorry!" she wailed. "I'm sorry!" Steve grabbed her up and rocked her in his arms.

"Kelly, it's okay. It's okay."

She was clutching her arm. Margaret pushed up the sleeve of the polo shirt and watched as the arm began to turn red in the same spot over the faint black and blue mark they had noticed when she returned home.

Margaret felt her mouth go dry. "That woman just pinched Kathy," she whispered. "I know she did. Oh, God, Steve, don't you get it? Give me the keys!"

He reluctantly pulled the car keys from his pocket, and she yanked them out of his hand and ran for the door. Fifteen minutes later, she was entering Abby's Discount on Route 7.

There were about a dozen people in the store, all of them women. Margaret walked up and down the aisles, looking for the clerk who had waited on her, but she did not see her anywhere. Finally, desperate for answers, she approached the cashier, who directed her to the manager.

"Oh, you mean Lila Jackson," the manager said when Margaret described the sales clerk. "It's her day off, and I know she took her mother into New York for dinner and a show. Any one of our other clerks will be happy to help you in any of . . ."

"Does Lila have a cell phone?" Margaret interrupted.

"Yes, but I really can't give that to you." The manager, a woman of about sixty, with frosted blond hair, suddenly became more formal and less cordial. "If you have a complaint, you can speak directly to me. I'm Joan Howell, and I'm in charge here."

"It's not a complaint. It's just that Lila Jackson was also waiting on another woman who bought outfits for twins and didn't know their size when I was here last week. I want to ask her about that woman."

Howell shook her head. "I can't give you Lila's cell phone," she said positively. "She'll be in at ten o'clock tomorrow morning. You can come back then." With a dismissive smile, she turned her back on Margaret.

Margaret caught Howell by the arm as she tried to walk away. "You don't understand," she pleaded, her voice rising. "My little girl is missing. She's alive. I've got to find her. I've got to get to her before it's too late."

She had drawn the attention of the other shoppers in the area. Don't make a scene, she warned herself. They'll think you're crazy. "I'm sorry," she stammered as she released Howell's sleeve. "What time is Lila coming in tomorrow?"

"Ten o'clock." Joan Howell's expression was sympathetic. "You're Mrs. Frawley, aren't you? Lila told me that you bought the birthday dresses for your twins here. I'm so sorry about Kathy. And I'm sorry I didn't recognize you. I'll give you Lila's cell phone number, but the odds are that she won't have taken it with her to the theatre, or at least she'll have turned it off. Please, come into the office."

Margaret could hear the whisperings of the shoppers who had heard her outburst. "That's Margaret Frawley. She's the one whose twins . . ."

In a rush of grief that staggered her with its violence, Margaret turned and rushed outside. In the car, she turned on the ignition key and floored the gas pedal. Not knowing where she was going, she began to drive. Later, she remembered being on I-95 North and going as far as Providence, Rhode Island. There, at the first sign for Cape Cod, she stopped for gas, and only then realized how far she had gone. She turned onto I-95 South, and drove until she saw the sign for Route 7, then followed it, sensing that she needed to find Danbury Airport. Reaching it finally, she parked near the entrance.

He carried her body in a box, she thought. That was her casket. He took her on the plane and flew over the ocean, then he opened the door or the window and dropped the body of my beautiful little girl into the ocean. It would have been a long fall. Did the box break? Did Kathy tumble out of it into the water? The water is so cold now.

Don't think about that, she admonished herself. Think about how much she loved diving into the waves.

I have to get Steve to rent a boat. If we go out on the ocean, and I drop some flowers, maybe then it will feel as though I can really say goodbye to her. Maybe . . ."

A light suddenly shone in the driver's window, and Margaret looked up.

"Mrs. Frawley." The state trooper's voice was gentle.

"Yes."

"We'd like to help you get home, ma'am. Your husband is terribly worried about you."

"I just ran an errand."

"Ma'am, it's eleven o'clock at night. You left the store at four o'clock."

"Did I? I guess that's because I stopped hoping."

"Yes, ma'am. Now let me drive you home."

53

Late Friday afternoon, Agents Angus Sommers and Ruthanne Scaturro went directly from Amy Lindcroft's home to the Park Avenue office of C.F.G.&Y. and requested an immediate meeting with Gregg Stanford. After a full half-hour wait, they were finally admitted to his office, which obviously had been furnished to reflect his own rather grand taste.

Instead of a typical desk, he had an antique writing table. Sommers, something of a furniture buff himself, recognized it as being early eighteenth century and probably worth a small fortune. Instead of book shelves, an eighteenth century *bureau-cabinet* on the left wall reflected the late afternoon sunlight that was filtering through a window that overlooked Park Avenue. In lieu of the usual executive desk chair, Sommers had opted for a richly upholstered antique armchair. In contrast, the seats in front of his desk were side chairs upholstered in a rather plain fabric, a clear indication to Sommers that visitors were not considered to be on the same social level as Gregg Stanford himself. A portrait of a beautiful woman in an evening gown dominated the wall to the right of the desk. Sommers was sure that the haughty, unsmiling subject of the portrait had to be Stanford's current wife, Millicent.

I wonder if he's gotten to the point where he orders his staff not to look him directly in the eye, Sommers thought. What a phony. And this office—did he rig it up like this on his own, or was the wife in on it? She's on a couple of museum boards, so she probably knows her stuff.

When the two agents had interviewed Norman Bond, he made the gesture of rising slightly from his chair when they entered his office. Stanford did not extend that courtesy to them. He remained seated, his hands clasped in front of him, until the agents sat down without being invited.

"Have you made any progress in your

search for the Pied Piper?" he asked abruptly.

"Yes, we have," Angus Sommers said promptly and convincingly. "In fact, we're closing in on him fast. More than that, I'm not at liberty to tell you."

He noticed that Stanford's mouth tightened. Nerves, he wondered? He hoped so. "Mr. Stanford, we have just come across some information that we need to discuss with you."

"I cannot imagine what you have to discuss with me," Stanford said. "I have made my position on the ransom payment eminently clear. That is obviously my only area of interest to you."

"Not quite," Sommers said slowly, taking satisfaction in drawing the words out. "When you learned that Lucas Wohl was one of the kidnappers, it must have been quite a shock to you."

"What *are* you talking about?"

"You must have seen his picture in the newspapers and on television?"

"I saw his picture, of course."

"Then you must have recognized that he was the ex-convict who was your chauffeur for several years."

"I don't know what you're talking about."

"I think you *do,* Mr. Stanford. Your second wife, Tina Olsen, was very active with a charity that helped ex-convicts get jobs. Through her, you met Jimmy Nelson, who at some time took on the name of his deceased cousin, Lucas Wohl. Tina Olsen had a longtime private chauffeur, but Jimmy—or Lucas or whatever you called him—drove you frequently during your marriage to her. Yesterday, Tina Olsen called your first wife, Amy Lindcroft, and told her that she believes Lucas continued to drive you long after the breakup of the marriage. Is that true, Mr. Stanford?"

Stanford stared first at one agent and then the other. "If there is anything worse than one woman scorned, it is two women scorned," he said. "During my marriage to Tina, I used a car service. Quite frankly I never established nor did I want to establish any kind of relationship with the various drivers who worked for that service. If you tell me that one of the kidnappers was one of those drivers, I accept it, although of course I am shocked. The idea that I saw his picture in the newspaper and should have recognized him is ludicrous."

"Then you don't deny that you know him?" Sommers asked.

"You could tell me that *any* person drove me from time to time, years ago, and I would not be able to either confirm or deny it. Now get out of here."

"We'll be going over the records Lucas kept; they go back quite a few years," Sommers said as he stood up. "I think he was your driver far more frequently than you have cared to admit, which leads me to wonder what else you have to conceal. We will find out what it is, Mr. Stanford. I can promise you *that.*"

54

"Now get this straight," Angie told Kathy at nine o'clock on Saturday morning. "Between the crying and the coughing, you kept me awake half the night, and I'm sick of it. I can't stay cooped up in this room all day and I can't shut you up by taping your mouth because with that cold you might not be able to breathe, so I'm taking you with me. I bought some clothes for you yesterday when I went out, but the shoes don't fit right. They're too small. So we're going to go back to Sears, and I'll go in and switch them for the next size, and *you* are going to stay on the floor of the van and say not one word, got it?"

Kathy nodded. Angie had dressed her in a polo shirt, corduroy overalls and a hooded jacket. Her short dark hair lay limply on her forehead and cheeks, still damp from the shower Angie had given her. An overflowing tablespoon of the cough syrup was already making her sleepy. She wanted so much to talk to Kelly, but twin talk was forbidden. That was why Angie had pinched her so hard yesterday.

"Mommy, Daddy," she whispered in her mind. "I want to come home. I want to come home." She knew she had to try not to cry anymore. She didn't *mean* to cry, but when she fell asleep and reached out for Kelly's hand and it wasn't there, and then she realized she wasn't in her own bed and Mommy wasn't coming in to make sure they were covered, she couldn't help it. That was when she started to cry.

The shoes Angie had bought for her were too small. They hurt her toes, and they didn't feel at all like her sneakers with the pink laces, or the party shoes she wore with the party dress. Maybe if she was very good, and didn't cry, and tried not to cough, and didn't talk twin talk, Mommy would come and take her home. And Angie was Mona's real name. That was what Harry had called her sometimes. And his name wasn't

Harry, it was Clint. That's what Angie called him sometimes.

I want to go home, she thought, as tears welled in her eyes.

"Don't start crying," Angie warned as she opened the door and pulled Kathy by the hand outside onto the parking lot. It was raining hard, and Angie put down the big suitcase she was carrying and yanked the hood of the jacket over Kathy's head. "You don't need a worse cold," she said. "You're sick enough as it is."

Angie carried the big suitcase into the car and then made Kathy lie down on the pillow on the floor, and covered her with a blanket. "That's something else. I have to get a car seat for you." She sighed. "God, you're more trouble than you're worth."

She slammed the back door, got in the driver's seat, and turned the key in the ignition. "On the other hand, I always wanted a kid," she said, talking more to herself than to Kathy. "That's what got me in trouble before. I think that little kid really *liked* me and wanted to stay with me. I almost went nuts when the mother picked him up. His name was Billy. He was cute, and I could make him laugh—not like you, always crying. God."

Kathy knew that Angie didn't like her anymore. She curled up on the floor and put her thumb in her mouth. She used to do that when she was a baby, but then she stopped. Now she couldn't *help* doing it—it made it easier not to cry.

As Angie drove out of the motel parking lot, she said, "Just in case you're interested, you're in Cape Cod, baby doll. This street leads to the docks where the boats go over to Martha's Vineyard and Nantucket. I went to Martha's Vineyard once, with the guy who brought me up here. I kind of liked him, but we never got together again. Boy, I wish I could tell *him* that I'm driving around with a million bucks in a suitcase. Wouldn't that be something?"

Kathy felt the car turn.

"Main Street, Hyannis," Angie said. "Not as crowded as it will be in a couple of months. By then we'll be in Hawaii. I mean, that's probably a lot safer than being in Florida."

They drove for a little while more. Angie began to sing a song about Cape Cod. She didn't know many of the words, so she'd hum and then sort of yell, "In Old Cape Cod." She sang those words over and over and over. Then, after a while, the car stopped, and Angie sang one more time, "Here in Old Cape Cod." Then she said, "Boy can I belt out a song," after which she leaned over the seat and looked down, a mean expression on her face. "Okay, we're here," she said. "Now listen, don't you dare get up, understand? I'm going to pull the blanket over your head, so that if anyone happens to look in, they won't see you. If I come out and find you moved one *inch,* you know what will happen, don't you?"

Kathy's eyes welled with tears, and she nodded.

"Okay. We understand each other. I'll be back fast, then we'll go to McDonald's or Burger King. You and me together. Mommy and Stevie."

Kathy felt the blanket being pulled over her head, but she didn't care. It felt good to be dark and warm, and anyhow, she was sleepy, and it was good to be asleep. But the blanket was fuzzy, and it tickled her nose. She could tell she was going to start coughing again, but managed not to cough until Angie got out of the car and had closed and locked the door.

Then she let herself cry and talk to Kelly. "I don't want to be in Old Cape Cod. I don't want to be in Old Cape Cod. *I want to come home.*"

55

"There he is," Agent Sean Walsh whispered to his partner, Damon Philburn. It was nine thirty on Saturday morning. He was pointing to the lanky figure of a man in a hooded sweatshirt who had parked near a condominium in Clifton, New Jersey, and was now walking up the path to the front door. The car the agents had been waiting in was parked on the opposite side of the street. In a swift, simultaneous movement, they were out of it and on either side of the man before he could even turn the key in the door.

Steve Frawley's half-brother, Richard Mason, the object of their surveillance, did not seem surprised to see them. "Come on in," he said. "But you're wasting your time. I had nothing to do with my brother's kids being kidnapped. Knowing the way you guys work, you probably had my mother's phone bugged when she called me after you came looking for me."

Neither agent bothered to reply as Mason turned on the foyer light and walked into the living room. To Walsh, it had the look of a motel unit: a couch upholstered in a brown-tweed pattern, two striped brown chairs, two end tables with matching lamps, a coffee table, beige carpeting. They had learned that Mason had been living there for the past ten months, but there was nothing in the room to suggest that this was his home. The built-in bookshelves did not hold a single book. There were no family pictures or personal items that might have suggested a hobby or any kind of leisure-time activity. Mason sat in one of the chairs, folded his legs, and took out a pack of cigarettes, lit one, glanced at the table next to the chair, and looked annoyed. "Threw out the ashtrays so that I wouldn't be tempted to smoke." Shrugging, he got up, disappeared into the kitchen, came back holding a saucer and resettled in the chair.

He's trying to show us how cool he is, Walsh thought. We can all play that game. He exchanged a quick glance with Philburn and knew they were of the same mind. The agents let the silence grow.

"Listen, I've done a lot of driving these past few days and need to get to bed. What do you want?" Mason asked, his tone insolent.

"When did you resume smoking, Mr. Mason?" Walsh asked.

"A week ago, when I heard my brother's twins were missing," Mason answered.

"It wasn't when you and Franklin Bailey decided to kidnap them, was it?" Agent Philburn asked matter-of-factly.

"You've got to be crazy! My brother's kids?"

Walsh watched as Mason turned his head to look at Philburn. He could see the deep flush that rose on his neck and colored his face. He had studied his mug shots and already noticed the strong physical resemblance to his half brother. But there the resemblance ends, he thought. He had seen Steve Frawley's appearances on television, and had been impressed by his emotional control, even though he was clearly under tremendous strain. Mason had gone to prison because he was a con man who bilked people out of their money. And he's trying to con us now, Walsh thought, by playing the part of the outraged uncle.

"I haven't spoken to Franklin Bailey in eight years," Mason said. "Considering the circumstances, I doubt very much that he would want to speak to me."

"Doesn't it seem quite a coincidence that he, a virtual stranger, rushed to offer his services as a go-between to the Frawleys?" Walsh asked.

"If I were to guess at all, from what I remember of Bailey, I'd say he loved the spotlight. He was mayor when he was investing in my company, and I remember he even joked to me that he'd go to the opening of an envelope if the press would cover it. When they finally voted him out of office, it just about broke his heart. I know he was looking forward to taking the witness stand at my trial and had to be disappointed when I took a plea deal. With all the liars the feds had lined up as witnesses, I didn't stand a chance if I went to trial."

"You visited your brother and his wife in Ridgefield shortly after they moved in a few months ago," Walsh said. "You didn't stop by Franklin Bailey's home for old times' sake?"

"That's a stupid question," Mason replied evenly. "He would have kicked me out."

"You've never been very close to your brother, have you?" Philburn asked.

"A lot of brothers aren't close. Even more half-brothers aren't close."

"You met Steve's wife, Margaret, before he met her. It was at a wedding, I believe. You phoned and asked her for a date, and she turned you down. Then she met Steve in law school. Did that bother you?"

"I never had trouble getting an attractive woman. I have two divorces from smart, attractive women to prove it. I never gave Margaret a second thought."

"You almost got away with pulling off a scam that would have made millions for you. Since Steve was hired in a job that amounts to a straight path to the top, has it occurred to you that once again he's bested you?"

"Never crossed my mind. And like I said, I never cheated anyone."

"Mr. Mason, a baggage handler has a pretty exhausting job. Somehow it doesn't seem to be the kind of occupation you'd choose."

"It's an interim position," Richard Mason replied calmly.

"Aren't you afraid of losing it? You didn't show up for work all week."

"I phoned in to say I wasn't feeling well and needed the week off."

"Funny, we weren't told that," Philburn commented.

"Then somebody messed up at the other end. I assure you I made the call."

"Where did you go?"

"I drove to Vegas. I was feeling lucky."

"It didn't occur to you to be with your brother while his children were missing?"

"He wouldn't have wanted me. I'm an embarrassment to him. Can't you just picture the ex-con brother hovering in the background with the media around? You said yourself, Stevie is going places with C.F.G.&Y. I bet he didn't put me down as a reference on his résumé."

"You are sophisticated about wire transfers and the kind of banks that will accept them, forward funds, and destroy the records, aren't you?"

Mason stood up. "Get out. Arrest me or get out."

Neither agent made a move. "Isn't it a coincidence that last weekend you visited your mother in North Carolina, the very weekend that your brother's children were kidnapped? Maybe you were trying to establish an alibi."

"Get out."

Walsh took out his notebook. "Where did you stay in Vegas, Mr. Mason, and who were some of the people who could verify that you were there?"

"I'm not answering any questions until I talk to a lawyer. I know you guys. You're trying to trap me."

Walsh and Philburn got up. "We'll be back," Walsh said, his tone even.

They left the apartment but stopped at Mason's car. Walsh took out a flashlight and played it on the dashboard. "Fifty thousand, six hundred and forty-six miles," he said.

Philburn jotted down the figure. "He's watching us," he commented.

"I want him to watch us. He knows what I'm doing."

"How many miles did the mother say was on the odometer?"

"In that wire-tapped phone call she made to him after we left, she reminded him that the stepfather had noticed that his car was coming up to fifty thousand miles, and his warranty would be expiring, so she urged him to get it checked for any problems. Sounds like Frawley senior may be a stickler on car maintenance."

"Mason's some six hundred miles over fifty thousand on this car. It's about six hundred miles from Winston-Salem. He never drove this car to Vegas for sure. So where do you think he was?"

"My guess is somewhere in the tristate area, babysitting," Philburn replied.

56

On Saturday morning, Lila Jackson couldn't wait to tell everyone at Abby's Discount how much she had enjoyed the play she and her mother had seen the night before.

"It was a revival of *Our Town*," Lila told Joan Howell. "To say it was wonderful just isn't enough. I loved it! That final scene, when George throws himself on Emily's grave! I can't tell you. The tears just rolled out of my eyes. You know, when I was twelve, we did that play at St. Francis Xavier. I played the first dead woman. My line was, 'It's on the same road we lived on. Um-hum.' "

When Lila was enthusiastic, there was no stopping her. Howell waited patiently for a pause in the narration, then said, "We had quite a bit of excitement around here late yesterday afternoon. Margaret Frawley, the mother of the kidnapped twins, came in here looking for you."

"She *what?*" Lila had been about to step out from the office to the sales floor. Now she took her hand from the door. *"Why?"*

"I don't know. She asked for your cell phone number, and when I wouldn't give it, she said something about her little girl being alive, and she had to find her. I think the poor thing is having a nervous breakdown. I don't blame her, of course, after losing one of her twins. She actually grabbed me, and for a minute, I thought I was dealing with a lunatic. Then I recognized her and tried to talk to her, but she started crying and ran out of here. This morning I heard on the news that there had been an alert out for her because she was missing, and that the police found her at eleven o'clock last night parked near the airport in Danbury. They said she seemed dazed and disoriented."

Lila had forgotten about the play. "I know why she wanted to talk to me," she said quietly. "There was another woman shopping here the same evening Mrs. Frawley was shopping for the birthday dresses last week. She was selecting clothes for three-year-old twins, and she didn't seem to have a clue what size to buy for them. I told that to Mrs. Frawley because I thought it was so unusual. I even . . ."

Lila let her voice trail off. She did not think that Joan Howell, a stickler for doing things according to the book, would like the idea that she had twisted the bookkeeper's arm to phone the credit card company and get the address of the woman who had bought clothes for twins, not knowing their size. "If it would help Mrs. Frawley to talk to me, I'd really like to talk to her," she finished.

"She didn't leave her number. I'd say, let it go." Joan Howell glanced at her watch, a clear indication to Lila that it was five minutes after ten and that as of ten A.M. she was being paid to sell Abby's Discount Clothes.

Lila remembered the name of the customer who hadn't known the size of the three-year-old twins. It's Downes, she thought as she headed for a sales rack. She signed the slip as Mrs. Clint Downes, but when I talked to Jim Gilbert about her, he told me her name is Angie, that she's not married to Downes, and that he's the caretaker at the Danbury Country Club, and they live in a cottage on the grounds of the club.

Aware that Joan Howell's eyes were on her, she turned to a woman at the sales rack who by now had several pantsuits over her arm. "May I put these aside for you?" she asked. At the customer's grateful nod, she took the garments, and, as she waited, thought about how convinced she had been that it wouldn't hurt to mention the incident to the police. They had been begging for anyone to report anything that might help them find the kidnappers.

Jim Gilbert made me feel like an idiot, she thought. Talked about how many phony clues the police were getting. And because he's a retired detective, I listened to him.

The shopper had found two more suits to try on and was ready to go to a dressing room. "There's an empty one right over here," Lila told her. I could talk to the police now, she thought, but they might just dismiss it the way Jim did. I've got a better idea. The country club is only ten minutes from here. On my lunch hour I'll drive over, ring the bell of the caretaker's cottage, and I'll say that I realized the polo shirts I sold her were defective, and I wanted to replace them. Then, if I still feel funny about anything, I will call the police.

At one o'clock Lila took two size 4 polo shirts to the cashier. "Kate, toss these in a bag," she said. "Ring them up when I get back. I'm in a hurry." She realized that for some reason she had a compelling feeling of urgency.

It had begun to rain again, and in her haste she had not bothered to take her umbrella with her. Oh, so what if I get wet, she thought as she ran across the parking lot to her car. Twelve minutes later, she was at the gate to the Danbury Country Club. To her dismay, she saw that it was padlocked. There's got to be another entrance, she thought. She drove around slowly, stopping at another locked gate before she found a service road with a bar across it and a box to punch in the code to raise the bar. In the distance, well to the right and behind the club house, she could see a small building which she knew might be the caretaker's cottage Jim Gilbert had mentioned.

The rain was getting heavier. I've come this far, Lila decided, I'm going ahead. At least I was smart enough to wear a raincoat. She got out of the car, ducked under the security arm, and, keeping as much as possible in the shelter of the evergreens, began to jog toward the cottage, the bag with the polo shirts cradled under her jacket.

She passed a one-car garage to the right of the cottage. The door was open, and she could see that the garage was empty. Maybe there's no one home, she thought. In that case, what do I do?

But as she got closer to the cottage she could see that there was a light on in the front room. Here goes nothing, she thought, as she went up the two steps to the small porch and rang the bell.

On Friday evening, Clint had gone out with Gus again, got home late, slept until noon, and now was hungover and nervous. While they were having dinner at the bar, Gus had said that when he'd phoned the other night and talked to Angie, he'd have sworn he heard two kids crying in the background.

I tried to make a joke of it, Clint thought. I told him he must have been drunk to think that there were two kids in this chicken coop. I told him that I don't mind that Angie makes money babysitting, but if she ever showed up with two kids, I'd tell her to hit the road. I think he bought it, but I don't know. He's got a big mouth. Suppose he mentions to someone else that he heard two crying kids who Angie was minding. Besides that, he told me about seeing Angie at the drug store buying the vaporizer and aspirin. For all I know, he could have told somebody else.

I've got to rent a car and get rid of that crib, he thought as he made coffee. At least I took it apart, but I have to get it out of here and ditch it in the woods somewhere. Why did Angie keep one of the kids? Why did she kill Lucas? If both kids had been returned, we'd have split the money with Lucas, and no one would be the wiser. Now the whole country is on the warpath because they think one of the kids is dead.

Angie will get sick of minding her. Then she'll dump her somewhere. I know she will. I just hope she doesn't . . . Clint didn't finish the thought, but the image of Angie leaning into the car and shooting Lucas was never far from his mind. She had shocked him, and now he was terrified of what else she might do.

He was hunched over the kitchen table, wearing a heavy sweatshirt and jeans; his hair was uncombed; a two-day growth of beard darkened his face; his second cup of coffee sat untouched in front of him. Then the doorbell rang.

The cops! It would be the cops, he was sure of it. Perspiration began to pour from him. No, maybe it's Gus, he thought, grasping at straws. He had to open the door. If it was the cops, they'd have seen that the light was on, and they wouldn't go away.

He was still barefoot when he padded across the living room, his thick feet noiseless on the shabby rug. He put his hand on the knob, turned it, and yanked the door open.

Lila gasped. She had expected that the woman who had shopped for the clothes would be standing there. Now she was faced with a heavy-set, sloppy man, who was glaring at her suspiciously.

To Clint, the reprieve of not being confronted by the police was replaced by fear that this was some sort of trap. Maybe she's an undercover cop nosing around, he thought. Don't look nervous, he told himself. If I didn't have anything to worry about, I'd be polite and ask her what I could do for her.

He forced something like a smile to cross his face. "Hello."

I wonder if he's sick, was Lila's first thought. He's perspiring so much. "Is Mrs. Downes, I mean, is Angie home?" she asked.

"No. She's away on a babysitting job. I'm Clint. Why do you want her?"

This is probably going to sound stupid, Lila thought, but I'm going to say it anyhow. "I'm Lila Jackson," she explained. "I work at Abby's Discount on Route 7. My boss sent me over to give Angie something. I'm expected back in a few minutes. Do you mind if I step in?"

As long as I give him the impression that people know where I am, it should be okay, she thought. She realized she could not leave until she was sure Angie wasn't hiding somewhere in the house.

"Sure, come in." Clint stood aside and Lila brushed past him. In a quick glance she saw that there was no one else in the living room, dining or kitchen area, and that the bedroom door was open. Clint Downes was apparently alone in the house, and if there had been children here, there was no sign of them now. She unbuttoned her coat, fished out the bag with the polo shirts, and handed it to him. "When Mrs. Downes, I mean

Angie, was in our store last week, she bought polo shirts for the twins," she said. "We received a notice from the manufacturer that the whole run of two of the shirts I sold her had defects, so I came over with replacements."

"That was very nice of you," Clint said slowly, his mind scrambling to explain the purchase. Angie had to have charged that stuff on my credit card, he thought. She was stupid enough to leave a paper trail. "My girlfriend babysits all the time," he explained to Lila. "She drove to Wisconsin with a family to help take care of their kids. She'll be there for a couple of weeks. She bought that stuff because the mother called ahead to say she forgot to bring one of their suitcases."

"The mother of the three-year-old twins?" Lila asked.

"Yeah. Actually from what Angie told me, the kids are less than a year apart. They're about the same size, though. The mother dresses them alike and calls them twins, but they're not really. Why don't you just leave the shirts here? I'm sending a package to Angie and I'll put them in it."

Lila did not know how to refuse the offer.

This is a wild goose chase, she decided. This guy looks harmless. People do jokingly call children who are very close in age twins. I know they do. She handed the bag to Clint. "I'll be on my way," she said. "Please apologize to Angie, or to her employer."

"Sure, glad to. No problem."

The phone rang. "Well anyhow, goodbye," Clint said as he hurried to pick up the receiver. "Hi," he said, his eyes fixed on Lila whose hand was now on the door knob.

"Why haven't you been answering my phone? I've called you a dozen times," a voice barked.

It was the Pied Piper.

For Lila's benefit Clint tried to sound casual. "Not tonight, Gus," he said. "I really want to take it easy."

Lila was opening the door slowly, hoping to hear what Clint was saying. But there was no way she could hang around, and besides, she clearly had rushed here on a fool's errand. Jim Gilbert had told her that Angie was a babysitter, and it was reasonable that the mother had asked her to pick up some extra clothes. Now I'm drenched and out the money for the shirts, she thought as she hurried back to the car.

"Who's there with you?" the Pied Piper was demanding.

Clint waited until he saw Lila pass the window, then said, "Angie took off with the kid. She didn't think it was safe to hang around here anymore. She has the cell phone you gave Lucas to pass on to me. She charged the clothes she bought for the kids to my credit card. Some woman was here from the store replacing shirts that were no good. I don't know whether or not she's on the level." He knew his voice was rising as he said, "I've got to figure out what to do. I don't even know where Angie is."

He heard the sharp intake of breath and knew that the Pied Piper was nervous, too.

"Take it easy, Clint. Do you think Angie will call again?"

"I think so. She trusts me. I think she knows she needs me."

"But you don't need *her.* What would happen if you told her a cop had come around looking for her?"

"She'd panic."

"Then tell her that. Arrange to meet her

wherever she is. And remember—what she did to Lucas, she could do to you."

"Don't think I'm not thinking about that."

"And while you're thinking about that, remember that if the child really is still alive, she could identify you, too."

57

"Everyone has a breaking point, Margaret," Dr. Sylvia Harris said gently early Saturday afternoon. It was one o'clock, and she and Kelly had just awakened Margaret.

Now Margaret was sitting up in bed, Kelly snuggled beside her. She tried to smile. "Whatever did you give me to knock me out like that? Do you realize I've been sleeping for twelve hours?"

"Do you realize how much sleep you've lost in the past week?" Dr. Harris's tone was light, but her eyes were watchful. Margaret's so thin, she thought, and so terribly pale. "I hated to wake you up even now, but Agent Carlson phoned. He wants to stop by. Steve is on his way over and asked me to wake you up."

"The FBI is probably trying to decide what

I was up to when I took off last night. I wonder if they think I'm crazy. Right after you left yesterday, I called Agent Carlson. I screamed at him that Kathy was still alive, and he had to find her." Margaret pulled Kelly into her arms. "Then I went over to the place where I bought the dresses and practically attacked the manager, or whoever she was. I just lost it, I guess."

"Do you have any idea of where you went after you left the store?" Dr. Harris asked. "Last night, you said it was a total blank."

"I don't really remember anything until I saw a sign for Cape Cod. That kind of woke me up, and I knew I had to turn around. I feel so guilty. Poor Steve has had enough stress without *me* going off the deep end."

Dr. Harris thought of the look of desperation she had seen on Steve's face last night when she returned to the house at eight o'clock and learned that Margaret was missing.

"Dr. Sylvia," Steve had explained, his voice agonized. "Right after I brought Kelly home from nursery school, as she was taking off her jacket, she let out a yell and grabbed her arm in that same spot where she had the bruise. She must have banged it on the leg of that table in the foyer. But Margaret went *nuts!* She was sure it meant that someone was hurting Kathy and that Kelly was feeling the pain with her. Margaret grabbed the car keys from me and told me she had to talk to someone in that store where she bought the birthday dresses. When she didn't come home, and when I couldn't remember the name of the store, I finally called the police and reported her missing. Dr. Sylvia, she wouldn't harm herself, would she? Do you think she would harm herself?"

It was three more agonizing hours before the call came that the police had found Margaret, sitting in her car near the Danbury airport. When they finally brought her home, she had not been able to tell them where she had been all that time. I gave her a strong sleeping pill, Dr. Harris thought, and it was the right thing to do. I can't lighten her grief, but I least I am able to give her a chance to escape it and rest.

She watched now as Margaret brushed her finger over Kelly's cheek.

"Hey, somebody's really quiet," Margaret said softly. "How are we doing, Kel?"

Kelly looked up at her solemnly but did not answer.

"Our little girl really has been pretty quiet all morning," Dr. Harris observed. "I slept in with you last night, didn't I, Kelly?"

Kelly nodded silently.

"Did she sleep well?" Margaret asked.

"She was having a little reaction to everything, I think. She was crying in her sleep and doing quite a bit of coughing. That's why I thought it best to stay with her."

Margaret bit her lip. Trying to keep her voice steady, she said, "She's probably getting her sister's cold." She kissed the top of Kelly's head. "We'll take very good care of that, won't we, Dr. Sylvia?"

"Indeed we will, but I can assure you that her chest is absolutely clear." In fact, Dr. Sylvia Harris thought, there is no reason for all that coughing. She doesn't have a cold. She stood up. "Margaret, why don't we give you a chance to shower and dress? We'll go downstairs, and Kelly will pick out whatever story she wants me to read to her."

Kelly hesitated.

"I think that's a wonderful idea," Margaret said firmly.

Silently, Kelly slid off the bed and reached

for Sylvia Harris's hand. They went downstairs to the study. There, Kelly selected a
book and climbed onto the doctor's lap.
The room was a little cool. Sylvia reached
for the afghan that was folded over the arm
of the couch and tucked it around Kelly. She
began to open the book, then pushed up
Kelly's sleeve for the second time that day.

The purple bruise on her forearm was in
almost exactly the same spot as the one
that was fading. It looks as though someone
pinched her hard, Sylvia thought. "You
didn't get that by hitting your arm against a
table, Kelly," she said aloud, and then wondered if it was possible. Is Margaret right
that Kelly was actually feeling Kathy's pain?
She could not stop herself from voicing the
question that was burning in her mind.

"Kelly," she asked, "can you sometimes
feel what Kathy feels?"

Kelly looked at her and shook her head,
her eyes frightened. "Ssshhh," she whispered, then rolled into a ball, put her thumb
in her mouth, and pulled the afghan over her
head.

58

Special Agent Connor Ryan had called a meeting in his New Haven office for eleven o'clock on Saturday morning. Grimly determined to track down the kidnappers, he, Agents Carlson and Realto, and Jed Gunther, a captain with the Connecticut State Police, were settled around a conference table, reviewing the status of the investigation.

As head of the Bureau in Connecticut, Ryan led the discussion. "Wohl, as he was known, *could* have killed himself. It was physically possible, but it's not the way most people do it. The typical suicide puts a gun in his mouth or to the side of his head and pulls the trigger. Take a look at these."

He passed the autopsy pictures of Lucas

Wohl to the other men. "From the angle of the bullet we can tell that he would have to be holding the gun above his head when he fired it."

"Then we have the suicide note, which is another problem," he said flatly. "Wohl's fingerprints are on it, but not all over it, the way they would be if he had rolled the sheet of paper into the typewriter and then removed it after he finished typing his confession. Unless, of course, he was wearing gloves when he did the typing." He handed the note to Carlson.

"Let's reconstruct," Ryan continued. "We know we have at least two people involved. One was Lucas Wohl. The night of the kidnapping, the babysitter was on her way to the twins' bedroom because one of them had cried out. Then she was grabbed from behind in the upstairs hallway. She believes that there has to have been someone in the room with the children when she was attacked. It makes sense, because we know that two men were seen carrying the ransom money."

"Do you think one of them was the Pied Piper?" Gunther asked.

"I think the Pied Piper was someone else,

a third man, the one who was calling the shots and not in on the actual kidnapping, but that's just a hunch."

"I believe there may have been another person involved," Walter Carlson said. "A woman. After Kelly got back home, she said two names in her sleep, 'Mona' and 'Harry.' The father was sitting by the bed and heard her. The Frawleys are positive they don't know anyone by either of those names. So Harry may be the name of the other kidnapper, and Mona might be a woman who was minding them."

"Then let's agree that we may be looking for at least two, and perhaps three people other than Lucas Wohl: the second kidnapper, a man whose name may be Harry, and a woman whose name may be Mona. And if neither one of these three was the Pied Piper, then we're also looking for a fourth person," Ryan said.

The slight nods of the heads of the other men told him that they were in agreement. "Which brings us to the persons of interest," he went on. "The way I see it, there may be four of them. There's Steve Frawley's half-brother, Richard Mason, who is jealous of Steve, may have had a thing for Margaret, knew Franklin Bailey, and was lying when he claimed he went to Vegas. Then there's Bailey himself. Also, Norman Bond, the man at C.F.G.&Y. who hired Steve, who lived in Ridgefield, whose early life parallels Steve's, who has had several breakdowns, and who referred to his missing ex-wife as 'his *late* wife.' "

Ryan's lips tightened. "Finally we have Gregg Stanford, who vigorously objected to voting to have C.F.G.&Y. pay the ransom, who may be in domestic trouble with his rich wife, and who at one time used Lucas Wohl as his personal driver.

"By the time we're finished checking out those four, Mason, Bailey, Bond, and Stanford, we'll know when they said their first baby word and what it was. I'm sure of that. But that doesn't mean we're not off base with all of them. There could be other people involved."

"Our guys are taking the position that somebody knew his way around the Frawley house that night," Gunther said. "We're going through all the real estate records of the selling broker to see if we can make some kind of connection. Beyond that, I was talking to the New York trooper who got to Kelly first. He made some interesting points. Kelly was wearing the pajamas that we now know she had on the night she was abducted, but they were fairly clean. No three-year-old kid I know could wear the same outfit for five days without it looking as though it had been worn for five months. That means someone either changed her into other clothes, or washed and dried those pajamas at least a couple of times. To me that sounds as though there was a woman involved in this."

"I've felt that," Carlson agreed. "Another question is, did Lucas carry Kelly to that parking lot in the stolen car? In that case she may have seen him shoot himself. Where were the other kidnappers? Isn't it reasonable to suppose that they didn't know that Lucas was planning to commit suicide and were following him to the parking lot with the idea of leaving Kelly, or perhaps both Kelly and Kathy, in the car and taking Lucas back with them? And remember, when the Pied Piper phoned Monsignor Romney, he said *both* girls were safe. At that point, he had no reason to lie. It may have been a shock for him to learn that Kathy was dead.

"Mind you, I think she *is* dead and that it happened the way Lucas described it. It was an accident. I believe he buried her body at sea. I talked to the mechanic who saw Wohl carrying the heavy box onto his plane, and I talked as well to the catering service driver who saw him get out of the plane an hour later without the box. We all know that professional kidnappers who are looking for a ransom don't deliberately hurt their victims, particularly children. Here's the scenario I think is possible: Lucas *did* accidentally kill Kathy and went off the deep end about it. He worried the others. I think they may have driven to the parking lot with him, and one of them killed him to keep him from getting drunk and talking. We've got to talk to Kelly and try to find out what she knows. She hardly said a word in the hospital the other day, and apparently she has been pretty quiet since she came home. But Thursday night, she did say those two names in her sleep, 'Mona' and 'Harry.' Maybe we can get her to say something else about what happened during the time she was gone. I want to talk to the parents about bringing in a child psychiatrist to question her."

"What about Margaret Frawley?" Ryan asked. "Tony, have you spoken to her husband today?"

"I spoke to him last night, after the cops took Margaret home. He told me she was in shock and that the doctor who is the twins' pediatrician gave her a strong sedative. She apparently didn't know where she'd been or even remember that she'd gone to that store where she bought the birthday dresses."

"What was her reason for going to the store?"

"I talked to the manager this morning. Margaret was pretty out of it when she was there yesterday. Wanted to talk to the sales clerk who sold her the dresses, then when the manager was about to give her the clerk's cell phone number, she broke down and ran out. God only knows what was running through her mind. But her husband told me she was insisting that a new bruise on Kelly's arm was caused by something that was happening to Kathy, and that Kelly was experiencing Kathy's pain."

"You don't believe that nonsense, do you, Tony?" Ryan was clearly incredulous.

"No, of course I don't. I don't think for

one minute that Kelly is in communication with Kathy, but I do want her to start communicating with *us,* and the sooner the better."

59

Norman Bond lived on the fortieth floor of an apartment building bordering the East River at Seventy-second Street in Manhattan. His panoramic, three-hundred-and-sixty-degree view had always enriched his solitary personal life. In the morning, he often got up in time to watch the sunrise. At night, he took particular pleasure in observing the brilliance of the lights on the bridges that spanned the river.

On Saturday morning, after the dreary weather of the past week, the day dawned crisp and clear, but even the bright sunrise did not lift his spirits. For hours he sat on the couch in his living room, methodically reviewing his options.

There weren't many, he decided. What's done is done and can't be changed. "The moving finger having writ . . . And neither piety nor wit . . . can move it to cancel nor yet replace a word of it," he recited to himself.

I haven't got the quote right, but it went something like that, he decided.

How could I be so stupid, he asked himself. How could I have slipped and referred to Theresa as "my late wife"?

The FBI agents had pounced on that. Long ago they had given up questioning him about Theresa's disappearance. Now it would start all over again. But when someone has been missing for seven years, and has been declared legally dead, isn't it natural to refer to that person as if she *was* dead? Theresa has been missing seventeen years.

Of *course* it is.

It was all right to wear the wedding ring he had given Theresa, the one she left for him on the dresser. But was it safe to continue wearing her other ring, the one her second husband gave her? He unfastened the chain from around his neck and held both rings in his hand, studying them intensely. LOVE IS ETERNAL was inscribed in tiny letters on the inside of both bands.

The one he gave her is all diamonds, Norman thought enviously. I gave her a plain silver ring. It was all I could afford at that time.

"My *late* wife," he said aloud.

Now, after all this time, the kidnapping of two little girls had brought him to the attention of the FBI again.

My late wife!

It would be dangerous to resign from C.F.G.&Y. and move abroad—too abrupt, too contradictory of all the plans he had talked about.

At noon, he became aware that he was still wearing just his underwear. Theresa used to get so irritated whenever he did that. "People who know anything don't sit around in their underwear, Norman," she used to tell him, her tone disdainful. "They just *don't*. Either put on a robe, or get dressed. One or the other."

She had cried and cried when the twins were born prematurely and didn't survive, but only a week later she had said something about "maybe it was for the best." Shortly after that, she left him, moved to California, got a divorce, and within the year was remarried. He had overheard some of the employees at C.F.G.&Y. laughing about it. "The guy she picked is from a different bolt of cloth than poor Norman," he heard one of them say.

He still winced at the hurt.

When they were married, he had told Theresa that someday he was going to be the chairman and CEO of C.F.G.&Y.

Now he knew, of course, that was never going to happen, but somehow it didn't matter anymore. He didn't need the grief of the job, and now he didn't need the money, either. But I can't stop wearing the rings, he thought as he clasped the chain around his neck again. They're what give me strength. They remind me that I am not just the insecure, compulsive hard worker that others assume me to be.

Norman smiled, remembering the terrified look on Theresa's face that night when she turned around and saw him hiding in the backseat of her car.

60

"These shoes are too big," Angie said, "but I'm not going to worry about it." She had parked outside McDonald's, near the mall where she'd bought the shoes, and now was fastening them on Kathy's feet. "Remember to keep your mouth shut, but if anyone asks your name, say it's 'Stevie.' Got it? Say it for me now."

"Stevie," Kathy whispered.

"You got it. Now come on."

The shoes hurt Kathy in a different way than the others Angie had bought for her. They made it hard to walk because her feet kept sliding and starting to come out of them. But Angie was pulling her along so fast, and besides, she was afraid to tell her that.

She felt her foot come out of one of the shoes.

Outside McDonald's, Angie stopped to buy a newspaper at a vending machine. Then they went inside and got on line. When she got their food, they sat at a table where Angie could see the van. "Never had to worry about minding that old rattletrap before," she said. "But with all that loot in the suitcase, it would be just my luck to have someone decide to steal it."

Kathy didn't want the egg sandwich and orange juice Angie had bought her. She wasn't hungry and really just wanted to sleep. But she also didn't want to make Angie mad, so she tried to eat some of the sandwich.

"I think from here we go back to the motel, then look up some places to buy a used car," Angie said. "Trouble is, having piles of fifty- and twenty-dollar bills to pay for it is going to attract attention."

Kathy could tell that Angie was getting mad and she watched as she opened the newspaper and said something under her breath that Kathy couldn't understand. Then she reached over and pulled the hood back over Kathy's head. "God Almighty, your face is all over this paper," she said. "Except for the hair, any dope would recognize you. Let's get out of here."

Kathy didn't want Angie to be mad at her again. She slid off the chair and reached for Angie's hand.

"Where's your other shoe, little boy?" asked a lady who was cleaning the next table.

"Her other shoe?" Angie asked, then looked down and saw that Kathy was wearing only one shoe. "Oh, hell," she said, "did you untie that again in the car?"

"No," Kathy whispered. "It fell off. It's too big."

"Your other one's too big, too," said the lady. "What's your name, little boy?"

Kathy tried hard, but she couldn't remember what Angie had told her to say.

"Tell me your name," the lady said.

"Kathy," she whispered, but then she could feel Angie squeezing her hand hard, and suddenly she remembered the name Angie had told her to say. "Stevie," she said. "My name is Stevie."

"Oh, I bet you have a pretend friend named Kathy," the woman said. "My granddaughter has a pretend friend, too."

"Yeah," Angie agreed hurriedly. "Well, we got to be on our way."

Kathy glanced back and saw the woman picking up a newspaper on the chair at the table she was cleaning. On it, Kathy could see her photograph, and Kelly's, too. She couldn't help it. She began to talk twin talk to Kelly, then felt Angie squeeze her hand very, very hard.

"Come on," Angie said, yanking her.

The other new shoe was still on the sidewalk where it had come off. Angie reached down and grabbed it, then opened the back door of the van. "Get in," she said angrily, tossing the shoe inside.

Kathy scrambled to get in, and, not waiting to be told, lay down on the pillow and reached for the blanket. But then she heard a man ask, "Where is the safety seat for your child, ma'am?"

Kathy looked up and saw that it was a policeman.

"We're on our way to buy a new one," Angie said. "I didn't lock the van when we stayed at a motel last night, and it was stolen."

"Where did you stay?"

"At the Soundview."

"Did you report the theft?"

"No," Angie said. "It was an old seat, not worth the effort."

"We want to know if there's theft going on in Hyannis. May I see your driver's license and registration, please?"

"Sure. Right here." Kathy watched as Angie pulled papers out of her wallet.

"Ms. Hagen, whose van is this?" the policeman asked.

"My boyfriend's."

"I see. Well, I'm going to give you a break. I want you to walk over to the mall and buy a new car seat. I will not allow you to drive with this child in the car without one."

"Thank you, officer. I'll do that right away. Come on, Stevie."

Angie leaned down and picked up Kathy, pressing her face against her jacket. She closed the door of the van and began to walk the block back to the mall.

"That cop is watching us," she hissed. "I don't know whether it was smart to give him Linda Hagen's driver's license. He looked at me kind of funny, but on the other hand I'm registered at the motel under Linda's name. God, this is a mess."

As soon as they were inside the mall, she

put Kathy down. "Here, let me put that other shoe on. I'll stuff a handkerchief in it. You've got to walk. I can't carry you all over Cape Cod. Now we've got to find a place to buy a car seat."

It seemed to Kathy that they walked forever. Then when they did find a store that sold car seats, Angie got mad at the man there. "Listen, open it up for me," she told him. "I'll carry it under my arm."

"It will set the alarm off," he told her. "I can open the box, but you'll have to leave the car seat in it until you're out of the store."

Kathy could tell that Angie was getting very angry, so she didn't want to tell her that even with the handkerchief in it, the shoe had come off again. Then, on the way back to the car, someone stopped Angie. "Your little boy has lost one of his shoes," she said.

Angie grabbed Kathy up. "The stupid clerk sold her the wrong size," she explained. "I mean him. I'll buy him another pair." She walked very quickly away from the lady who talked to them, then stopped, holding Kathy in one arm and dragging the car seat with the other. "Oh, God, that cop is still hanging around. Don't *dare* answer if he talks to you." She got to the car and put Kathy down on the front seat, then tried to attach the car seat in the back. "I'd better have this right," she said. She lifted Kathy around to sit in it. "Turn your head," she whispered. "Turn it now. Don't look at him."

Kathy was so scared of Angie that she began to cry.

"Shut up!" Angie whispered. "Shut up! That cop is watching us."

She slammed the back door and got in the driver's seat. Finally they drove off. On the way back to the motel, she screamed at Kathy. "You said your name! You were doing that twin talk stuff! I told you to shut up! *I told you to shut up!* You could have made a lot of trouble. Not another word. Do you hear me? The next time you open your mouth, I'll slap you silly."

Kathy squeezed her eyes shut and held her hands over her ears. She could tell that Kelly was trying to talk to her, but she knew she must not talk back to her anymore, or Angie would hurt her.

When they got back to the room, Angie dropped Kathy on the bed and said, "Don't move a muscle or say a word. Here, have some more cough medicine. And swallow this aspirin. You feel hot again."

Kathy drank the cough medicine and swallowed the aspirin and closed her eyes, trying not to cough. A few minutes later, before she drifted off, she could hear Angie talking on the phone.

"Clint," Angie was saying. "It's me, honey. Listen, I'm kind of scared. People notice the kid when I'm out with her. Her face is all over the newspapers. I think you were right. I should have let her go home with the other one. What should I do about it? I've got to get rid of her. How should I do it?"

Kathy heard the sound of the buzzer, then Angie's scared voice trying to whisper, "Clint, I have to call you back. There's someone at the door. Oh, God, suppose it's that cop."

Kathy buried her face in the pillow as the phone snapped shut. Home, she thought as she fell asleep. I want to go home.

61

On Saturday morning a wildly restless Gregg Stanford went to his club for a game of squash then returned to the Greenwich estate that was his wife's main residence. He showered, dressed, and ordered lunch served to him in the study. With its paneled walls, antique tapestries and carpets, Hepplewhite furniture and sweeping views of Long Island Sound, it was his favorite room in the mansion.

But even the perfectly cooked salmon served with a bottle of Château Cheval Blanc, 1st Grand Cru Classé neither relaxed nor comforted him. The seventh anniversary of his marriage to Millicent was next Wednesday. Their pre-nuptial agreement read that if they were either legally separated or divorced before that anniversary, he would receive nothing from her. If their marriage lasted past the seventh anniversary, he would irrevocably receive twenty million dollars even if they were to break up anytime after that.

Millicent's first husband had died. Her second marriage lasted only a few years. She had divorce papers served on her third husband only a few days before the seventh anniversary. I have four more days to go, he thought. Even in the beautiful room, he started to sweat at the idea.

Gregg was sure Millicent was playing a cat-and-mouse game with him. She had been traveling in Europe visiting friends for the past three weeks, but she had phoned from Monaco on Tuesday and approved the stand he took about paying the ransom. "It's a miracle twenty other children of our employees haven't been kidnapped already," she'd said. "You showed good sense."

And when we're out together she seems to enjoy being with me, Gregg thought in an effort to reassure himself.

"Considering your roots, it's a miracle how much polish you've managed to acquire," she had told him.

He had learned to accept her barbs with

a dismissive smile. The very rich are different. He had learned that since his marriage to Millicent. Tina's father had been rich, but he'd made his way up by the bootstraps. He lived extremely well but was a candle to a star when compared with Millicent's lifestyle. Millicent could and did trace her ancestry back to England before the *Mayflower* sailing. And, as she scornfully pointed out, unlike the hordes of impoverished well-bred aristocrats, generation after generation of her family had always had money, a great, great deal of money.

The terrible possibility was that Millicent had somehow learned about one of his affairs. I've been discreet, he thought, but if she found out about any of them, it would be the end of me.

He was pouring his third glass of wine when the phone rang. It was Millicent. "Gregg, I haven't been very fair to you."

He felt his mouth go dry. "I don't know what you mean, dear," he said, hoping the tone of his voice sounded amused.

"I'll be honest. I thought you might be cheating on me, and I simply could not tolerate that. But you've been given a clean bill of health so . . ." here Millicent laughed, "when I get back, how about celebrating our seventh anniversary and toasting the next seven?"

This time Gregg Stanford did not need to fake the emotion in his voice. "Oh, my dear!"

"I'll be back on Monday. I . . . I'm really quite fond of you, Gregg. Goodbye."

He hung up the phone slowly. As he suspected, she had been having him watched. It was a stroke of luck that instinct had made him stop seeing any woman these past few months.

Now nothing could stand in the way of the seventh anniversary celebration. It was the climax of everything he had worked toward all his life. He knew that a lot of people were wondering if Millicent was going to stay with him. Even Page Six of the *New York Post* had run an item headlined GUESS WHO'S HOLDING HIS BREATH? With Millicent behind him, his position on the board was solidified. He would be first in line for Chairman and CEO.

Gregg Stanford looked around the room, at the paneling and the tapestries, at the Persian carpet and the Hepplewhite furniture. "I'll do anything not to lose all this," he said aloud.

62

During the past week, which felt interminable, it seemed to Margaret that Agents
Tony Realto and Walter Carlson had become friends, although she never forgot
that they were law enforcement officers as
well. When they arrived today, the fatigue
and concern in their eyes gave her a mea-
sure of comfort. She knew that to them, the
failure to rescue Kathy was deeply personal
as well as professional.

*It's ridiculous to be embarrassed because
I crashed last night,* she thought, cringing at
the memory of grabbing the arm of the
manager of Abby's Discount. *I know I'm
grasping at straws.*

Or am I?

Realto and Carlson introduced her to the
man who was with them, Captain Jed Gun-

ther of the Connecticut State Police. He's about our age, she thought. He must be pretty smart to be a captain already. She knew that the state police had been working round the clock with the Ridgefield police, going door-to-door, asking if anyone had seen strangers loitering in the neighborhood. She also knew that the night of the kidnapping, and the day after, they had taken clothing of the twins, and had searched the town and all the parks in the surrounding area with their trained dogs, looking for any scent to follow.

With Dr. Sylvia following, she and Steve brought the investigators into the dining room—our "command post," she thought. How many times in this past week have we sat around this table waiting for a phone call, praying that we'd get the twins back?

Kelly had brought down the matching baby dolls and teddy bears that were the twins' favorite toys. She'd laid them on doll blankets on the living room floor and was now setting up the play table and chairs for a tea party. She and Kathy loved to play together at serving afternoon tea, Margaret thought. Across the table, she exchanged a glance with Dr. Sylvia. She's thinking the same thing. Sylvia always asked the girls about their tea parties when we went to her office.

"How are you feeling, Margaret?" Agent Carlson asked sympathetically.

"I'm okay, I guess. I'm sure you heard that I went to the dress shop where I bought the birthday dresses and asked to speak to the clerk who waited on me."

"She wasn't there, we understand," Agent Realto said. "Can you tell us your purpose in seeking to speak to her?"

"Only that she said she had just waited on a woman who was buying clothes for twins and that it seemed peculiar that the woman didn't know their sizes. I just had the crazy thought that maybe someone was buying those clothes, anticipating kidnapping my children and . . . and . . ." She swallowed. "The clerk wasn't there, and at first the manager wouldn't give me her cell phone number. I realized I was making a scene, so I ran out. Then I guess I just kept driving. When I saw a sign for Cape Cod, I came to my senses somewhat and turned around. The next thing I remember is a policeman shining a light in my face. I was parked at the airport."

Steve drew his chair closer to hers and put an arm around her shoulder. She reached up and linked her fingers with his.

"Steve," Agent Realto said, "you've told us that Kelly said the names 'Mona' and 'Harry' in her sleep, and that you are positive you don't know anyone with those names."

"That's right."

"Has Kelly said anything else that might be helpful in identifying the people who were holding her?"

"She said something about a crib, which gave me the impression that Kathy and she were kept in a crib. But that's all that really made sense."

"What *didn't* make sense to you, Steve?" Margaret asked intently.

"Marg, honey, if I could only hope with you, but . . ." Steve's face crumbled, and tears welled in his eyes. "I wish to God I could believe there was even a *possibility* that she's alive."

"Margaret, you called me yesterday and told me you believe that Kathy is still alive," Carlson said. *"Why* do you believe that?"

"Because Kelly told me she is. Because at Mass yesterday morning she said Kathy wants to come home, too, right now. Then, at breakfast, when Steve said that he would read a book to her, and pretend he was reading to Kathy, too, Kelly said something like, 'Oh, Daddy, that's silly. Kathy is tied up on the bed. She can't hear you.' And a few times Kelly has tried to talk twin talk to Kathy."

"Twin talk?" Gunther asked.

"They have their own special language." Sensing that her voice was about to start rising, Margaret stopped. Then, as she looked around the table, whispered imploringly, "I've told myself that this is simply a grief reaction, but it *isn't.* If Kathy were dead, I would know it, but she isn't. Don't you *see?* Don't you understand?"

She glanced into the living room. Then, before any of them could speak, she raised her finger to her lips and pointed. They all turned to observe Kelly. She had placed the teddy bears on chairs at the table. The doll that had been Kathy's was lying on a blanket on the floor. Kelly had tied a sock around its mouth. Now she was sitting by it, her own doll in her arms. She was stroking the cheek of Kathy's doll and whispering. As if she sensed that they were watching her, she looked up and said, "She's not allowed to talk to me anymore."

63

After the visit of Agents Walsh and Philburn, Richie Mason made coffee and coldly considered his options. The FBI was watching him. The irony of how it had all gotten out of control hit him in waves, provoking him to fury. Everything had been clicking along so smoothly, and then the one weak link in the chain, the one he always knew was a problem, had indeed become the problem.

Now the feds were closing in. The fact that they still didn't know how close they were to learning the truth was a miracle. The fact that they were concentrating on Bailey's connection to him was a distraction that was giving him time, but he knew they'd soon move on.

I am *not* going back to prison, he thought. The image of the tiny, crowded cell, and the

uniforms, and the terrible food, and the mo-
notony of prison life made him shiver. For
the tenth time in the last two days, he
looked at the passport that would ensure
his safety.

Steve's passport. He had stolen it from
the dresser drawer that day he'd been in
Ridgefield. He looked enough like Steve to
pass without anyone asking questions. All I
need to do is have a nice, warm smile like
baby brother when they check it, he
thought.

There was always the danger of an immi-
gration clerk saying, "Wasn't it your twins
who were kidnapped?" In that case he'd
simply say that it was his cousin who had
the tragedy. "We both were named after our
grandfather," he would explain. "And we
look enough alike to be brothers."

Bahrain had no extradition agreement
with the United States. But by then he'd
have a new identity, so it shouldn't matter.

Should he be satisfied with what he had,
or should he go for the rest of the pot of
gold?

Why not? He asked himself. And anyhow
it was always better to tie up loose ends.

Satisfied with the decision, he smiled.

64

"Mrs. Frawley," Tony Realto said slowly, "I cannot act on your belief that Kelly is in touch with her sister. However, the only indicators that Kathy is dead are the suicide note and the fact that Lucas Wohl was seen carrying a heavy box with him onto the aircraft. According to the note, he dropped Kathy's body into the sea. I'm going to be absolutely honest with you. We are not completely satisfied that Lucas either typed that note, or that he shot himself."

"What are you *talking* about?" Steve snapped.

"What I am saying is that if Lucas was shot by one of his cohorts, then that note might be a phony and may have been left there to give the impression that Kathy is dead."

"Are you finally starting to believe that she's alive?" Margaret asked imploringly.

"We are starting to believe that there may be a slight possibility that she is alive," Tony Realto said, emphasizing the words "slight possibility." "Frankly, I do not have faith in twin telepathy, but I do believe that Kelly may be able to help us. We need to question her. You say she did talk about 'Mona' and 'Harry.' She might let another name slip or give us some indication where they were kept."

They watched as Kelly picked up a doll's washcloth and went into the kitchen. They heard her pull a chair over to the sink. When she came back, the washcloth was wet. She knelt down and put it on the forehead of Kathy's baby doll. Then she began to speak, and they all got up and moved closer to hear what she was saying.

She was whispering, "Don't cry, Kathy. Don't cry. Mommy and Daddy will find you."

Kelly looked up at them. "She's really, really coughing. Mona made her take medicine, but she spit it up."

Tony Realto and Jed Gunther exchanged glances, disbelief in their eyes.

Walter Carlson was studying Sylvia Harris. She's a doctor, he thought. Her specialty is twin telepathy, and from her expression, he could tell that she believed the twins were communicating.

Margaret and Steve were clinging to each other, both of them now weeping.

"Dr. Harris," Carlson said quietly. "Will you talk to Kelly?"

Sylvia nodded and sat on the floor next to Kelly. "You're taking good care of Kathy," she said. "Does Kathy still feel sick?"

Kelly nodded. "She can't talk to me anymore. She told her real name to some lady, and Mona got mad and scared. She has to tell everyone her name is Stevie. Her head is *sooo* hot."

"Is that why you're putting a cool cloth on it, Kelly?"

"Yes.

"Does Kathy have something tied around her mouth?"

"She did, but she started to get sick, so Mona pulled it off. Kathy's falling asleep now."

Kelly untied the sock from the mouth of the doll, then laid her own doll next to it. She covered them with the same blanket, making sure their fingers were touching.

65

It was the manager of the motel, David Toomey, who rapped on Angie's door. A slightly built man in his mid-seventies, he had probing eyes that peered at her through rimless glasses. He introduced himself, then, with annoyance in his voice asked, "What's this about your car seat being stolen from your van last night? Officer Tyron from the Barnstable police stopped by to find out if any other cars had been broken into."

Angie tried to think fast. Should she tell him that she had lied, that she had forgotten to bring the car seat? That might make for more trouble. The cop might come around and give her a ticket. And ask questions. "It's not a big deal," she said. She glanced at the bed. Kathy was facing the wall. Only

344 Mary Higgins Clark

the back of her head, with its dark brown hair, was showing. "My little guy has a bad cold, and I was just concerned about getting him inside."

She watched as Toomey's eyes darted around the room. She could read his mind. He didn't believe her. She had paid cash for a two-night stay. He sensed that something was peculiar. Maybe he could hear Kathy wheezing.

He *had* heard her. "Maybe you should take your son to the emergency room at Cape Cod Hospital," he suggested. "My wife always gets asthma after a bronchitis attack, and he sounds as though he's building up to an asthma attack."

"That's what I was thinking," Angie said. "Can you give me directions to the hospital?"

"It's ten minutes from here," Toomey told her. "I'd be happy to drive you."

"No. No. That's fine. My . . . my mother will be here around one o'clock. She'll go with us."

"I see. Well, Ms. Hagen, I suggest that you get medical treatment for that child promptly."

"You bet I will. Thanks a lot. That's really

nice of you. And don't worry about the car seat. I mean, it was old anyway. You know what I mean."

"I know what you mean, Ms. Hagen. There was no theft. But I gather from Office Tyron that you do have a car seat now." Toomey did not bother to hide the sarcasm in his voice as he closed the door behind him.

Angie immediately double-locked the door. He's gonna be watching me, she thought. He knows I didn't have a car seat, and he's mad because it makes his place look bad if there's a complaint about a theft. That cop. He's suspicious, too. I've got to get out of here, but I don't know where to go. I can't pull out with all my stuff—he'll know I'm taking off. Now I have to look as though I'm waiting for my mother. If I run out right away, he'll know there's something up. Maybe if I just wait a while, then carry out the kid and put her in the car seat in the back, then go back—like for my pocketbook. From the office he can only see the passenger side of the car. I can put a blanket over the suitcase with the money and slip it in on the other side. I'll leave all the other stuff here so he'll think I'm coming back. If he talks to me, I'll tell him that my mother called and is meeting me at the hospital. But maybe with any luck, somebody will want to check in or out of this dump, and I can sneak out while he's busy.

Facing left from the window she could see the driveway in front of the office. She waited there forty minutes. Then, as Kathy's breathing became heavier and the wheeze became stronger, she decided she had to break open one of the penicillin capsules, dissolve some of it in a spoon, and force her to drink it. I've got to get rid of her, she thought, but I don't want her to die on my hands. Both furious and nervous, she opened her shoulder bag, got out the bottle of capsules, broke one open, poured it into a glass from the bathroom, diluted it with a little water, and grabbed a plastic spoon from the coffee machine on the counter. She shook Kathy, who stirred, opened her eyes, and immediately began to cry.

"Geez, you're burning up," Angie snapped. "Here, drink this."

Kathy shook her head, and as the first taste of the liquid touched her tongue, she pressed her lips shut. "I said, *drink* it!" Angie shouted. She managed to force some of the liquid into Kathy's mouth, but Kathy gagged, and the medication trickled out onto her cheek. She began to wail and cough. Angie grabbed a towel and tied it around her mouth to quiet the sound, then realized that Kathy might suffocate and pulled it off. "Keep quiet," she hissed. "You hear me good. Don't make another sound or I'll kill you right now. All this is your fault. Every *bit* of it."

She looked out the window and saw that several cars were now parked in front of the office. This is my chance, she thought. She picked up Kathy, ran outside, opened the door of the van, and strapped her in the car seat. Then, in a quick movement, she ran back inside the motel, grabbed the blanket-wrapped suitcase and her shoulder bag, and tossed them in beside Kathy. Thirty seconds later she was backing out of the parking space.

Where do I go? she wondered. Should I get off the Cape right away? I haven't called Clint back. He doesn't even know where I am. In case that cop is suspicious and starts looking for me, he has my license plate number. So does the guy at the motel. I've got to tell Clint to come up here in a rental car or something. It isn't safe for me to be driving this thing any longer.

But where should I go?

The weather had continued to clear, and the afternoon sun was bright. The thought that the cop who had made her buy the car seat might pull up in a squad car beside her made Angie want to scream in frustration at the slow-moving traffic. At the base of Main Street the traffic became one-way, and she was forced to turn right. I need to get out of Hyannis, and in case that cop is really suspicious and sends out an alarm, I don't want to get caught at one of the bridges. I'll take Route 28, she thought.

She glanced back at Kathy. The girl's eyes were closed, and her head was on her chest, but Angie could see that she was breathing in gasps through her mouth, and that her cheeks were flushed. I've got to find another motel and check in, she thought. Then I'll call Clint and tell him to get up here. Since I left that stuff in the Soundview, that nosey manager will probably think we're coming back. At least he'll think that until we don't show up by late tonight.

Forty minutes later, shortly after she passed the sign for Chatham, she spotted the kind of motel she was looking for. It had a flashing VACANCY sign and was next to a diner. "The Shell and Dune," she said, reading the name aloud. "It'll do." She turned the van off the road and pulled into a parking spot near the office door, but not where Kathy could be seen from inside the office.

The sallow-faced clerk at the desk was on the phone with his girlfriend and barely glanced up as he handed her a registration form. Again, on the chance that the Hyannis cop might send out an all-points bulletin, she decided not to use Linda Hagen's name. But if he asks for an ID, I have to show him something, she thought, reluctantly pulling out her own driver's license. She made up a license plate number and scrawled it on the slip. She was sure the clerk, deep in his conversation, wouldn't bother to check it. He took the cash for an overnight stay and tossed her a key. Feeling somewhat more secure now, Angie got back in the van, drove around to the back of the motel, and went into the room.

"Better than the last place," she said aloud as she hid the suitcase under the bed. She went back outside for Kathy, who did not wake up as she was taken from the car seat. Boy, that fever is getting worse, Angie thought. At least she doesn't fight the baby aspirin. She probably thinks it's candy. I'll wake her up and make her take some now.

But first I'd better call Clint.

He answered on the first ring. "Where the hell are you?" he barked. "Why didn't you call back sooner? I've been sweating here, wondering if you were in jail."

"The manager of the motel I was in was too nosy. I got out of there fast."

"Where are you?"

"I'm on Cape Cod."

"What?"

"It seemed like a good place to hide. And I know my way around here."

"Clint, the kid is really sick, and that cop I was telling you about, the one who made me buy the car seat, has the license number of the van. He smells something fishy. I know he does. I was afraid I'd be stopped at the bridge if I tried to leave the Cape. I'm in a different motel. It's on Route 28, in a town called Chatham. You told me you came up here when you were a kid. You probably know where it is."

"I know where it is. Look, you stay there. I'll fly up to Boston and rent a car. It's three thirty now. I should make it there by nine or nine thirty."

"Did you get rid of the crib?"

"I took it apart and put it in the garage. I don't have the van to move it, remember? I'm not worried about the crib now. You know what you've pulled on me, don't you? I couldn't leave because this is the only phone where you could reach me. I don't have more than eighty bucks and my credit card. Now you've attracted the cops up there, and that sales clerk where you bought the kids clothes—and used my credit card—smelled a rat and was nosing around here."

"Why would she come to the house?" Angie's voice was loud and fearful.

"She claimed she wanted to replace two of the shirts, but as far as I'm concerned, she came here to snoop around. That's why I've got to get out of here. And why you have to stay put until I get up there. Got it?"

I'm sitting here packed, waiting all this time, scared I'm gonna find out some cop has grabbed you and the kid, not to mention the suitcase full of money, Clint thought. *She screwed this up good. I can't* wait *to get my hands on her.*

"Yeah. Clint, I'm sorry I shot Lucas. I mean I just thought it would be nice to have a kid and the whole million to ourselves. I know he was your friend."

Clint did not tell her that he was afraid the FBI would start looking for him once they learned that years ago he and Lucas had shared a cell in Attica. As Clint Downes, he was safe. But if they ever checked his fingerprints, they would learn right away that Clint Downes didn't exist.

"Forget about Lucas. What's the name of the motel?"

"The Shell and Dune. Isn't that corny? I love you, Clint-man."

"Okay, okay. How's the kid?"

"She's really, *really* sick. She's got a big fever."

"Give her some aspirin."

"Clint, I don't want to be stuck with her anymore. I can't stand her."

"You've got your answer. We'll leave her in the van when we sink it somewhere. In case you haven't noticed, there's a lot of water around there."

"Okay. Okay. Clint, I don't know what I'd do without you. Honest to God. You're smart, Clint. Lucas thought he was smarter than you, but he wasn't. I can't wait for you to get here."

"I know. You and me. The two of us. That's the way it's gotta be." Clint hung up the phone. "And if you believe that, you're even dumber than I thought," he said aloud.

66

"I still don't believe that Kelly is actually in touch with her sister," Tony Realto had said bluntly before he and Captain Gunther left the family home at three o'clock. "But I do believe that she may be able to tell us something about the people she was with or where she was kept, something that will help us. That is why, awake or asleep, someone should be catching every word she says and should follow up with questions if she comes out with anything that may relate to the kidnapping."

"Do you at least accept that Kathy may be alive?" Margaret had pressed.

"Mrs. Frawley, from this point in the investigation we are going to proceed, not on the *likelihood,* but on the *premise* that Kathy is alive. However, I don't want this to be known. Our one advantage is that whoever has her believes that we think she is dead."

After they were gone, Kelly began to fall asleep in the living room next to the dolls. Steve slipped a pillow under her head and covered her, then he and Margaret sat cross-legged beside her.

"Sometimes she and Kathy talk in their sleep," Dr. Harris explained to Walter Carlson.

Harris and Carlson were still at the table in the dining room. "Dr. Harris," Carlson said slowly, "I am a skeptic, but that doesn't mean that Kelly's behavior hasn't shaken all of us. I asked you this before, but now I'm asking it in a different way. I know you have begun to believe that the twins are in contact with each other, but isn't it possible that everything Kelly has been saying and acting out is simply her own recollection of what happened to them during the days she was away?"

"Kelly had a bruise on her arm when she was taken to the hospital after she was found," Sylvia Harris said flatly. "When I saw it, I said that it was the result of a vicious pinch and that from my experience that sort of punishment is inflicted by a woman. Yesterday afternoon, Kelly began to scream.

Steve thought she had hit her arm against the table in the hall. Margaret recognized that she was reacting to Kathy's pain. That was when Margaret rushed to see the sales clerk. Mr. Carlson, Kelly has another nasty bruise, a new one that I would swear is the result of a pinch Kathy received yesterday. Take it or leave it."

Through his Swedish ancestors and his FBI training, Walter Carlson had learned to keep his emotions from showing. "If you are right . . ." he began, speaking slowly.

"I *am* right, Mr. Carlson."

". . . then Kathy may be with an abusive woman."

"I'm glad you recognize that. But equally serious, she is *very* ill. Think of what Kelly was doing with Kathy's doll. She is treating the doll as if she has a fever. That's why Kelly was putting a wet cloth on her forehead. Margaret does that sometimes if one of the twins is running a temperature."

"One of the twins? You mean they don't both get sick at the same time?"

"They are two individual human beings. Having said that, I must tell you that Kelly coughed frequently last night, but she absolutely does not have a cold. There was no need whatsoever for her to cough, unless she was identifying with Kathy. I am desperately afraid that Kathy is seriously ill."

"Dr. Sylvia . . ."

They looked up as Margaret came back into the dining room.

"Did Kelly say anything?" Sylvia Harris asked anxiously.

"No, but I want you to sit next to her with Steve. Agent Carlson—I mean, Walter—will you drive me back to the shop where I bought the girls' birthday dresses? I've been thinking and thinking. I was half-crazy when I went over there yesterday because I knew someone had hurt Kathy, but I *have* to talk to that clerk who waited on me. I still think she felt something was wrong about the woman who bought clothes for twins almost at the same time I was there. That clerk was off yesterday, but today, if she's not there and you're with me, I know they can't refuse to give us her phone number and address."

Carlson stood up. He recognized the expression on Margaret Frawley's face. It was that of a zealot, convinced of her mission.

"Let's go," he said. "I don't care where that clerk is. We'll find her and talk to her face to face."

67

The Pied Piper had been calling Clint every half hour. Fifteen minutes after Angie phoned, he tried him again. "Have you heard from her again?" he asked.

"She's on Cape Cod," Clint said. "I'm going to fly up to Boston and rent a car to drive there."

"Where is she?"

"Hiding in a motel in Chatham. She already had a run-in with a cop."

"What motel?"

"It's called the Shell and Dune."

"What are you going to do when you get there?"

"Just what you think. Listen, the cab driver is blowing the horn. He can't get past the gate."

"Then this is it for us. Good luck, Clint." The

Pied Piper broke the connection, waited, then dialed the number of a private plane service. "I need a plane to leave in one hour from Teterboro, to land at the airport nearest to Chatham on Cape Cod," he ordered.

68

Sixty-four-year-old Elsie Stone didn't get a chance to look at a newspaper all day. Her job at McDonald's, near the Cape Cod Mall, didn't allow for leisure reading, and this Saturday she had rushed to her daughter's house in Yarmouth to pick up her six-year-old granddaughter. As Elsie liked to put it, she and Debby were "thicker than thieves," and she willingly babysat at any time.

Elsie had followed the Frawley kidnapping with rapt attention. The thought of someone kidnapping Debby, then killing her, was just too horrible for her to allow to cross her mind. At least the Frawleys got *one* back, she thought, but oh, dear God, how awful for them.

Today she and Debby went back to her house in Hyannis and baked cookies. "How's your pretend friend doing?" she asked as Debby spooned the batter filled with chocolate morsels onto the baking pan.

"Oh, Nana, you forgot. I don't have a pretend friend anymore. I had her when I was little." Debby shook her head emphatically, causing her light brown hair to bounce on her shoulders.

"Oh, that's right." Elsie's eyes crinkled when she smiled. "I guess I was thinking of your pretend friend because there was a little boy in my restaurant today. His name was Stevie, and he has a pretend friend named Kathy."

"I'm going to make this a really big cookie," Debby announced.

So much for her interest in pretend friends, Elsie thought. Funny how that little kid sticks in my mind. The mother was in some kind of hurry. She didn't let the poor child eat more than a few bites.

When they put the baking pan in the oven, she said, "All right, Debs, while we're waiting, Nana's going to sit down and read the paper for a few minutes. You start coloring the next page in your Barbie doll book."

Elsie settled in her La-Z-Boy recliner and opened the newspaper. A follow-up story on the Frawley twins was on the front page. MASSIVE FBI SEARCH FOR KIDNAPPERS was the headline. A picture of the twins in front of their birthday cake brought tears to Elsie's eyes. She began to read the article. The family was in seclusion. The FBI had confirmed that the suicide note left by the man known as Lucas Wohl had contained his confession to unintentionally killing Kathy. Wohl's fingerprints identified him as being Jimmy Nelson, a convicted felon who had served six years in Attica for a series of burglaries.

Shaking her head, Elsie closed the paper. Her eyes strayed back to the front page and the picture of the twins. "Kathy and Kelly on their third birthday" was the caption. What is it . . . ? she wondered, staring at the photograph, trying to figure out why something about it seemed so familiar.

Just then the oven timer went off. Debby dropped the crayon she was holding and looked up from the coloring book. "Nana, Nana, the cookies are finished," she called as she ran to the kitchen.

Elsie let the newspaper slide to the floor and got up to follow her.

69

When Captain Jed Gunther left the Frawley home, he drove directly to the Ridgefield police station. More shaken by what he had witnessed than he had allowed the Frawleys or the FBI agents to see, he reminded himself that he did not believe that there was anything to twin talk or twin telepathy. He did believe that Kelly was acting out the memory of her own experience with the kidnappers, but that was all.

He was also now firmly convinced that Kathy Frawley had been alive when Kelly was left in the car with the body of Lucas Wohl.

He parked in front of the police station and hurried through the steady rain across the pavement to the front door. Clearing by early afternoon, he thought dismissively of the earlier weather report. Tell me about it.

The desk sergeant confirmed that Captain Martinson was in his office, then dialed his extension. Gunther took the phone. "Marty, it's Jed. I just left the Frawleys and I'd like to see you for a couple of minutes."

"Sure, Jed. Come on in."

Both now thirty-six years old, the two men had been friends since kindergarten. In college they had independently decided to opt for careers in law enforcement. The leadership qualities they possessed had resulted in early and regular promotions, Marty in the Ridgefield Police Department and Jed with the Connecticut State Troopers.

Over the years they had dealt with many tragedies, including the heartbreaking accidents that claim young victims, but this was the first ransom kidnapping either of them had ever encountered. Since the night the 911 call came in from the Frawley home, their departments had been working closely together, in conjunction with the FBI. The lack of any lead so far that would help to solve the crime was agonizing to both of them.

Jed shook Martinson's hand and took the chair nearest his desk. He was the taller of the two by three inches, and his hair was thick and dark, while Martinson's was already receding and showing premature hints of silver. Still, an observer would have recognized the characteristics they shared. They both exuded intelligence and self-confidence.

"How is it going at the Frawleys'?" Martinson asked.

Jed Gunther gave a brief account of what had transpired earlier, finishing with, "You know how suspect Wohl's confession is. I absolutely believe now that Kathy was still alive early Thursday morning when we found her sister in the car. When I was in the house today, I took another look around. It's plain that two people had to have taken part in the actual kidnapping."

"I keep going over it, too," Martinson agreed. "There were no curtains or drapes in the living room, only shades that were partially lowered. They could have looked in the windows and seen the babysitter on the couch, talking on the cell phone. A credit card would have opened that old lock on the kitchen door. The back staircase is next to the door, so they could have counted on getting upstairs quickly. The question is whether or not they made one of the children cry to lure the babysitter upstairs. My guess is that that's the way it happened."

Gunther nodded. "That's how I see it. They turned off the upstairs hall light and were carrying the chloroform to knock out the girl, and they may have been wearing masks in case she had a chance to see them face to face. They never could have risked walking around upstairs looking to see which room the children were in. They must have known their way around, so one of them has to have been in the house before that night.

"The question is, *when* was one of the kidnappers in there?" he continued. "The Frawleys bought an 'as is' house from the estate after old Mrs. Cunningham died, which is why they got it for the price they did."

"But no matter how 'as is' it was, it had to pass an inspection before the mortgage went through," Martinson pointed out.

"That's why I'm here," Gunther told him. "I've read the reports, but I wanted to go over them with you. Your guys know this town inside out. Do you think there is *any* chance that someone was in the house and got the layout of it just before the Frawleys moved in? That's a long hall upstairs, and the floorboards creak. The doors of the three bedrooms the family isn't using are always kept closed. The hinges creak. The kidnappers had to have known the twins were in one of the two bedrooms at the very end of the hall."

"We spoke to the house inspector," Martinson said slowly. "He's lived here thirty years. Nobody came in while he was there. Two days before the Frawleys moved in, the real estate agent sent over one of those local services to do a thorough cleaning. It's a family-owned business. I'll vouch for them myself."

"What about Franklin Bailey? Was he any part of this?"

"I don't know what the feds think, but in my opinion, absolutely not. From what I hear, the poor guy is on the verge of a heart attack."

Jed got up. "I'm going back to my office to see if I can find anything we missed in our files. Marty, I'll say again that I don't believe in telepathy, but remember how Kathy was coughing when we heard her on that tape? If she *is* alive, she is one sick kid, and what scares me is that the so-called suicide note may turn out to be a self-fulfilling prophecy. They may not *mean* to kill her, but it's a cinch they're not going to take her to a doctor. Her face has been in every newspaper in the country. And without medical attention, I'm worried that she won't live."

70

At LaGuardia Airport, Clint had the driver leave him at the drop-off for Continental Airlines. If the feds were closing in on him, the last thing he needed was for them to know he had been left at the entrance to the shuttle, a dead giveaway that he was heading for either Boston or Washington.

He paid the taxi fare with his credit card. Even as the driver zapped it through, he found himself sweating that Angie had done more shopping on it before she took off, and the card was maxed out. If that happened, every nickel of the eighty dollars he had in his pocket would be gone.

But it went through. He sighed with relief.

His anger at Angie was building, like the rumbling that precedes a volcanic eruption. If they had left both kids in the car and split the million, Lucas would be running his limo service and driving Bailey around just like always. And by next week, he and Angie would have been on their way to the phony job in Florida, with no one the wiser.

Now, not only had she killed Lucas, she had also blown his cover. How soon before they caught on to his old cellmate pal who had dropped out of sight? he wondered. *Very* soon. Clint knew how the feds thought. Then Angie, in her dumb, stupid way, had charged those clothes for the kids on his credit card, and even that dopey sales clerk had been smart enough to know that something phony was going on.

Carrying the small bag that held just a couple of shirts, some underwear, socks, and his toothbrush and shaving kit, Clint walked into the terminal, then went outside again and waited for the bus that would take him to the terminal where he could get the US Airways shuttle. There he purchased an electronic ticket. The next plane for Boston was leaving at six P.M., giving him forty minutes to kill. He hadn't eaten any lunch, so he walked back to a service bar and ordered a hot dog, French fries, and coffee. He'd have loved a scotch, but that would be his reward later.

When the food arrived, he took a huge bite of the hot dog, and washed it down with a gulp of the bitter coffee. Was it only ten nights ago that he and Lucas had sat at the table in the cottage splitting the bottle of scotch, feeling good about how smoothly the job had gone?

Angie, he thought, as the rumbling anger intensified. She's already had a run-in with a cop on the Cape, and now he knows the license plate on the van. For all I know, he's looking for her right now. He ate quickly, looked at the check, and slapped worn single-dollar bills on the counter, leaving the server a thirty-eight cent tip. He slid off the stool. His jacket had ridden up over his stomach while he was seated, and he yanked it down as he shuffled toward the gate for the Boston-bound plane.

With contempt in her eyes, Rosita, the third-year college student who had waited on him, observed his departure. He still has mustard on that pudgy face, she thought. Boy I'd hate to think that guy was coming home to me at the end of the day. What a slob. Oh, well, she thought with a shrug, at least you don't have to worry about him being a terrorist. If anyone is harmless, that jerk is.

71

Alan Hart, the evening manager of the Soundview Motel in Hyannis, came on duty at seven o'clock. The first thing David Toomey, the motel manager, did was to brief him on the theft of the car seat that Linda Hagen, the woman in A-49, had reported to Officer Tyron. "I'm sure she was lying," Toomey said. "I'd bet the rest of my life that she never had a car seat. Al, did you by any chance get a look at her van when she checked in last night?"

"Yeah, I did," Hart told him, a frown on his thin, intense face. "I always give a once-over to the vehicle, you know that. That's why I installed that new light outside. That stringy brunette checked in sometime after midnight. I could see her van plainly, and I didn't even know she had a kid. It must have been asleep in the backseat, but it sure wasn't in a car seat."

"I was really bugged when Sam Tyron stopped by," Toomey snapped. "He wanted to know if we've been having any other problems with thefts. I talked to the Hagen woman after he left. She's got a little boy, not more than three or four years old from what I could see. I told her to take him to the hospital. He had one heck of an asthmatic wheeze."

"Did she do it?"

"I don't know. She claimed she was waiting for her mother to go with them to the hospital."

"She's booked until tomorrow morning. She paid in cash with a wad of twenties. I figured she might be meeting a boyfriend up here, and she was the one financing it. Has she come back with the kid?" Hart asked.

"I don't think so. Maybe I'll just knock on the door and inquire about him."

"You really think there's something fishy about her?"

"I don't give a damn about her, Al. I just think she doesn't realize how sick that child is. If she's not there, I'll keep on going. But I will stop at the police station and let them know that we did *not* have a theft here last night."

"Okay. I'll keep an eye out to see if she shows up."

With a wave of his hand, David Toomey went outside, turned right and walked to the ground-floor unit with the number A-49 on the side of the door. He could see that there was no light shining behind the drawn shade. He knocked, waited, then after only a brief hesitation, took out his master key, unlocked the door, opened it, turned on the light, and stepped inside.

It was apparent to him that Linda Hagen was planning to return. There was an open suitcase on the floor with women's clothing stuffed inside it. There was a child's jacket on the bed, which made Toomey raise his eyes. It had been there in the same spot earlier that afternoon. Was it possible that she hadn't put it on the little boy when she took him out? Maybe she had just wrapped him in a blanket. He looked in the closet and found that the extra blanket was missing. He nodded. A good guess.

A quick look into the bathroom showed makeup and toiletries scattered on the sink. She plans to come back, he thought.

Maybe they kept the child at the hospital. I hope so. I'll be on my way. As he started to walk back through the bedroom, something on the floor caught his eye. He bent down to examine it. It was a twenty-dollar bill.

The bed's faded orange and brown dust ruffle behind the bill was hiked up. As Toomey knelt down to straighten it, his eyes widened. There were at least a dozen twenty-dollar bills scattered under the bed. Not touching any of them, he got up slowly. That woman is some dingbat, he thought. She must have kept her money in a bag under the bed, and never even realized she was missing some of it.

Shaking his head, he walked to the door, turned out the light, and left. He had been on his feet all day and was looking forward to getting home. I could just phone the station, he thought, then decided to go ahead and take the time to stop there. I want it on record that there was no theft at my motel, and if they want to go after that Hagen woman for lying to an officer, let them do it.

72

"Lila left early today," Joan Howell, the manager of Abby's Discount, explained to Margaret Frawley and Agent Carlson. "She ran out at lunchtime to do some shopping or something. When she came back, her hair was soaking wet. I asked her what was so important to make her rush out, and she said it was a fool's errand. But she left early because she felt chilled and thought maybe she was getting sick."

Wanting to scream, Margaret pursed her lips together. She had just endured Howell's sympathetic questions about how she felt today, and her expressions of condolences over the loss of Kathy.

Walter Carlson had already presented his credentials. When Howell stopped for breath, he broke in. "Ms. Howell, I need Ms.

Jackson's cell phone number, home phone number, and address immediately."

Howell looked flustered. She glanced around the sales floor. It was busy with Saturday afternoon shoppers. She realized that the nearby ones were watching them with obvious curiosity. "Of course," she said, "of course. I mean, I hope Lila isn't in any kind of trouble. She's the nicest girl you'd ever want to meet. Smart! Ambitious! I tell her, 'Lila, don't you dare open your own shop and run us out of business. Hear me?' "

A glance at the expressions on the faces of Margaret Frawley and Agent Carlson made her cut off her next anecdote about Lila's promising future. "Just follow me into the office," she said.

The office, Walter Carlson observed, was just barely big enough to hold a desk, chair, and file cabinets. A gray-haired woman in her sixties, reading glasses perched on the end of her nose, looked up.

"Jean, right away, will you please give Lila's address and telephone numbers to Mrs. Frawley." Howell said. Her tone indicated that Jean had better be fast about it.

The impulse to tell Mrs. Frawley how happy she was that she had gotten one of her twins back but how heartbroken she was for her about the other one died on Jean Wagner's lips as she observed the steely expression on Margaret's face. "I'll jot it down for you," she said briskly.

Trying not to snatch it from the woman's hands, Margaret murmured a quick thank you and was gone, with Carlson right behind her.

"What was *that* all about?" Jean Wagner asked Howell.

"That was an FBI agent with Mrs. Frawley. He didn't bother to give any explanation to me. But yesterday when Mrs. Frawley came in, all upset, she said something about Lila selling outfits for twins, and the woman buying them didn't seem to know the size. I don't know why that's so important to them right now. Between us, I think that poor Margaret Frawley should be put to bed and given something that will let her forget all her sorrow until she can begin to cope with it. That's why we have a bereavement group at our church. When my mother died, it was the most wonderful help to me. Otherwise I don't know how I could have gotten through it."

Behind Howell, Jean Wagner raised her

eyes to heaven. Howell's mother was ninety-six years old, and had been driving Joan crazy before she mercifully had been called to her Maker. But the rest of what Howell had been saying was even more startling to her.

Lila thought there was something wrong about that woman, Jean thought. I got her address from the credit card company for her. I remember it: Mrs. Clint Downes at 100 Orchard Avenue in Danbury.

Howell had opened the door and was on her way out. Wagner started to call after her, then stopped. Lila will tell them who the woman is, she decided. Joan's getting in a bad mood. She won't like it that I broke rules to get Lila that address. I'd better mind my own business.

73

Angie placed Kathy on a pillow on the floor of the bathroom. Then she plugged up the tub and turned on the shower full blast, so that the small room would fill with steam. She had managed to get Kathy to chew and swallow two more orange-flavored baby aspirin.

As each minute passed, she was becoming more and more nervous. "Don't you dare die on me," she told Kathy. "I mean, that's just what I need, another nosy motel guy banging on the door, and you not breathing. I wish I could get some more of that penicillin into you."

On the other hand, she was beginning to wonder if maybe Kathy had been allergic to the penicillin she had swallowed. There were red spots showing up on her arms and

chest, lots of them. Belatedly, Angie remembered that a guy she had lived with
once had been allergic to penicillin. He had
broken out in red spots the first time he took
it, too.

"Geez, is that what's happening to you?"
Angie asked Kathy. "It was a lousy idea to
come to Cape Cod. I forgot that if I hit any
trouble there are only two bridges I can use
to get away, and now they could be watching for me there. Forget old Cape Cod."

Kathy did not open her eyes. She was
finding it hard to breathe. She wanted
Mommy. She wanted to be home. In her
mind, she could see Kelly. She was sitting
on the floor with their dolls. She heard Kelly
ask her where she was.

Even though she wasn't allowed to talk to
her, she moved her lips and whispered,
"Cape Cod."

Kelly had awakened but did not want to get
up from the living room floor. Sylvia Harris
brought in a tray with milk and cookies and
put it on the play table where the teddy
bears were propped in chairs, but Kelly ig-
nored it. Sitting cross-legged on the carpet,

Steve had not moved from his position across from her.

He broke the silence. "Dr. Sylvia, do you remember when they were born—Margaret had to have a C-section, and there was a tiny piece of membrane that had to be cut off between Kelly's right thumb and Kathy's left thumb?"

"Yes, I do, Steve. In that real sense of the word, they were not only identical, but conjoined twins."

"Sylvia, I don't want to let myself believe . . ." He paused. "You know what I mean. But now, even the FBI guys admit it's a possibility that Kathy is alive. My God, if we only knew where she is, where to look for her. Do you think it's possible that Kelly knows?"

Kelly looked up. "I *do* know."

Sylvia Harris raised her hand as a warning to Steve. "Where is she, Kelly?" she asked quietly, her tone not betraying any emotion.

"Kathy's in old Cape Cod. She just told me."

"When Margaret was in bed with Kelly this morning, she was talking about driving during her blackout last night and told me that when she saw the sign for Cape Cod, she knew she had to turn around," Sylvia whispered to Steve. "That's where she heard about Cape Cod."

Kelly went into a spasm of coughing and gagging. Sylvia grabbed her, threw her across her lap, and hit her sharply between the shoulder blades.

As Kelly began to wail, Dr. Harris turned her around and nestled her head against her neck. "Oh, sweetheart, I'm sorry," she said soothingly. "I was so afraid you had put something in your mouth and were choking."

"I want to go home," Kelly sobbed. "I want Mommy."

74

Agent Carlson rang the bell at Lila Jackson's modest home in Danbury. In the car on the way there, he had tried to reach her by phone, but her land line was busy, and she did not answer her cell phone. "At least we know someone's in the house," he said, trying to reassure Margaret as he drove the three-mile distance well in excess of the speed limit.

"She has *got* to be home," Margaret had said in the car. Now, as they heard footsteps approaching the door, she whispered, "Oh, God, please let her be able to tell us something."

Lila's mother answered the door. Her welcoming smile disappeared as she saw the two strangers on the porch. In a quick movement, she partially closed the door and slipped on the security chain.

Before the woman could speak, Carlson had his FBI identification in his hand and was extending it to her to examine. "I am Agent Walter Carlson," he said briskly. "This is Margaret Frawley, the mother of the twins who were kidnapped. Your daughter Lila sold her the twins' birthday dresses. We have just left Abby's Discount. Ms. Howell told us that Lila left early because she didn't feel well. We *must* speak with her."

The chain slipped off, and Lila's flustered mother stammered her apologies. "I am so sorry. In this day and age you just can't be too careful. Come in. Please come in. Lila is on the couch in the den. Come in."

She has got to be able to tell us something that will help, Margaret thought. Dear God, please, please, please. She caught a glimpse of herself in the mirror opposite the door in the tiny foyer. Earlier that day she had twisted her hair into a bun, but the wind had blown strands loose, and they were hanging on her neck. Dark shadows under her eyes contrasted with her pasty-white complexion, and her eyes looked dull and fatigued. A nerve on the side of her mouth was causing her face to quiver. She had bitten her bottom lip so often that it was swollen and cracked.

No wonder the sight of me made this woman lock the door, she thought, but then forgot any consideration of her appearance as she went into the study and saw the bundled-up figure sitting on the couch.

Lila was wearing her favorite fleece-lined bathrobe and had a blanket tucked around her. Her feet were stretched out on an ottoman, and she was sipping hot tea. She looked up and recognized Margaret immediately. "Mrs. Frawley!" She leaned over to put the cup she was holding on the coffee table.

"Please, don't get up," Margaret said. "I'm sorry to burst in like this, but I have to talk to you. It's about something you said when I was buying the birthday dresses for my twins."

"Lila talked about that," Mrs. Jackson exclaimed. "In fact she wanted to go to the police about it, but my friend Jim Gilbert, who knows what he's talking about, told her to forget it."

"Ms. Jackson, what did you want to tell

the police?" Walter Carlson's tone demanded an instant, straightforward answer.

Lila looked from him to Margaret. She recognized the hungry hope in Margaret's eyes. Knowing she was about to disappoint her, she answered directly to Carlson. "As I told Mrs. Frawley that night, I had just sold some outfits to a woman who wanted them for her three-year-old twins, but she said she didn't know what size to buy. After the kidnapping, I looked up her name, but then, as my mother just said, Jim, who is a retired detective here in Danbury, didn't think it was worth reporting." She looked at Margaret. "This morning, when I heard that you had come to the store looking for me yesterday, I decided I would go talk to that woman on my lunch hour."

"You know where she is?" Margaret asked, gasping.

The manager of the store told us Lila said she had been on a fool's errand, Carlson remembered grimly.

"Her name is Angie. She lives with the caretaker of the country club in a cottage on the club grounds. I made up a story to tell her—I said that two of the polo shirts I sold her were damaged. But the caretaker told me what happened. Angie babysits and was hired to drive to Wisconsin with a mother and her two children. He told me they're not really twins, just close in age. The mother was on her way to pick up Angie when she realized she had forgotten one of the suitcases and phoned ahead to have Angie run out and buy some of the things they'd need. That's why she wasn't that sure of the size, you see."

Margaret had been standing. Her knees suddenly weak, she sank down onto the chair opposite the couch. A dead end, she thought. Our only chance. She closed her eyes, and, for the first time, began to give up hope that she was going to find Kathy before it was too late.

Walter Carlson, however, was not yet satisfied. "Was there any indication that children had been staying in that house, Ms. Jackson?" he asked.

Lila shook her head. "It's a really small place; living room, dining area to the left that's separated from the kitchen by a divider. The door to the bedroom was open. I'm sure that Clint guy was alone there. I got the impression that the woman Angie was babysitting for had picked her up and kept going."

"Did this guy Clint seem nervous to you in any way?" Carlson asked.

"Jim Gilbert knows the caretaker and his girlfriend," Lila's mother chimed in. "That's why he said to forget it."

This is useless, Margaret thought. Useless and hopeless. She felt the tension in her body being replaced by a dull ache. I want to go home, she thought. I want to be with Kelly.

Lila then answered Carlson's question. "No, I wouldn't say that Clint, or whatever his name is, was nervous exactly. I mean, he was sweating a lot, but I assumed that he was the kind of heavyset guy who naturally sweats a lot." An expression of distaste came over her face. "His girlfriend should treat him to a case of deodorant. He stank like a locker room."

Margaret stared at her. "What did you say?"

Lila looked uncomfortable. "Mrs. Frawley, I'm sorry. I don't mean to sound flippant. I only wish to God I could have helped you."

"You did!" Margaret cried, her face suddenly alive. "You did!" She jumped up from the chair, turned to Carlson and saw at once that he, too, had recognized the importance of Lila's off-hand remark.

The only impression Trish Logan, the babysitter, had of the man who had grabbed her was that he was heavyset and stank of perspiration.

75

Even though he was frantic to get to Cape Cod, the Pied Piper had taken the time to dig out a hooded sweater to wear under his jacket, as well as an old pair of dark glasses that covered half his face. He drove his car to the airport, parked, and went inside the small terminal where he found the pilot waiting for him. Their exchange was brief. He was told that the plane was waiting on the tarmac. As he had requested, a car with a map of the area would be ready for him at the Chatham airport. The pilot would wait to fly him back later tonight.

Just over an hour later, the Pied Piper was getting off the plane. It was seven o'clock. The unexpectedly crisp, dry air on the Cape and the star-filled sky made him uneasy. Somehow he'd been expecting to find the same overcast sky and steady rainfall that was blanketing the New York area. But at least when he got to the car it was exactly the kind he wanted, a black mid-sized sedan, a look-alike for half the vehicles on the road. A study of the map showed him that he could not be very far from the Shell and Dune Motel on Route 28.

I've got at least an hour to kill, maybe more, he thought. Clint might have made the Delta Shuttle at five thirty. Otherwise he'd be on the US Air Flight at six. Right now, he's probably in Boston, renting a car. The pilot said the drive to Chatham from Boston should take about an hour and a half. I'll park somewhere around the motel and wait for him.

On the phone call with Clint, he had wanted to ask the license number of the van, but he knew that would have made Clint suspicious. Lucas had described it as old and beat-up. Of course it had Connecticut license plates. It shouldn't be that hard to find in the motel parking lot, he reasoned.

Even though Lucas had somewhat derisively described Clint and Angie to him, he had never met either one of them. Was he taking an unnecessary risk by coming up here and not just letting Clint finish Angie and the kid off? So what if he got to keep the million dollars? But if all of them are dead, I can sleep at night, he thought. Lucas knew who I am. They don't. But how do I know that he didn't tell Clint? I don't need to have him looking me up after he's run through his share of the ransom. He just might start to think he should share the other seven million with me.

The traffic on Route 28 was heavier than he had expected. I guess the Cape is like a lot of other summer vacation places, he thought. More and more people are living here year-round now.

Who cares?

He spotted the large Shell and Dune Motel sign with the flashing VACANCY beneath it. The exterior was white clapboard with green shutters. It looked to be a cut above the run-of-the-mill motels situated along most major highways. He saw that after the entrance sign, the driveway split. One side went under the overhang at the office, the other around it. He turned right off Route 28 and followed the lane that avoided the office. Not wanting to attract attention, he drove at what he hoped was a normal pace, his eyes darting back and forth, looking for the van. He was almost certain it was not in front of the motel facing Route 28. He drove around to the back. A lot more cars were parked in that area, most likely the ones belonging to people who had rooms on the second floor. In a way, that was good, he decided. When he found the van, he could look for a spot near it.

If Angie had any brains, she wouldn't park too near the building. Because of the lights near the entrance, the license plates on the cars parked there were clearly visible. The Pied Piper slowed to a crawl as he studied the vehicles he was passing.

Finally he spotted the one that almost certainly was hers, a dark brown van, at least ten or twelve years old, with a dent on the side and Connecticut license plates. There was an empty space about five cars away in the next row. The Pied Piper parked there, got out of the sedan, and walked over to inspect the van. The light was sufficient to see the car seat in the back.

He checked his watch. He had plenty of time, and he was hungry. He could see the diner next door. Why not? he asked himself as he took out the dark glasses, slipped them on, and began to walk across the parking lot. When he got to the diner, he saw that it was crowded. All to the good, he thought. The only seat at the counter was next to the take-out section. He sat down, and as he reached for the menu, the woman standing next to him began placing her order for a hamburger, black coffee, and a dish of orange sherbet to go.

The Pied Piper turned his head abruptly, but even before he saw the thin woman with the stringy brown hair, he recognized her harsh, aggressive voice.

He buried his face in the menu. He knew he was not mistaken.

It was Angie.

76

The office of A-One Reliable Cleaning Service was located in the basement of Stan Shafter's home. An hour after his exchange with Jed Gunther, Marty Martinson decided to have another talk with Shafter. He had reviewed the statements given by Stan's two sons and by the longtime women employees who had done the actual work of washing and dusting and scrubbing and polishing the Frawley home the day before the family moved in. They had all stated that no one other than they had been in the house when they were there.

When Marty reread the statements from Shafter's employees, he had been struck by one omission. Not one of them had mentioned that Stan himself had stopped in while they were cleaning, yet he had said that he had made his usual inspection. If they hadn't thought to mention him, was it possible they had inadvertently missed someone else? It was certainly worth a person-to-person talk, Marty decided.

Stan Shafter answered the door himself. A short but powerful-looking man in his late fifties, with a full head of carrot-red hair and lively brown eyes, and it was said of him that he always gave the impression of being in a hurry. Marty noticed that he was wearing his heavy outside jacket. Either he was on his way out or had just returned home.

His eyebrows lifted when he saw his visitor. "Come on in, Marty, or should I say Captain?"

"Marty's fine, Stan. I need just a couple of minutes of your time, unless you have to be somewhere."

"I just got back three minutes ago; I'm in for the rest of the day. Sonya left me a note saying that the business phone has been ringing all afternoon, so I've got to call the answering service and collect the messages."

As Marty followed him down the stairs, he thanked his stars that Stan's wife was out. A nonstop talker and world-class gossip, she would have peppered him with questions about the investigation.

The walls of the basement office were covered in knotty pine, a finish that reminded Marty of his grandmother's recreation room. The large clipboard behind Shafter's desk was filled with cartoons depicting home-cleaning situations.

"I've got some new ones, Marty," Shafter said. "Really funny. Take a look."

"Not now," Marty responded. "Stan, I need to talk to you about the Frawley house."

"Fine, but your guys grilled all of us after the kidnapping."

"I know they did, but there're still things to cover. We're following any inconsistency, no matter how trivial, in our hunt for those kidnappers. You can understand that."

"Yes, I can, but I hope you're not insinuating that any of my people lied to you." The bristling tone in Stan's voice, and the way his barrel chest suddenly swelled as he straightened up in the chair, reminded Marty of an angry rooster.

"No, I'm not looking at your people, Stan," Marty reassured him quickly. "And this is probably just one more of the many dead ends we've been running into. To put it simply, we believe that someone staked out the house and learned beforehand which bedroom the twins would be in. As you know, the house is a lot bigger than it looks from the outside. There are five bedrooms, anyone of which would have been appropriate for the little girls, yet someone knew *exactly* where to go. The Frawleys moved in the day after your people did the cleanup. Margaret Frawley tells us there were no strangers in the house before the kidnapping. We doubt that someone would have had the nerve to try to sneak in and case the place."

"You mean . . ."

"I mean someone knew exactly where to go upstairs. I believe that your staff would never deliberately lie, but on the other hand, in your statement you said you had stopped in to inspect the house near the end of the day. Not one of your people mentioned that."

"They must have thought you were asking if an outsider came in. They count me as part of the crew. Go talk to any of them again. They'll be back soon to pick up their cars."

"Did any of you know which room had been selected for the children?"

"We all knew. The parents were driving up that night to paint it. The cans of blue paint were stacked in the big back room, and the white carpet was rolled up in the corner. They'd even dropped off some of the toys and a hobby horse, and they were in there as well."

"Did you discuss that with anyone, Stan?"

"Only Sonya. You know my wife, Marty. She could be an investigator for you. She was in that house years ago when old Mrs. Cunningham had some charity event there. If you can believe it, she was trying to get me to consider buying it when Mrs. Cunningham passed on. I told her to forget it."

Stan Shafter smiled, indulgently. "Sonya was excited when she heard that identical twins were going to live there. She wanted to know which room the twins would be in, or if they had separate rooms, and if they had put up Cinderella wallpaper for them because that's what she would have done. I told her the twins were in the same room, the big one in the back corner, and I told her it was going to be painted sky blue and have a white carpet. Then I said, 'Sonya, now let me have a beer in peace with Clint.' "

"Clint?"

"Clint Downes. He's the caretaker at the Danbury Country Club. I've known him for years. We do a general housecleaning there every season before the club opens. Clint happened to be here when I got back from the Frawley house, and I asked him to stay for a beer."

Marty stood up and reached for his uniform hat. "Well, if anything occurs to you, give me a call, Stan. Okay?"

"Sure. I look at our grandkids and try to think of one of them being gone for good. I can't handle it."

"I understand." Marty climbed the first few stairs, then turned. "Stan, this guy, Downes. Do you know where he lives?"

"Yeah, in the cottage on the grounds of the club."

"Does he regularly drop in on you?"

"No. He wanted to tell me that he's accepted a job in Florida and would be leaving soon. He thought I might know someone who'd like to apply for the job at the golf club." Stan laughed. "I know Sonya can wear most people down, but Clint was polite enough to act real interested in what I was telling her about the Frawley home."

"Okay. See you."

Back in his car, returning to the station house, Marty thought about what Shafter had told him. Danbury isn't my jurisdiction, but I think I'll call Carlson and pass this onto him, he decided. It's probably another dead end, but since we're all grasping at straws, we might as well give this guy the once-over, too.

77

On Saturday evening, dressed in casual clothes, seeking to blend in with the dozens of other passengers, Agents Sean Walsh and Damon Philburn stood in the Galaxy Airlines baggage collection area at the international arrivals terminal of Newark Liberty Airport.

They both wore the exasperated expressions of travelers who, after a long flight, can't wait to see their bags tumble onto the carousel. In fact, they were actually watching a thin-faced, middle-aged man who was there waiting for his luggage. When he reached down and plucked a nondescript black suitcase from the carousel, they moved immediately to either side of him.

"FBI," Walsh told him. "Do you want to come quietly or make a scene?"

Without answering, the man nodded and fell in step with them. They herded him to an office in a private area of the terminal where other agents were guarding Danny Hamilton, a frightened twenty year old who was wearing the uniform of a baggage handler.

When the man accompanied by Walsh and Philburn saw Hamilton in handcuffs, he turned ashen and blurted, "I'm not saying anything. I want a lawyer."

Walsh laid the suitcase on a table and snapped open the locks. He put the neat piles of folded underwear, shirts, and slacks on a chair, then took out a pocket knife and slit the edges of the false bottom of the suitcase. When he ripped it off, the hidden contents of the bag were revealed, large packages of white powder.

Sean Walsh smiled at the courier. "You're going to need a lawyer."

Walsh and Philburn could not believe the turn of events. They had come here to speak to Richie Mason's co-workers to see if they could learn any shred of information that might connect him to the kidnapping. They started to talk to Hamilton and had immediately sensed that he was unduly nervous.

When they pressed him, he adamantly denied any knowledge of the kidnapping but then broke down and admitted that he knew Richie Mason was getting cocaine shipments at the airport. He said that Richie had given him five hundred dollars on three or four occasions to keep quiet about it. He'd told them that late this afternoon Richie had called to tell him that a shipment was coming in, but he couldn't be there to meet it.

Richie had told Hamilton to meet the courier at the carousel. From Richie's description, he would recognize him because he had seen him at the airport with Richie before. He had instructed Hamilton to give the code words "Home Free," and the courier would then know that it was safe to give the suiticase containing the cocaine to him. Hamilton said that Richie had told him to hide the bag at his apartment and that he would contact him in the next few days and let him know how he would retrieve the bag.

Sean Walsh's cell phone rang. He opened it and listened, then turned to Philburn. "Mason's not at his Clifton apartment. I think he's taken off."

78

"Margaret, this may be another blind alley," Agent Carlson warned as they drove from Lila Jackson's home to the caretaker cottage where Clint Downes lived.

"It's not another blind alley," Margaret insisted. "The one impression Trish had before she was knocked out was that of perspiration on a heavyset man. I knew, I knew, I just knew that if I spoke to that sales clerk, she would be able to tell me something that would help. Why didn't I do it sooner?"

"Our office is having a check run on Downes," Carlson said as he drove through downtown Danbury, headed toward the club grounds. "We'll know soon if he's ever been in trouble. But you've got to realize that if he's not home, we have no grounds for breaking into that house. I don't want to wait for one of our agents to get here, so I'm having a squad car from the Danbury police meet us there."

Margaret did not respond. Why did it take me so long to go back and talk to Lila? she thought, castigating herself. Where is that woman, Angie? Is Kathy with her?

Overhead, the clouds were finally clearing, blown away by the crisp late-afternoon wind. But it was after five o'clock, and darkness was setting in. Margaret called home during the drive to the golf club and learned from Dr. Harris that Kelly had fallen back asleep. Then the doctor told her that Kelly seemed to be communicating with Kathy and added that she had experienced a severe coughing spell.

Lila Jackson had told Carlson they would have to park at the service road gate. As they got out of the car, the agent ordered Margaret to wait in the car. "If this guy is connected to the kidnapping, he could be dangerous."

"Walter," Margaret said, "if that man is there, I am going to talk to him. Unless you're planning to restrain me physically, you'd better just accept that fact."

A squad car pulled up beside them, and

two cops immediately got out, one with sergeant's chevrons on his jacket. They listened to Carlson's brief rundown about the clothing purchase at Abby's Discount and how the impression the babysitter had the night of the kidnapping coincided with the way the sales clerk described Clint to them—heavyset and perspiring.

Like Carlson, they tried to persuade Margaret to wait in the car, but when she would not be dissuaded, they told her she would have to stand back until they were sure there would not be any resistance from Clint Downes to letting them in and to answering their questions.

As they approached the cottage, it was obvious to all of them that their precautions were unnecessary. The building was in darkness. The open door of the garage showed them that there was no vehicle inside. Bitterly disappointed, Margaret watched as the police went from window to window of the cottage, shining lights inside. He was here this afternoon around one o'clock, she thought. That was only four hours ago. Did Lila frighten him off? Where would he have gone? Where did that woman Angie go?

She walked over to the garage and

flipped on the light. Inside, to the right, she saw the crib that Clint had taken apart and stacked against the wall. The size of the mattress caught her eye. It was nearly twice the size of the mattress of a standard crib. Had it been bought because someone knew that two children would be sleeping on it? As the FBI agent and the Danbury police officers hurried over from the cottage, Margaret walked to the mattress and put her face against it. The faint familiar odor of Vick's VapoRub filled her nostrils.

She spun around and screamed at the law enforcement officers, "They were here! This is where they kept them! Where did they go? You've got to find out where they took Kathy!"

79

At Logan Airport, Clint went directly to the area where the car rental agencies were located. Crushingly aware that if Angie had maxed out the card, he might not be able to rent a car, he carefully studied the rates before he selected the cheapest service and the cheapest car.

A million dollars in cash, he thought, and if the credit card for the rental doesn't go through, I'll have to steal a car to get to the Cape.

But it did go through.

"You got a map for Maine?" he asked the clerk.

"Right over there."

An indifferent hand pointed to a rack holding a collection of maps. Clint picked up his copy of the rental receipt and walked over to the display. Carefully blocking his choice from the possible observation of the clerk, he grabbed a map of Cape Cod and shoved it in his jacket. Twenty minutes later he was squeezing his body into the driver's seat of a budget compact. He turned on the overhead light and studied the map. It was just about as far as he remembered—about an hour and a half drive from Boston. Shouldn't be too much traffic at this time of the year, he thought.

He started the car. Angie remembered him telling her that he'd been on the Cape before. She forgets nothing, he thought. What I didn't tell her was that I was here on a job with Lucas. Lucas had driven some big shot up here for a weekend, then had to stay in a motel and wait around for him. That gave him a chance to look the place over. We came back a couple of months later and hit a house in Osterville, Clint remembered. Swanky neighborhood, but we didn't get as much as Lucas expected. In fact, he gave me peanuts for my share. That's why I demanded an even split on this job.

Clint drove out of the airport. The map had indicated that he should turn left into the Ted Williams Tunnel and then watch for signs to Cape Cod. If I got it straight, Route 3 takes me directly to the Sagamore Bridge, he thought. Then the map says I take the Mid-Cape Highway to Route 137, which will take me to Route 28.

He was glad that the weather in Boston was clear. It made it easier to follow the signs. On the other hand, clear weather might be a problem later but not a problem that couldn't be solved. Should he stop somewhere and phone Angie, he wondered. Let her know that he'd definitely be there by nine thirty or so?

Once again he cursed her for taking the cell phones with her.

A few minutes after emerging from the tunnel, he spotted the Cape Cod sign. Maybe it's good that I don't have a phone, he thought. In her own crazy way, Angie is a smart babe. She just might start to figure out that it's just as easy for her to get rid of the kid on her own, and then take off again with the money, as it is to wait for me.

The thought made him slam his foot down on the gas pedal.

80

On weekends, when he could get away, Geoffrey Sussex Banks would race down from Bel-Air to his home in Palm Springs, California. Having stayed in Los Angeles this Saturday, however, he returned from a round of golf in late afternoon to learn from his housekeeper that an FBI agent was waiting for him. "He gave me his card, sir. Here it is," she said. As she handed it to him, she added, "I'm sorry."

"Thank you, Conchita."

He had hired Conchita and Manuel years ago, when he and Theresa were first married. The couple had adored Theresa, and when they got news eight months later that she was expecting twins, they had been thrilled. When Theresa disappeared shortly thereafter, they kept alive the hope that one day a key would turn in the door and she would be there. "And maybe she had the babies and just forgot her past and then all of a sudden remembered and came home and your little boys were with her." That was Conchita's prayer. But now Conchita knew that if the FBI was here it was only to ask more questions about Theresa's disappearance or, worse, to confirm after all these years that her remains had been found.

Geoff braced himself for the news as he walked down the hall to his library.

Dominick Telesco was from the Los Angeles FBI headquarters. An agent for ten years, he had often read stories in the business section of the *L.A. Times* about Geoffrey Sussex Banks, international banker, philanthropist, handsome socialite whose young, pregnant wife had disappeared on her way to her baby shower seventeen years ago.

Telesco knew that Banks was fifty years old. That means he was my age, thirty-two, when his wife disappeared, he thought as he looked out the window that faced the golf course. Wonder why he's never remarried? Women must be falling all over him.

"Mr. Telesco?"

Somewhat embarrassed at not hearing Banks come into the room, the agent turned quickly. "Mr. Banks, I apologize. I just watched someone hit a fabulous shot, and I didn't hear you come in."

"I bet I know who it might be," Banks said with a hint of a smile. "Most of our members find the sixteenth hole a problem. Only one or two have mastered it. Please sit down."

For an instant the two men studied each other. Telesco had dark brown hair and eyes, a rangy build, and was wearing a pin-striped business suit and tie. Banks was wearing a golf shirt and shorts. His patrician features were slightly sunburned. His hair, more silvery than dark blond, showed signs of thinning.

It was obvious to Agent Telesco that, at least at first impression, the reports that Banks possessed that rare combination of authority and courtesy were justified.

"Is it about my wife?" Banks asked, getting directly to the point.

"Yes, sir. It is," Telesco said, "although what brings me here is actually her possible connection to another case. You may have read about the Frawley kidnapping in Connecticut?"

"Of course. I understand that one of the twins was returned."

"Yes." Telesco did not share the news that a memo circulated through the Bureau indicated that the second twin might still be alive. "Mr. Banks, are you aware that Norman Bond, your wife's first husband, is on the board of C.F.G.&Y., and that the board voted to pay the ransom money for the return of the Frawley twins?"

"I know that Norman Bond is on the board of C.F.G.&Y."

Telesco did not miss the anger in Banks's voice. "Mr. Banks, Norman Bond hired the twins' father, Steve Frawley, for a job at C.F.G.&Y., and he did it under rather unusual circumstances. Three other mid-level executives at the company were the leading candidates for the position, yet Frawley was chosen. Note that Steve Frawley is the father of identical twins, and he lives in Ridgefield, Connecticut. Norman Bond and his wife were living in Ridgefield, Connecticut, when she gave birth to identical twins."

Geoff Banks's sunburn could not conceal that the color was draining from his face. "Are you suggesting that Bond had something to do with the Frawley kidnapping?"

"In light of the suspicions you have voiced about your wife's disappearance, do you think Norman Bond would be capable of planning and executing a kidnapping?"

"Norman Bond is evil," Banks said flatly. "I am absolutely certain that he was responsible for my wife's disappearance. It is a matter of record that he was wildly jealous when he learned that she was pregnant again with twins. When she disappeared, I put my life on hold, and it will remain on hold until I know exactly what happened to her."

"I've investigated the case thoroughly, sir. There isn't a shred of evidence to tie Norman Bond to your wife's disappearance. Witnesses saw him in New York that night."

"Witnesses *thought* they saw him in New York that night, or maybe he hired someone to do the job for him. I said it then and I say it now, he was responsible for whatever happened to Theresa."

"We talked to him last week. At that time, Bond referred to your wife as his 'late wife.' We wondered if that was a slip of the tongue, or perhaps more incriminating."

"His '*late* wife.'" Geoffrey Banks exclaimed. "Look through your notes. All these

years, that man told everybody that he believed Theresa was still alive, and he said she
wanted to get away from me. You will never
once hear of him referring to her as if she
were dead. Are you asking me if he is capable
of kidnapping the children of someone who is
living the life he wanted and expected to live?
You bet he is. *You bet he is.*"

When he was back in his car, Dominick
Telesco looked at his watch. It was a little
after seven on the East Coast. He put a call
in to Angus Sommers in the New York office
and related his conversation with Banks. "I
think it would be a good idea to start tailing
Bond, 24/7," he said.

"So do I," Sommers agreed. "Thanks."

81

"Lila Jackson told us the garage was empty," Agent Carlson said to the Danbury police officers. "She also told us that Clint Downes had received a phone call from someone named Gus while she was in the cottage. She would have reported her suspicions earlier, but one of your retired detectives, Jim Gilbert, stopped her. He claimed he knew Downes and his girl-friend. Maybe this Gus is the one who picked up Downes there earlier. Maybe Gilbert knows who Gus is."

Margaret could not keep her eyes off the dismantled crib. That's where they kept my babies, she thought. Those sides are so high—it's like a cage! The morning Mon-signor said Mass for Kathy, Kelly described it, talking about the big crib. I've got to go home. I've got to question her. She's the only one who can tell us where Kathy is now.

82

The Pied Piper put the menu down and slipped off the seat. He needed to know where in the motel Angie was staying. As the curious eyes of the counterman caught his gaze, he pulled his cell phone from his pocket. Hating to attract attention to himself, he flipped it open and made a gesture of answering it, listening intently as he walked outside.

He was standing in the shadow of the diner when Angie came out, a bag of food in her hand. Looking neither to the left nor the right, she darted through the diner parking lot and over the curb that separated it from the motel property. As his gaze followed her, the Pied Piper observed that Angie was intent on getting back inside the motel. She doesn't expect Clint for another hour and a half, he reasoned, and maybe she thinks she's safe holed up here.

To his satisfaction, she opened the door to a ground-floor unit. Easier to keep an eye on, he thought. Did he dare to go back to the diner and have something to eat? No, better to follow her example and order take-out. It was seven twenty. With any luck, Clint would be here between eight thirty and nine.

The shade on the window of Angie's room was fully drawn. The Pied Piper rolled up the collar of his jacket. The hood pulled up, his dark glasses on, he walked slowly past it, hesitating only as long as it took for him to catch the repetitive, hiccuping wail of a child who clearly had been crying for a long time.

He hurried back to the diner, ordered himself a hamburger and coffee to go, grabbed it, and once again walked past Angie's motel room. He was not sure he could still hear the child, but the sound of a rerun of *Everybody Loves Raymond* assured him that Angie was still there, waiting for Clint to arrive.

Everything was going according to plan.

83

Gus Svenson was sitting at his usual perch in the Danbury Pub when two men appeared on either side of him. "FBI," one man told him. "Get up."

Gus was on his third beer. "Who you kidding?"

"We're not." Tony Realto looked at the bartender "Run a tab for him."

Five minutes later, Gus was in the Danbury police station. "What's going on?" he demanded. Gotta clear my head, he told himself. These guys are crazy.

"Where did Clint Downes go?" Realto snapped.

"How do I know?"

"You called him at about quarter after one this afternoon."

"You're nuts. At quarter past one this afternoon I was fixing the mayor's plumbing. Call him if you don't believe me. He was there."

Agents Realto and Carlson exchanged glances. *He's not lying,* they communicated to each other. "Why would Clint act as if he's talking to you?" Carlson asked.

"Ask *him.* Maybe he didn't want his girl-friend to know another dame phoned him."

"His girlfriend, Angie?" Realto asked.

"Yeah, that nutcase."

"When was the last time you saw Clint?"

"Let me see. Today's Saturday. He and I had dinner last night."

"Did Angie go with you?"

"Nah. She was away on a babysitting job."

"When was the last time you saw her?"

"Clint and I went out for a couple of beers and a burger on Thursday night, too. Angie was in the house when I picked him up. She was minding a kid. His name was Stevie."

"You saw the child?" Carlson could not hide the rush of excitement in his voice.

"Yeah. Not much of a look. He was wrapped in a blanket. I saw the back of his head."

"Could you see what color hair he had?"

"Dark brown. Short."

Carlson's cell phone rang. The ID showed that it was from the Ridgefield police station. "Walt," Marty Martinson began, "I've been wanting to talk to you for the last couple of hours, but we had an emergency. Teenage drivers in a bad accident; fortunately they'll mend. There's a name I want to pass on to you in the Frawley case. It's probably another waste, but I'll tell you why I think it's worth checking."

Even before Martinson continued, Agent Carlson was sure that the name he was going to hear was Clint Downes.

Across the table, a suddenly sobered Gus Svenson was telling Tony Realto, "I hadn't been out to dinner with Clint for months. Then I ran into Angie at the drugstore. She was buying a bunch of stuff like a vaporizer and cough drops for a kid she was minding who was sick. And I . . ."

As the agents listened, Gus willingly poured out anything he remembered about his recent contacts with Clint and Angie. "I called Clint Wednesday night to see if he wanted to go out for a couple of beers, but Angie said he was out looking at a new car.

She was babysitting and the kids were crying so we didn't stay long."

"The *kids* were crying?" Realto snapped.

"Oh, wrong. I thought I heard two of them, but I couldn't be sure. When I asked, Angie just about hung up on me."

"Let's get this straight. The last time you saw Angie was Thursday night, and the last time you saw Clint was last night?"

"Yeah. I picked him up and then dropped him off later—he said he had no way to get around. He told me Angie was in Wisconsin babysitting, and that he'd sold the van."

"Did you believe him?"

"Listen, what do I know? I can't figure why he'd sell one car before he got something else to drive."

"You're positive his van wasn't there last night?"

"Swear to God. But it was in the garage when I picked him up Thursday night, and Angie was there then with the kid she was minding."

"Okay. Just stay there, Gus. We'll be right back." The agents walked outside and stood in the corridor. "What do you think, Walt?" Realto asked.

"Angie must have taken off with Kathy in

the van. Either they split the money and have separated, or he's meeting her somewhere."

"That's what I think, too."

They went back into the office where Gus was sitting. "Gus, by any chance did Clint have a lot of cash with him when you went out?"

"Nah. He let me pick up the check both nights."

"Do you know anyone else who might have given him a ride somewhere today?"

"No."

The sergeant from the Danbury police who had visited the cottage at the golf club had been making his own inquiries. He walked into the office in time to hear the last question. "Clint Downes was driven by Danbury Taxi to the Continental Airlines drop-off at LaGuardia," he said. "He got there about five thirty."

Only two hours ago, Walter Carlson thought. We're tightening the net on him, but will we be fast enough to close it before it's too late for Kathy?

84

At the police station in Hyannis, the desk sergeant, Ari Schwartz, listened patiently to David Toomey's irate protest that there had been no theft in the parking lot of his motel. "I've worked at the Soundview for thirty-two years," Toomey declared vehemently, "and I'm not going to let that conniver, who doesn't even have the brains to take care of a sick kid, lie to Sam Tyron about a car seat that she never owned being stolen."

The sergeant knew and liked Toomey. "Dave, take it easy," he said soothingly. "I'll talk to Sam. You say your night manager swears the woman didn't have a car seat in the car?"

"Absolutely."

"We'll make sure that the record is corrected."

Somewhat mollified by the promise, Toomey turned to go, then hesitated. "I really worry about that little boy. He was one sick kid. Would you mind phoning over to the hospital and see if he's a patient, or if maybe he was treated in the emergency room? His name is Steve. The mother is Linda Hagen. I could do it, but they'll pay a lot more attention if the call comes from you."

Schwartz did not let the flash of irritation he felt show on his face. It was nice of Dave Toomey to be concerned about the kid, but, on the other hand, checking it out was going to be difficult. The mother could have taken the child to any one of a dozen urgent care centers on the Cape. He could have pointed that out to Dave, but instead he made the call to the hospital.

No pediatric patient by that name had been admitted to the hospital.

Anxious as he was to get home, Toomey was still reluctant to go. "There's something that bothers me about her," he said, as much to himself as to the sergeant. "If that was my grandson, my daughter would be frantic with worry." He shrugged. "I'd better mind my own business. Thanks, Sarge."

* * *

Four miles away, Elsie Stone was turning the key in the door of her white frame house. She had taken Debby home to Yarmouth but turned down the offer to stay for dinner with her daughter and son-in-law. "I'm feeling my age," she said cheerfully. "I'll go on home, heat up some of my vegetable soup, and enjoy it while I'm reading the paper and watching the news."

Not that the news is something you want to see, she thought as she turned on the foyer light. But much as that kidnapping makes me heartsick, I do want to see if they're any closer to catching those terrible people.

She hung up her coat and went straight into the den to turn on the television. The anchorman on the six-thirty news was saying, "An unnamed source has revealed that the FBI are now operating under the assumption that Kathy Frawley may still be alive."

"Oh, praise God," Elsie said aloud. "Lord, let them find that poor little lamb."

Turning up the sound of the television so as not to miss a word, she went into the kitchen. As she poured her homemade vegetable soup into a bowl and put it in the microwave, she realized that the name "Kathy" was running through her mind.

"Kathy . . . Kathy . . . Kathy . . ." What was it? she wondered.

85

"She was there," Margaret cried as Steve held her tightly. "I saw the crib they kept the twins in. The mattress smelled of Vick's, just as Kelly's pajamas did when we got her back. All those days, they were so near, Steve, so near. That woman who bought the clothes the night I bought the birthday dresses is the one who has Kathy now. And Kathy is sick. She is sick! *She is sick!*"

Ken Lynch, a rookie cop from the Danbury police force, had driven Margaret home and was surprised to see that the block was thick with media trucks. His hand under her arm, he had rushed her into the house, past Steve who was holding the door open for them. Now feeling helpless, he stepped through the archway and entered the living room. There, he stopped and turned.

This must be the room where the babysitter was on the phone and heard one of the twins cry out, he thought. Then, as his eyes darted around, absorbing all the details so he could share them with his wife, he saw the dolls on the floor in the center of the room. Identical baby dolls, covered by the same blanket, their fingers touching. A child's table and chairs in front of the fireplace was set for a tea party. Two identical teddy bears sat at the table, facing each other.

"Mommy, Mommy."

From upstairs he heard the excited cry, then the sound of feet rushing down the uncarpeted steps. He watched as Kelly threw herself into Margaret's arms. Feeling uncomfortably like a voyeur, Ken could not resist studying the anguish on the mother's face as she hugged her daughter to her.

That has to be the pediatrician who's staying with them, he thought, as an older woman with silver hair hurried down the stairs.

Margaret put Kelly down and knelt beside her, her hands on Kelly's shoulders. "Kelly," she said softly, "have you been talking to Kathy again?"

Kelly nodded. "She wants to come home."

"I know, darling, I know she does. I want her to come home, too, just as much as you do. Do you know where she is? Did she tell you?"

"Yes, Mommy. I told Daddy. And I told Dr. Sylvia. And I told you. Kathy is in old Cape Cod."

Margaret gasped and shook her head. "Oh, sweetheart, don't you remember, when you were in bed with me this morning, I was the one who talked about Cape Cod. That's where you heard about it. Maybe Kathy told you she was at some other place. Can you ask her now?"

"Kathy is very sleepy now." With an injured look, Kelly turned and walked past Officer Lynch. She sat down on the floor by the dolls. As Lynch stared, transfixed, he heard her say, "You *are* *so* on old Cape Cod." Then, though he strained to hear, he could not make sense of the gibberish she was whispering.

86

Eating the hamburger and drinking the coffee made Angie feel better. I didn't know how hungry I was, she thought resentfully, as she sat in the one comfortable chair in the motel room, ignoring Kathy. The sherbet Angie had given her was untouched, and she was lying on the bed with her eyes closed.

I had to drag the kid out of McDonald's because that nosy old waitress started talking to her, Angie thought, mentally reviewing the difficult day. "What's your name, little boy?" "My name is Kathy. My name is Stevie." "Oh, my granddaughter has a pretend friend, too." And all the while there's a picture of the twins lying there on the table. My God, if Grandma had looked closely, she'd have been yelling for that cop.

What time would Clint get here? she wondered. The earliest would have to be about nine o'clock. He sounded sore. I should have left him some money. But he'll get over it. I did make a mistake using the credit card to buy that stuff at Abby's Discount. I should have used the cash Lucas gave me. Oh, well, it's too late to worry about it now. I should be okay here until Clint shows up. Whatever car he rented, he'll probably ditch, then steal another one to use until we can get off the Cape.

And then we'll have a million bucks to ourselves. *A million bucks!* I'm going to have a real makeover, Angie promised herself as she reached for the television remote. She glanced at the bed. And no more big ideas about having a kid of my own. They're too damn much trouble.

87

The various law enforcement agencies had established a command post in the FBI's Danbury office. Agents Tony Realto and Walter Carlson, along with Captain Jed Gunther and the Danbury police chief were in a conference room.

"We're now certain that Clint Downes and Lucas Wohl were cellmates in Attica," Realto said. "They both broke parole as soon as they were released from prison, assumed new identities, and somehow have managed to stay under the radar for all these years. We now know how Bailey's credit card got used to hire the Excel car. Lucas knew the number since he often drove Bailey, and Bailey paid him by credit card."

Realto had given up smoking when he was nineteen, but he now found himself longing for a cigarette. "According to Gus Svenson, Angie has been living with Downes for the last seven or eight years," he continued. "Unfortunately there isn't a single picture of either one of them anywhere in the cottage. You can bet the old mug shot of Downes doesn't even look like him anymore. The best we can do is give the media an artist's sketch and description of both of them."

"Someone's been leaking to the press," Carlson said. "The rumor is already out that Kathy is alive. Are we going to comment on it?"

"Not yet. I'm afraid if we say that we think she is alive, it might be a death sentence for the kid. By now, Clint and Angie probably suspect that we're looking for them, and if they realize every cop in America is studying the face of every three-year-old they come in contact with, they could panic and decide to get rid of her. As long as they think we actually believe she is dead, then they might very well try to travel as a family."

"Margaret Frawley swears that the twins are communicating," Carlson said. "I was hoping I'd hear from her. If Kelly had said anything significant, I know she would have called me. Is the officer who drove her home still around?"

"That would be Ken Lynch," the Danbury police chief said. "I know he's back from the Frawleys." He picked up the phone on his desk. "Radio Lynch to get over here."

Fifteen minutes later, Lynch walked in. "I swear Kelly is in touch with her sister," he told them flatly. "I was right there, and she insisted that Kathy is on Cape Cod."

88

The traffic was light on the Sagamore Bridge. As he crossed the Cape Cod Canal, Clint drove with increasing impatience, constantly glancing at the speedometer to be sure he wasn't going too fast. He knew he had narrowly escaped being stopped by a cop on Route 3, when he'd been doing seventy in a fifty-five-mile-an-hour zone.

He looked at his watch. It was exactly eight o'clock. It's at least another forty minutes more before I get there, he thought. He turned on the radio just in time to hear the excited voice of the newscaster say, "The rumors continue that the suicide confession to the death of Kathy Frawley may be a hoax. While authorities will neither confirm nor deny the truth of the rumor, they have just released the names of two suspects in the kidnapping of the Frawley twins."

Clint felt perspiration begin to pour from his body.

"An all-points bulletin has been issued for the arrest of an ex-convict named Ralph Hudson. Using the alias of Clint Downes, he was most recently employed as the caretaker of the Danbury Country Club in Danbury, Connecticut. Also named in the warrant is his live-in girlfriend, Angie Ames. Downes was reportedly last seen when he was dropped off at LaGuardia Airport sometime after five P.M. The woman, Angie Ames, has not been seen since Thursday evening. She is believed to be traveling in a twelve-year-old, dark brown Chevy van with Connecticut plate number . . ."

It won't take them anytime to trace me to the shuttle, Clint thought frantically. The next thing, they'll trace me to the rental agency and get the description of this car. I have to dump it fast. He drove off the bridge onto the Mid-Cape Highway. At least I was smart enough to ask the guy behind the rental counter for a map of Maine, he thought. That may buy me a little time. I've got to think. What should I do?

I have to take a chance and stay on the highway, he decided. The closer I get to Chatham, the better. If the cops suspect we're on the Cape, they'll be checking motels—if they're not already checking them, he thought grimly.

His eyes darted over the road as he passed the exits, searching for police cars. The landscape became more familiar to him as he reached Exit 5 for Centerville. That's where we did the job, he thought. Exit 8, Dennis/Yarmouth. It seemed to him to be an interminable time before he finally got to Exit 11, Harwich/Brewster, and turned on to Route 137. I'm almost at Chatham, he thought, trying to reassure himself. It's time to dump this car. Then he spotted what he was looking for, a movie complex with a crowded parking lot.

Ten minutes later, parked two rows back, he watched as a pair of teenagers left an economy sedan and walked into the lobby of the theatre. He got out of the rental car and followed them into the lobby, standing in a corner as he watched them get on the ticket line. He waited until he saw the usher tear their tickets, then watched them disappear down a corridor before he went back outside. They didn't even bother to lock the door, he thought, as he tried the handle of the boy's car. Don't make it too easy for me. He got in the car, then waited a moment until he was sure no one was nearby.

He bent down under the dashboard and, with deft, practiced movements, attached wires together. The sound of the engine turning over gave him his first feeling of relief since he had heard the broadcast. He turned on the lights, put the car in gear, and began the final phase of his trip to Chatham.

89

"Why is Kelly so quiet, Sylvia?" Margaret asked, fear in her voice.

Kelly was sitting on Steve's lap, her eyes closed.

"It's all reaction, Margaret." Sylvia Harris tried to sound convincing. "Besides, she's having an allergic reaction to something." She reached over and pulled up the sleeve of Kelly's polo shirt, then bit her lip. The bruise was turning purple, but that was not what she wanted Margaret to see. It was the sprinkling of red marks on Kelly's arm.

Margaret stared at them then glanced back and forth between Dr. Harris and Steve. "Kelly doesn't get allergies," she said. "It's one of the few ways she and Kathy are different. Is it possible that Kathy is having some kind of allergic reaction?"

Her insistent tone demanded an answer.

"Marg, Sylvia and I have talked about it," Steve said. "We're starting to believe that it's possible that Kathy may be having an allergic reaction to something she's been given, maybe to some medication."

"You don't mean—not *penicillin?* Sylvia, remember when Kathy was so allergic to even the test drops of penicillin that you tried on her? She broke out in red spots, and her arm got swollen. You said that if you'd given her an injection of it, you might have killed her."

"Margaret, we simply don't know." Sylvia Harris tried to keep her own fearful anxiety out of her voice. "Even too much aspirin can cause a reaction." Margaret was at the breaking point—or beyond it—she thought. And now a new worry, one too frightening to even consider, was pulsing through her mind. Kelly was becoming so listless. Was it possible that Kathy and Kelly's vital functions were so entwined that if anything happened to Kathy, Kelly's reaction would be to follow her?

Sylvia had already shared that awful possibility with Steve. Now she could see that it was occurring to Margaret as well. Margaret was seated beside Steve on the couch in the living room. She reached over and took Kelly from him. "Sweetheart," she implored, "talk to Kathy. Ask her where she is. Tell her Mommy and Daddy love her."

Kelly opened her eyes. "She can't hear me," she said drowsily.

"Why, Kelly? Why can't she hear you?" Steve asked.

"She can't wake up anymore," Kelly said with a sigh as she curled into a fetal position in Margaret's arms and went back to sleep.

90

Slouched down in the car, the Pied Piper listened to the radio. The breaking news, being repeated every few minutes, was that Kathy Frawley might still be alive. Two suspects were being sought, an ex-convict going by the name of Clint Downes and his girlfriend, Angie Ames. She was believed to be traveling in a twelve-year-old, dark brown Chevy van with a Connecticut license number.

After the first moment of panic passed, the Pied Piper weighed his options. He could drive to the airport and get back on the plane, which was probably the smartest thing to do. But there was always that chance, that one single chance, that Lucas had revealed his identity to Clint Downes. If the feds arrest Clint, he'll give me up for a lighter sentence, he thought. I can't take that chance.

Cars began to arrive and depart from the motel parking lot. With any luck, I'll see Clint before he gets too near to Angie's room, he thought. I've got to talk to him first.

An hour later, his patience was rewarded. A sedan drove slowly around the parking lot, up one row and down the other, then pulled into the vacant spot near Angie's van. A heavyset figure climbed out. In an instant, the Pied Piper was out of his car and positioned by Clint's side. Clint spun around, his hand reaching for his jacket pocket.

"Don't bother to pull out a gun," the Pied Piper said. "I'm here to help you. Your plan won't work. You can't drive around in that van."

He watched as Clint's startled look was replaced by one of cunning understanding. "You're the Pied Piper."

"Yes."

"With all the risks I took, it's about time I met you. Who are you?"

He didn't have a clue, the Pied Piper realized, and now it's too late. I have to see it through. "She's in there," he said, pointing to Angie's room. "You have to tell her that I came up here to help you get away. What car are you driving?"

"I helped myself to it. The people who own it are at the movies. I'm safe for a couple of hours."

"Then get her and the child in that car and get out of here. Make arrangements for them as you see necessary. I'll follow you and then I'll take you to my plane. I'll drop you off in Canada."

Clint nodded. "She's the one who ruined it all."

"Not yet, she hasn't," the Pied Piper assured him. "But get her out of here before it's too late."

91

The taxi driver who had driven Clint to La-Guardia Airport was in the Danbury police station.

"The guy I picked up at the service road of the country club had a real small bag," he told the FBI agents and the police chief. "He paid with his credit card. Gave me a lousy tip. If he had money, I sure didn't see it."

"Angie must have taken off in the van with the ransom money," Carlson said to Realto. "He's got to be planning to meet her."

Realto nodded.

"He gave no indication of where he was going?" Carlson persisted. It was a question he'd asked the driver before but still was hoping against hope that maybe he'd spark some response that would be useful.

"Just to leave him at the Continental drop-off. That's all he said."

"Did he use a cell phone at all?"

"No. And didn't say one word to me except to tell me where to go."

"All right. Thank you." Frustrated, Walter Carlson looked at the clock. After Lila Jackson went to the house, Clint knew that it would be only a matter of time before we got to him, he thought. Was he meeting Angie at LaGuardia? Or did he take another cab, maybe to Kennedy, and get on an overseas flight? And what about Kathy?

Carlson knew that Ron Allen, the FBI agent in charge of the Bureau's operations at LaGuardia and JFK, was directing the investigation at both airports. If Clint was listed as a passenger on any plane leaving from either one of them, he would be sure to find out soon.

Fifteen minutes later, the call came from Allen. "Downes took the six P.M. shuttle to Boston," he said, crisply. "I've alerted our guys to look for him at Logan."

92

"We've got to try to keep her awake," Sylvia Harris said, not bothering to conceal the anxiety in her voice. "Put her down, Margaret. Hold her hand. You, too, Steve. Make her walk with you."

Her lips white with fear, Margaret obeyed. "Come on, Kelly," she urged. "You and Daddy and Kathy and I love to take a walk together. Come on, darling."

"I . . . can't. . . . No . . . I don't want . . ." Kelly's voice was fretful and sleepy.

"Kelly, you must tell Kathy that she has to wake up, too," Dr. Harris urged.

Kelly's head was drooping on her chest, but she began to shake it in protest. "No . . . no . . . no more. Go away, Mona."

"Kelly, what is it?" Help me, God, Margaret thought. Let me break through to

Kathy. That woman, Angie, must be the one Kelly called "Mona." "Kelly, what is Mona doing to Kathy?" she asked desperately.

Stumbling between Margaret and Steve, half carried by them, Kelly whispered. "Mona's singing." Her voice trembling, off-key, she sang, "No . . . more . . . Old Cape Cod."

93

"I'm afraid they're going to think I'm just one of those people who want to get their names in the paper," Elsie Stone confided to her daughter. She was holding the telephone in one hand and the *Cape Cod Times* in the other. On the television screen, pictures of the Frawley twins were being shown over and over again. "The woman told me the child was a boy, but I'm convinced she's a girl. And Suzie, as God is my witness, I swear that child was Kathy Frawley. I mean, she had a hood on, and it just showed some dark brown hair, but looking back, I knew there was something phony about the hair. You know what I mean, like when you see a bad dye job like your uncle Ray has. And when I asked her name, she said it was Kathy, but then I could see the scowl that woman gave her, and the kid looked real scared and said it was Stevie."

"Mom," Suzie broke in. "Are you sure you're not getting carried away?" She looked at her husband and shrugged. They had waited to have a late dinner after they put Debby to bed. Now, the loin lamb chops on her plate were cooling, and Vince, her husband, was making a slashing motion across his neck, meaning she should cut it short.

Vince was genuinely fond of his mother-in-law, but he did say that Elsie had a tendency to "reiterate again."

"I mean I don't want to make a fool of myself, but just suppose . . ."

"Mom, I'm going to tell you what to do, then I'm going to hang up and sit down before Vin has a heart attack. Call the Barnstable police. Tell them *exactly* what you told me, then leave it in their hands. I love you, Mom. Debby had a wonderful time with you today, and the cookies she brought home are heaven. Goodbye, Mom."

Elsie Stone kept the receiver in her hand as she debated what to do. Should I call that tipster number or the police? she wondered. They're probably getting a lot of crank calls on the tipster phone.

"If you do not wish to make a call, please hang up." The buzz of the computer voice was the catalyst that strengthened Elsie's resolve. "I wish to make a call," she said. She pushed the Off button, waited a moment, pushed the Talk button and dialed information.

When another computer voice asked for the city and state, she said hurriedly, "Barnstable, Massachusetts."

"Barnstable, Massachusetts, is that right?" repeated the mechanical voice.

Suddenly aware that if what she had to say had bearing on the Frawley case, then it was very important to get it to the right people quickly, she snapped, "Yes, that's right, and for heaven sake why do I have to waste my time with you?"

"Business or home?" the computerized voice asked.

"The Barnstable Police Department."

"The Barnstable Police Department, is that right?"

"Yes. Yes. Yes."

After a pause, a human operator's voice asked, "Is this an emergency, ma'am?"

"Put me through to the police station."

"Right away."

"Barnstable Police, Sergeant Schwartz speaking."

"Sergeant, this is Mrs. Elsie Stone." Elsie's diffidence was a thing of the past. "I am a waitress at McDonald's near the mall. I am almost certain I saw Kathy Frawley there this morning and this is why." She then began to recount the events of that morning.

At the police station, they had been talking about the breaking news in the Frawley situation. Now as Sergeant Schwartz listened, he was comparing Elsie Stone's story with David Toomey's annoyed account of the nonexistent theft at the Soundview Motel.

"The child said her name was Kathy and then corrected herself and said it was Stevie?" he verified.

"Yes. And all day it's been bothering me, until I really studied the newspaper picture of those darling little girls and saw their picture again on television. It's the same face. I swear on my immortal soul, it was the same face, and she said her name was Kathy. I just hope you don't dismiss me as a crank."

"No, Ms. Stone. I'm not dismissing you as a crank. I'm calling the FBI immediately. Please stay on the line. They may want to talk to you."

94

"Walter, this is Steve Frawley. Kathy is on Cape Cod. You've got to start looking there."

"Steve, I was about to phone you. We know Downes took the shuttle to Boston, but when he rented a car he asked for a map of Maine."

"Forget Maine. Kelly has been trying to tell us since yesterday that Kathy is on Cape Cod. What we missed is that she wasn't just saying 'Cape Cod.' She was even trying to sing that song, 'Old Cape Cod.' That woman the twins call Mona is singing it to Kathy now. Believe me. *Please* believe me."

"Steve, take it easy. We'll tell our guys to put out a special bulletin to the Cape, but I have to tell you, we know that an hour and a half ago, Clint Downes was standing at the window of the rental agency in Logan Airport and asking for a map of Maine. We're learning more about the girlfriend, Angie. She was brought up in Maine. We think she may be hiding out there with friends."

"No. The Cape! Kathy is on the Cape!"

"Hold on, Steve. There's a call I've got to take." Carlson put Steve on hold, answered the other call, then listened silently for a minute. After hanging up, he got back on with Frawley. "Steve, you may be right. We have an eyewitness who claims to have seen Kathy this morning in a McDonald's in Hyannis. As of now, we're concentrating the search in that area. An FBI plane is picking up Carlton and me in fifteen minutes."

"We're coming, too."

When Steve hung up the phone, he rushed back into the living room where Margaret and Dr. Sylvia were forcing Kelly to walk back and forth with them. "Kathy was seen on Cape Cod this morning," he said. "We're flying there now."

95

"You're here in Old Cape Cod," Angie sang, throwing her arms around Clint's neck. "Boy have I missed you, Big Man."

"You have, huh?" Clint was about to push her away from him, but then remembered that he could not let her become suspicious. Instead, he hugged her back. "And guess who missed you, little songbird?"

"Clint, I know you have to be mad at me for taking off with the money, but I started to worry that if anyone connected you to Lucas, it would be better if I was out of the way."

"It's okay. It's okay. But we've gotta get out of here. Have you been listening to the radio?"

"No. I've been watching *Everybody Loves*

Raymond. I gave the kid more cough medicine, and she finally fell asleep again."

Clint's glance darted to Kathy, who was lying on the bed, one shoe on, her damp hair clinging to her face. He could not stop himself from saying, "If we did it the way we were supposed to do it, that kid would be home right now. And we'd be on our way to Florida with half a million and not have the whole country looking for us."

He did not see the expression on Angie's face. It would have told him that she'd just realized she had made a mistake by letting him know where she was staying. "What makes you think the whole country is looking for us?" she asked.

"Listen to the radio. Switch channels. Forget your reruns. You're big news, baby. Like it or not, you're big news."

With a deliberate click of the remote, Angie turned off the television. "So what do you think we should do?"

"I've got a safe car. We get out of here and dump the kid where she won't be found. Then you and I get off the Cape."

"But we'd planned to get rid of the kid *and* the van."

"We leave the van here."

I'm registered here under my own name, Angie thought. If they really are looking for us, they'll be here soon enough. But Clint doesn't have to know that. I can tell he's lying to me. He's sore, and when dopey Clint gets sore, he gets nasty.

He wants to get rid of me.

"Clint, honey," she said. "That cop in Hyannis has the license plate of the van. By now, every cop on the Cape knows I was in Hyannis this afternoon. If they think I'm still around, they'll be looking for this van. If they find it in this parking lot, they'll know we can't have gone far. I used to work at a marina not five minutes from here, and I know it's closed this time of year. I can drive the van onto the pier with the kid in it, then jump out of it while it's still moving and let it keep going off the end. The water's plenty deep enough to cover it. They won't find it for months. Come on, honey, we're wasting time."

She watched as Clint looked uncertainly at the window. With a chill, she realized that someone else was out there, waiting to follow him, and that he had not come there to escape with her, but to kill her.

"Clint, you know I can read you like a

book," she said cajolingly. "You're mad at me for getting rid of Lucas and taking off. Maybe you're right. Maybe you're not. Tell me something. Is the Pied Piper up here with you?"

She could tell from the expression on his face that she was right. He started to speak, but she stopped him. "Don't answer, because I know. Have you seen him?"

"Yeah."

"Do you know who he is?"

"No, but he looks familiar, like someone I've seen before. I can't place him, though. I've got to figure it out."

"So you'd be able to identify him?"

"Yeah."

"Do you really think now that you've seen him, he's going to let you stay alive? I'll tell you something—he won't! I bet he told you to get rid of me and the kid, and that then you two would be pals. It don't work that way. Believe me, it don't. You're better off trusting me. We get out of this place—and we will—and we're half a million bucks ahead of what we would have been with Lucas around. Then when we figure who this guy is, we start reminding him that we deserve a bigger share. Or else."

She could see the anger draining out of Clint's face. I could always twist him around my little finger, she thought. He's so dumb. But once he figures out who this guy is, we're set for life. "Honey," she said. "You take the suitcase. Put it in the car you're driving. But hold on a minute—is it rented in your name?"

"No, but now that they're looking for us, they'll be able to trace the credit card to the rental agency. I was smart though. I asked for a map of Maine, and I switched cars at the movies."

"Good for you. Okay. I'll take the kid. You take the money. Let's get out of here. Is the Pied Piper gonna follow us?"

"Yeah. He thinks that I'll get in his car and drive with him to where he has a plane waiting."

"And instead of that," Angie said, "when we dump the van, you and I take off in your car. You don't think he's going to chase us and risk having the cops stop him, do you? Then we get off the Cape. We change cars again and drive to Canada, get a plane out of there, and disappear."

Clint thought for a moment, then nodded his head. "All right. Get the kid." When

Angie picked up Kathy, he noticed that the one shoe she was wearing fell off. So what, he thought. She won't need it anymore.

Three minutes later, at nine thirty-five, with Kathy wrapped in a blanket and lying on the floor, Angie drove the van out of the parking lot of the Shell and Dune Motel. Clint followed her in his stolen car. Directly behind, unaware that Angie and Clint had teamed up again, the Pied Piper followed. Why is she in that van? he asked himself. But he's carrying a suitcase, and the money has to be in it. "It's all or nothing now," he said aloud as he took his place at the rear of the deadly procession.

96

Officer Sam Tyron arrived at the Soundview Motel twelve minutes after receiving a terse phone call from the Barnstable Police Department. On the way there he angrily berated himself for not following his instinct to investigate further the woman he had stopped because of the lack of a car seat in her van.

It even crossed my mind that she didn't look that much like her photo ID, he thought. That bit of information, however, he did not intend to share with his superiors.

He arrived to find the motel swarming with police. The realization that the second Frawley twin was not only still alive, but had been spotted in Hyannis, had brought out all the brass. They were clustered in the motel room where the woman who registered as Linda Hagen had stayed. The twenty-dollar bills found scattered under the bed were a strong indication that this was indeed where the kidnapper had stayed. Kathy Frawley had been lying on that bed only hours before.

An excited David Toomey had responded to a call from the night manager and returned to the motel. "That child is very, very sick," he warned. "You can bet she hasn't seen a doctor. She was coughing and wheezing and should have been taken to the emergency room. You'd better find her soon or it'll be too late. I mean . . ."

"When was the last time you saw her?" the Barnstable police chief asked, urgency in his voice.

"It would have been about twelve thirty. I don't know what time she took off."

That's seven and a half hours ago, Sam Tyron thought. She could be in Canada by now.

The chief voiced that possibility, then added, "Just in case she's still here, though, we'll send a message to all the motels on the Cape to be on the lookout for her. The state police will put up road blocks at the bridges."

97

Other than their efforts to keep Kelly awake, everyone on the plane remained silent. Kelly, her eyes closed, was in Margaret's arms. Totally lethargic, her head resting against Margaret's heart, she was becoming less and less responsive.

Agents Carlson and Realto were in the plane with them. They had been in touch with FBI headquarters in Boston. Their counterparts there would be at the Cape to take over the investigation. An FBI car would meet them at the airport and take them to police headquarters in Hyannis, which would be the command center for the search. Before they boarded the plane the two men had quietly agreed that they had actually witnessed Kelly in communication with Kathy. They also believed that, judging by the way Kelly was behaving now, it might be too late to save her twin.

The plane held eight passengers. Carlson and Realto sat side by side, each caught up in his own thoughts, each filled with chagrin because they had missed Clint Downes by only hours. Even if Angie was on the Cape this morning, she was probably meeting him in Maine, Carlson thought. It made sense. He got a map for Maine from the car rental. She was raised there.

Realto was mentally analyzing what he would do if he were in Clint and Angie's position. I'd get rid of the van and the rental car, and I'd also get rid of the child, he decided. With every cop in the country on the lookout for her, Kathy's too much of a liability. If only they have the decency to leave her where she can be found quickly.

But that would give us the exact location from which to begin tracking them, he concluded grimly. Something tells me these people are too desperate and too evil to have any decency in them.

98

Every cop on the Cape is on the lookout for this van, Angie thought, biting her lip as she drove nervously along Route 28 from Chatham. But the marina is only a little past the town line into Harwich, and once we dump this wreck, we'll be okay. Geez, to think I wanted this kid. What a mess she ended up causing. I don't blame Clint for being mad at me.

She glanced up at the sky, noticing that the stars had been replaced by clouds. The weather sure changed quickly, she thought, but that's the way it happens up here. And it could be a good thing. Now I've gotta watch for that turn.

With her nerves on edge because any minute she expected to hear a siren, Angie reluctantly began to slow up. The turn is right along here, she thought. Yeah, not this one, the next one. A moment later, heaving a sigh of relief, she turned left off Route 28 and drove the winding road toward Nantucket Sound. Most of the houses along the road were hidden from view behind high shrubbery. The ones she could see were in darkness. Probably closed for the winter, she decided. It's a good spot to dump the van, she thought. I hope Clint realizes that.

She went around a final bend with Clint right behind her. The Pied Piper wouldn't have the nerve to get too close, she figured. I guess by now he knows that I'm no dope. The pier was directly ahead, and she was just about to drive on to it when she heard the faint, brief tap of a horn.

Stupid, stupid Clint. What the heck was he blowing a horn for? Angie wondered. She stopped the van, and, livid with anger, watched as he got out of his stolen car and rushed up to her. She opened the door. "You wanna kiss the brat goodbye?" she snapped.

The odor of acrid perspiration was the last thing she remembered as Clint's fist flew through the space between them and pummeled her into unconsciousness. As she slumped over the wheel, Clint put the car in gear and placed her foot on the accelerator. He closed the door just as the van began to move along the pier. He watched as it reached the end where it balanced for an instant, then dropped out of sight.

99

Phil King, the clerk at the Shell and Dune Motel, kept his eye on the clock. He went off duty at ten and was anxious to be on his way. He had spent all his spare time that day patching up a fight he'd had with his girlfriend, and she had finally agreed to meet him for a quiet drink in the bar at the Impudent Oyster. Only ten minutes to go, he noted with anticipation.

There was a small television set behind the desk, company for whoever was working the late-night shift. Remembering that the Celtics were playing the Nets in Boston, Phil flipped on the set, hoping to catch the score.

Instead he caught a breaking news story. Police had confirmed that Kathy Frawley had definitely been seen on the Cape that morning. Her abductor, Angie Ames, was driving a twelve-year-old dark brown Chevy van with Connecticut plates. The announcer gave the license plate number.

Phil King did not hear it. He was staring openmouthed at the television. Angie Ames, he thought. *Angie Ames!* His hand trembling, he grabbed the phone and dialed 911.

When the operator answered, he shouted, "Angie Ames is staying here! Angie Ames is staying here! I saw her van drive out of our lot not ten minutes ago."

100

Clint watched the van disappear, then, with grim satisfaction, he got back in his stolen car and made a sharp U-turn. In the beams of his headlights he caught the startled look on the face of the Pied Piper who was walking toward him. Just like I expected, he's got a gun, he thought. Sure, he was going to share with me. Real sure. I could run him over, but that would be too easy. It would be more fun to play with him.

He drove straight at him, then watched with glee as the Pied Piper dropped the pistol he was holding and jumped out of the car's path. Now I get me off the Cape, Clint thought, but first I gotta ditch this car. Those kids will be coming out of the movie in less than an hour, and then the police will be looking for this car.

He raced back along the quiet road until he came to Route 28. He figured the Pied Piper might try to chase him, but he knew he had too great a lead. He'll think I'm heading for the bridge, he decided, but what could he do—that was the best way to go. He turned left. The Mid-Cape Highway would be faster, but he decided to stay on Route 28. By now, they probably know that I flew to Boston and rented a car, he thought. I wonder if they fell for my asking for the map to Maine.

He turned on the radio in time to hear an excited announcer report that Kathy Frawley had definitely been sighted in Hyannis. With her was her abductor, Angie Ames, who also used the name Linda Hagen. Road blocks were being set up.

Clint gripped the wheel. I've got to get out of here fast, he thought. I can't waste any time. The suitcase with the money was on the floor of the backseat. The thought of it and what he could do with one million dollars kept Clint from dissolving into panic as he drove through South Dennis, then Yarmouth, and finally to the outskirts of Hyannis. Twenty more minutes and I'm at the bridge, he thought.

The sound of a police siren made him cringe. Can't be me, I'm not going too fast, he thought, then watched aghast as one police car swerved ahead of him and cut him off, while another pulled up behind him.

"Get out of the car with your hands up." The command came from a loudspeaker in the squad car behind him.

Clint felt rivulets of perspiration run down his cheeks as he slowly opened the car door and stepped out, his thick arms high over his head.

Two policemen, guns drawn, approached him. "You're out of luck," one of them said amiably. "The kids didn't like the movie and left in the middle of it. You are under arrest for possession of a stolen motor vehicle."

The other cop shone his flashlight in Clint's face, then did a double take. Clint knew he was comparing him with the description the police undoubtedly had of him.

"You're Clint Downes," the cop said positively, then angrily demanded, "Where is that little girl, you bum? Where's Kathy Frawley?"

101

Margaret and Steve and Dr. Harris and Kelly were in the police chief's office when the news came that Angie Ames had registered under her own name in a motel in Chatham and that the clerk had seen the van pull out only ten minutes ago.

"Was Kathy in it?" Margaret whispered.

"He doesn't know. But there was a child's shoe on the bed, and there was an indentation on the pillow. It seems probable that Kathy had been there."

Dr. Harris was holding Kelly now. Suddenly she began to shake her. "Kelly, wake up," she demanded, "Kelly, you must wake up." She looked at the police chief. "Get a respirator," she demanded. "Get one now!"

102

The Pied Piper had watched as the squad cars cut off Clint's stolen vehicle. He doesn't know my name, but as soon as he describes me, the FBI will be on my doorstep, he thought. And to think I didn't have to come here, he reproached himself—Lucas hadn't told him who I am.

He forced back the burst of blinding anger that made his hands tremble so much that he could hardly grasp the wheel. I've got seven million dollars, less the bank cut, waiting for me in Switzerland, he thought. The passport is in my pocket. I've got to get on an overseas flight right away. I'll have the plane fly me to Canada. Clint may not give me up right away since he can use me as a bargaining chip. I'm his ace in the hole.

His mouth dry, his throat choked with

terror, the Pied Piper turned off Route 28 North. Even before a handcuffed Clint was led to a police car, the Pied Piper was on Route 28 South, heading for Chatham Airport.

103

"We know your girlfriend left the Shell and Dune Motel twenty minutes ago. Was Kathy Frawley with her?"

"I don't know what you're talking about," Clint said, his voice a monotone.

"You know what we're talking about," FBI Agent Frank Reeves of the Boston office snapped. He, Realto, Carlson, and the Barnstable police chief were in the interview room of the Barnstable police station. "Is Kathy in that van?"

"You just read me my rights. I want a lawyer."

"Clint, listen to me," Carlson urged. "We believe that Kathy Frawley is very sick. If she dies, you've got two murder raps going. We know your pal Lucas didn't commit suicide."

"Lucas?"

"Clint, the twins' DNA must be all over that cottage in Danbury. Your friend Gus told us he heard two children crying when he was on the phone with Angie. Angie charged the clothes she bought for the twins on your card. A Barnstable policeman saw her this morning with Kathy. So did a waitress at McDonald's. We've got all the proof we need. Your only chance for any kind of leniency is to come clean now."

A scuffling outside the door caused them all to turn abruptly. Then they heard the voice of the sergeant at the desk. "Mrs. Frawley, I'm sorry you can't go in there."

"I have to. You have the man who kidnapped my children."

Reeves, Realto, and Carlson exchanged glances. "Let her in," Reeves shouted.

The door burst open, and Margaret rushed in, her blue eyes now coal black, her face deathly pale, her long hair a wild tangle. She looked around, then went directly to Clint and dropped on her knees before him. "Kathy is sick," she said, her voice quivering. "If she dies, I don't know whether Kelly will live. I can forgive you everything if only you will let me have Kathy back now. I will plead for you at your sentencing. I promise. I promise. Please."

Clint tried to look away, but found himself compelled to look into Margaret's blazing eyes. They have me cold, he reasoned. I won't give up the Pied Piper yet, but maybe there's another way to avoid having a murder charge thrown at me. He waited a long minute, quickly rehearsing his story, then said, "I didn't want to keep the other kid. That was Angie's doing. The night we dropped them off, she shot Lucas and left that phony note. She's crazy. Then she took off with all the money and didn't tell me where she'd gone. She phoned me today and asked me to meet her up here. I told her that we'd ditch the van and get off the Cape in the car I'd grabbed. But it didn't work out that way."

"What happened?" Realto asked.

"Angie knows the Cape. I don't. She knew a marina not far from that motel where we could drive the van down the pier and let it go over into the water. I was following her, but then something went wrong. She didn't get out of the van in time."

"The van went off the pier with her in it?"

"Yeah."

"Was Kathy in the van?"

"Yeah. Angie didn't mean to hurt her. We were gonna take her with us. We wanted to be a family."

"*A family! A family!*" The door to the interview room was still open. Margaret's heartrending cry echoed through the corridor.

Steve, already on his way to be with her, knew what her scream meant. "Oh, God," he prayed, "help us to bear it." In the interrogation room, he saw Margaret lying at the feet of the pudgy man who had to be the kidnapper. He hurried over, picked her up in his arms, and looked at Clint Downes. "If I could get my hands on a gun, I would kill you right now," he said.

The police chief grabbed the phone after Downes described the location. "The Seagull Marina, get diving equipment," he ordered. "Get a boat." He looked at the agents. "There's a loading dock under that pier," he said, then looked at Margaret and Steve. The last thing he wanted to do was to offer them false hope. In the winter the dock is supposed to have a chain across it. Maybe, maybe, there'll be a miracle, and the chain stopped the van from going completely into the water. But the tide is coming in fast, and even if the van stopped, the lower dock will be submerged within twenty minutes.

104

We've got all the airports covered, Realto thought as he rode with Reeves, Walter Carlson, and the Barnstable police chief down Route 28 toward Harwich. Downes claims he's not the Pied Piper but says he can give him to us as a bargaining chip in case anyone tries to slap him with the death penalty. I believe him. He's not smart enough to have engineered the whole kidnapping. Once the Pied Piper knows we have Downes, he'll realize it's only a matter of time until Downes gives him up. He has seven million dollars stashed somewhere. The only thing he can do now is to get out of the country before it's too late.

Beside him sat Walter Carlson, uncharacteristically silent, his hands folded, his eyes straight ahead. Kelly had been rushed with

Dr. Harris to Cape Cod Hospital, but Margaret and Steve had insisted on getting in a squad car and driving to the marina. I wish they hadn't come, he thought. They should not have to watch Kathy being removed from a car that has been dragged up from Nantucket Sound.

The traffic scrambled out of the way of the caravan of police cars. In only nine minutes time, they were turning right off Route 28 and racing down the narrow road that led to the marina.

The Massachusetts state police were already there. Through the murky fog, spotlights were shining on the pier. In the distance a boat was racing through the heavy waves.

"There is just one hope that we may not be too late," Chief O'Brien said prayerfully. "If the van landed on the loading dock and they weren't killed in the fall . . ." He did not complete the sentence.

With a squeal of brakes, the squad car stopped halfway down the pier. The men tumbled out and began racing ahead, their feet pounding the wooden planks. At the end of the pier they stopped and looked down. The back of the van was sticking out of the water, the wheels caught by the heavy linked chain. The front wheels, however, were already in the water, and heavy waves were smashing over the hood. Realto saw that the weight of the two cops and heavy grappling equipment on the loading dock was causing it to tip forward. As they watched, one of the rear wheels rolled over the chain and the van sagged further into the water.

Realto felt himself being pushed aside, and an instant later, Steve Frawley was at the edge of the pier. He looked down, then ripped off his jacket and dove into the water. He came up by the side of the van.

"Get the spotlight inside the car," Reeves barked.

The other back wheel was being lifted by the tide. It's too late, Realto thought. There's too much pressure from the water. He can't open that door.

Margaret Frawley had run up as well and was standing at the edge of the pier.

Steve was looking inside the van. "Kathy's on the floor in the back," he shouted. "There's a woman in the driver's seat. She's not moving." Frantically, he tugged at the back door and realized that it was impossible to open it. He drew his fist back and punched it against the window but could not break it. The waves were pulling him away from the van. He grasped the door handle with one hand and again and again slammed his fist against the window.

A splintering, crashing sound erupted as the glass finally gave. Heedless of his broken and bloody hand, Steve pushed the rest of the glass out of his way and thrust first his arms, and then his head and shoulders inside the van.

The final wheel was now free of the chain, and the van started to lurch forward into the water.

The Coast Guard boat reached the pier, and as it pulled up beside the van, two men leaned over and grabbed Steve around the waist and legs, dragging him back into the boat. His arms were tightly wrapped around a small, blanketed figure. As he fell against his rescuers, the van tipped over the edge and disappeared into the churning water.

He's got her! Realto thought. He's got her! If only we're not too late.

Margaret's cry, "Give her to me, give her to me," was drowned out by the wail of an arriving ambulance.

105

"Mom, I've been listening to the radio. I hear that there's a good chance Kathy is alive. I just want you to know, I had nothing to do with Steve's kids being kidnapped. My God, do you think I'd do anything like that to my brother? He's always been there for me."

Nervously, Richie Mason looked around the departure lounge at Kennedy Airport. He listened impatiently to his mother's tearful assurances that she knew perfectly well he'd never have anything to do with harming his brother's children. "Oh, Richie, if they can save Kathy, we'll fly up for a wonderful family reunion, dear," she said.

"You bet, Mom," he responded, cutting her off. "I've got to go. I've been offered a new job that really is going to be great. I'm flying out right now to the company headquarters in Oregon. They're about to start loading the plane. Love you, Mom. I'll stay in touch."

"We are beginning the boarding process for Continental flight 102 to Paris," the announcement began. "Our first-class passengers and those needing assistance . . .'"

With a last, furtive glance around the departure lounge, Mason presented his ticket and walked on the plane to settle in seat 2B. At the last minute he had decided to skip picking up the final shipment of cocaine from Colombia. With the FBI questioning him about the missing kids, instinct warned him it was time to get out of the country. Luckily, he could count on that kid Danny Hamilton to pick up the suitcase wih the cocaine and hide it for him. He still hadn't figured out which distributor he could trust to pick it up from Danny and forward his payment to him, but he'd make that decision later.

Hurry up, he wanted to yell as the plane began to fill. I'm okay, he tried to assure himself. Like I told Mom, big brother Steve has always been helpful to me. Because we look pretty much alike, his passport worked like a charm. Thanks, Steve.

The hostess had already given the departure speech. Let's go, let's go, he thought as he sat with his head down and his fists clenched. Then his mouth went dry as he heard footsteps racing up the aisle. They stopped at his seat.

"Mr. Mason, will you please accompany us quietly?" a voice asked.

Richie looked up. Two men were standing there. "FBI," one of them said.

The stewardess was about to collect Richie's glass. "There must be a mistake," she protested. "This is Mr. Steven Frawley, not Mr. Mason."

"I know what it says on the passenger manifest," FBI Agent Allen said pleasantly. "But right now, Mr. Frawley is on Cape Cod with his family."

Richie took a last gulp of the single malt scotch that he had been nursing. That's my last scotch for a very, very long time, he thought as he stood up. His fellow passengers were staring at him. He gave them a friendly wave. "Enjoy the trip," he said. "Sorry I can't join you."

106

"We have stabilized Kelly, but even though her lungs are clear, she still is having difficulty breathing," the doctor in pediatric intensive care said gravely. "Kathy, though, is much worse. She is a very, very sick little girl. The bronchitis has developed into pneumonia, and she has obviously been given heavy doses of adult medicine which has depressed her nervous system. I wish I could be more optimistic, but . . ."

Steve, his arms heavily bandaged, sat with Margaret next to the crib. Kathy, almost unrecognizable with her short dark hair and the oxygen mask on her face, was lying perfectly still. The alarm monitoring her respiration had already gone off twice.

Kelly's crib was down the hall in the pediatric wing. Dr. Harris was with her.

"Kelly must be brought in here right away," Margaret ordered.

"Mrs. Frawley. . . ."

"Right away," Margaret said. "Kathy needs her."

107

Norman Bond had stayed in his apartment all day Saturday, spending much of the time sitting on the couch, staring out over the East River and catching updates of the Frawley kidnapping on television.

Why did I hire Frawley? he wondered. Was it because I wanted to pretend I could start all over again, that I could turn back time, and be in Ridgefield with Theresa? Did I want to pretend that our twins had lived? They'd be twenty-one years old now.

They think I had something to do with the kidnapping. I was such a fool to refer to Theresa as "my late wife." I've always been careful to say that I believed she was alive, and that she'd dumped Banks the same way she dumped me.

Ever since the FBI had questioned him,

Bond hadn't been able to get Theresa out of his mind, not for one single minute. Before he killed her, she had begged for the life of the twins she was expecting the way Margaret Frawley had begged for the safe return of her children.

Maybe Frawley's other child was still alive. It's all about the ransom, Norman thought. Someone was counting on the company paying it.

At seven o'clock, he made himself a drink. "A suspect in the kidnapping was believed to have been spotted on Cape Cod," a news brief reported.

"Norman . . . please . . . don't . . ."

Weekends are always the hardest, he thought.

He had given up going to museums. They bored him. Concerts were tedious, a form of torture. When Theresa and he were married, she would tease him about his restlessness. "Norman, you'll do very well in business and may even become a patron of the arts, but you'll never understand why a sculpture or a painting or an opera is a thing of beauty. You're hopeless."

Hopeless. Hopeless. Norman made himself another drink, then sipped it as he ran his hand over Theresa's wedding rings that he kept on the chain around his neck—the one he had given her that she'd left on the dresser, and the circle of diamonds her rich, cultured, second husband had given her. He remembered how he had to struggle to pull that one off her finger. Her slender fingers were swollen because of the pregnancy.

At eight-thirty he decided to shower and dress and go out for dinner. Somewhat unsteady on his feet, he got up, went to the closet, and laid out a business suit, white shirt, and one of the ties the Paul Stuart salesman had assured him complemented the suit.

Forty minutes later, as he was leaving his apartment building, he happened to glance across the street. Two men were getting out of a car. The street light shone on the face of the driver. He was the FBI agent who had come to his office and who had become hostile and suspicious when he'd made his slip about "my late wife." In a sudden panic, Norman Bond darted uncertainly down the block, then dashed across Seventy-second Street. He did not see the vehicle that was making a U-turn.

The impact of the truck hitting him was an

explosion that seemed to rip him apart. He felt himself lifted into the air, then the awful pain as his body crashed against the sidewalk. He tasted blood gushing from his mouth.

He heard the clamor around him and the demands for an ambulance. The face of the FBI agent was swimming above him. The chain with Theresa's rings, he thought. I've got to get rid of it.

But he could not move his hand.

He could feel his white shirt becoming soaked with blood. The oyster, he thought. Remember when it slithered off that fork and all the sauce dripped on my shirt and tie? The memory usually brought a wave of shame, but now he felt nothing. Nothing at all.

His lips formed her name: "Theresa."

Agent Angus Sommers was kneeling beside Norman Bond. He put his finger on Bond's neck. "He's gone," he said.

108

Agents Reeves, Carlson, and Realto entered Clint's holding cell.

"They got the little girl out of the car, but she may not make it," Carlson said angrily. "Your girlfriend, Angie, is dead. They'll do an autopsy, but you know what? We think she was already gone before she hit the water. Someone punched her hard enough to kill her. I wonder who that was."

Feeling as if he'd been hit by a cement block, Clint realized that it was all over for him. He bitterly decided that he wasn't going down alone. Telling them who the Pied Piper is may or may not help me with my sentence, he thought, but I'm *not* going to rot in prison while he lives it up on seven million bucks.

"I don't know the Pied Piper's name," he

told the agents, "but I can tell you what he looks like. He's tall, I'd guess a couple of inches over six feet. Sandy blond hair. Classy looking. Early forties. When he wanted me to dump Angie, he told me that I should follow him to Chatham Airport where he had a plane waiting."

Clint paused. "Wait a minute!" he exclaimed. "I *do* know who he is. I thought I had seen him someplace before. He's the big shot from that company that paid the ransom. He was on TV saying that he shouldn't have paid it."

"Gregg Stanford!" Carlson said as Realto nodded in agreement.

Reeves was instantly on his cell phone.

"If only we can grab him before his plane takes off," Carlson said. With contempt and fury in his voice, he told Clint, "You better get down on your knees, you lowlife, and start praying that Kathy Frawley pulls through."

109

"The Frawley twins have been rushed to Cape Cod Hospital," the announcer on channel 5 reported. "The condition of Kathy Frawley is extremely critical. The body of one of the kidnappers, Angie Ames, has been recovered from the sunken van at the Harwich marina. Her accomplice Clint Downes, in whose Danbury, Connecticut, home the twins were kept, is under arrest in Hyannis. The man believed to be the mastermind of the kidnapping, the 'Pied Piper,' is still at large."

They don't say that I'm on the Cape, the Pied Piper thought frantically as he sat in the departure lounge of Chatham airport and watched the breaking news on television. That means Clint hasn't described me to them yet. I'm his bargaining chip. He gives me up in return for a lighter sentence.

I've got to get out of the country now. But the drenching rain and enveloping fog was temporarily grounding all the planes. His pilot had told him that he hoped that the delay wouldn't be much longer.

Why did I panic and come up with that crazy idea of kidnapping those kids? he asked himself. I did it because I was scared. I did it because I was afraid Millicent might have had me followed and discovered that I was fooling around with other women. If she had decided to dump me, I'd be out of a job, and I don't have a nickel in my own name. I did it because I thought I could trust Lucas. He knew how to keep his mouth shut. He'd never give me away, no matter how much someone offered him. In the end he still didn't give me away. Clint had no idea who I am.

If only I hadn't come to Cape Cod. I could have been out of the country by now with all those millions waiting for me. I have my passport. I'll have the plane take me to the Maldives. There's no extraditon there.

The door of the lounge burst open and two men rushed in. One slipped behind him and ordered him to stand with his hands spread out. Quickly he frisked him.

"FBI, Mr. Stanford," the other one said. "What a surprise. What brings you to the Cape this evening?"

Gregg Stanford looked directly at him. "I was visiting a friend, a young woman. A private matter which is none of your business."

"By any chance was her name Angie?"

"What are you talking about?" Stanford demanded. "This is outrageous."

"You know exactly what we're talking about," the agent replied. "You won't be catching a plane tonight, Mr. Stanford. Or perhaps I should ask, would you prefer to be addressed as the Pied Piper?"

110

Kelly, still in her crib and accompanied by Dr. Harris, was wheeled into the intensive care unit. Like her sister, she was wearing an oxygen mask. Margaret stood up. "Disconnect her mask," she said. "I'm putting her in the crib with Kathy."

"Margaret, Kathy has pneumonia." The protest died on Sylvia Harris's lips.

"Do it," Margaret told the nurse. "You can hook it up again as soon as I settle her."

The nurse looked at Steve. "Go ahead," he told her.

Margaret picked up Kelly, and for an instant held her head against her neck. "Kathy needs you, baby," she whispered. "And you need her."

The nurse rolled down the side of the crib, and Margaret placed Kelly next to her twin, with Kelly's right thumb touching Kathy's left one.

It's where they were conjoined, Sylvia thought.

The nurse reattached Kelly's mask to the oxygen.

In silent prayer, Margaret, Steve, and Sylvia kept a heartsick vigil by the crib all night. The twins did not stir from their deep sleep. Then, as the first light of dawn filtered into the room, Kathy stirred, moved her hand, and entwined her fingers in Kelly's.

Kelly opened her eyes and turned her head to look at her sister.

Kathy's eyes opened wide. She looked around the room, going from one person to another. Her lips began to move.

A smile lit Kelly's face, and she murmured something in Kathy's ear.

"Twin talk," Steve said softly.

"What is she telling you, Kelly?" Margaret whispered.

"Kathy said that she missed us very, very much, and that she wants to go home."

Epilogue

Three weeks later, Walter Carlson sat at the dining room table with Steve and Margaret, lingering over second cups of coffee. All through dinner, he kept thinking of the first time he had seen them, the handsome young couple in evening clothes who had arrived home to learn that their children were gone. In the following days they had become shadows of their former selves, pale and gaunt, clinging to each other in despair, their eyes red rimmed and swollen.

Now Steve's manner was relaxed and confident. Margaret, lovely in a white sweater and dark slacks, her hair loose around her shoulders, a smile on her lips, was a different person from the half-crazed woman who had pleaded with them to believe that Kathy was alive.

Even so, Carlson noticed how, during dinner, her eyes often darted to the living room, where the twins, dressed in their pajamas, were having a tea party with their dolls and teddy bears. She needs to keep reassuring herself that they're both still there, he thought.

The Frawleys had invited him to dinner to celebrate their return to normal life, as Margaret had put it. But now, inevitably, it was natural to let them in on some of the information revealed through the confessions of Gregg Stanford and Clint Downes.

He had not intended to talk about Steve's half brother, Richard Mason, but when Steve mentioned that his mother and father had been up for a visit, he asked about them.

"You can understand how tough it is for my mother to know that Richie is in trouble again," Steve said. "Smuggling cocaine is even worse than that scam he was involved in years ago. She knows the kind of prison term he's facing and, like all mothers, she's trying to figure what she did wrong to make him turn out like this."

"She didn't do anything wrong," Carlson

said bluntly. "He's a bad apple, pure and simple."

Then, with a final sip of coffee, he said, "If there's anything good that came out of all this, it's that we know that Norman Bond killed his ex-wife, Theresa. Her wedding ring given her by her second husband was on a chain around his neck. She was wearing it the night she disappeared. At least now her second husband can get on with his life. For seventeen years he's held on to the hope that she's still alive."

Carlson could not stop glancing at the twins. "They're as alike as two peas in a pod," he said.

"Aren't they?" Margaret said in agreement. "Just last week we took Kathy to the hairdresser and got rid of that terrible dye job and then I had them cut Kelly's hair so that now they both have the same pixie cut. It's sweet on them, isn't it?"

She sighed. "I get up at least three times a night and check on them, just to be sure they're still here. We have a state-of-the-art alarm system, and at night it's set on 'instant,' so if a door or window is opened, the noise it makes would wake up the dead. But even with that protection, I still can't bear to have them out of my sight."

"That will ease," Carlson assured her. "Maybe not for a while, but it will get better in time. How are the girls doing?"

"Kathy still has nightmares. In her sleep she says, 'No more Mona. No more Mona.' Then, the other day when we were out shopping, she saw a thin woman with messy long brown hair who, I guess, reminded her of Angie. Kathy started shrieking and threw her arms around my legs. It just about broke my heart. But Dr. Sylvia has recommended a wonderful child psychiatrist, Dr. Judith Knowles. We'll be taking the twins to her every week. It will take time, but she assured us they'll be fine eventually."

"Is Stanford going to plea bargain?" Steve asked.

"He hasn't got much to bargain with. He plotted the kidnapping because he was panicking. He was afraid his wife had found out about his philandering and was going to divorce him. If she had, he wouldn't have a penny. He was in on some of the company's financial problems last year and was still afraid of being caught. He had to have a back-up fund, and, Steve, when he met you at the office and you were showing pictures of the twins, he hatched his scheme.

"Lucas Wohl and he had a strange relationship," Carlson continued. "Lucas was his trusted driver when he had his little affairs. Then one day during his second marriage, Stanford came home unexpectedly and found Lucas jimmying the safe in which his wife kept her jewels. He told him to go ahead with the robbery, but he had to cut him in on the proceeds. After that, he sometimes would tip Lucas off on houses to rob. Stanford always has lived on the edge. What I like about the way this played out is that he might have gotten away with all of it if he had trusted Lucas not to tell Clint who he was. He was high on our list of suspects and he'd been under surveillance, but we didn't really have anything on him. That's what's going to haunt Stanford for the rest of his life when he wakes up every morning in a prison cell."

"What about Clint Downes?" Margaret asked. "Has he confessed?"

"He's a kidnapper and murderer. He's still trying to say Angie's death was an accident, but lots of luck with that one. The federal courts will deal with him. I'm sure he's had his last beer at the Danbury Pub. He'll never get out of prison again."

The twins had finished the tea party and scampered into the dining room. A moment later, a smiling Kathy was on Margaret's lap and a giggling Kelly was being lifted up by Steve.

Walter Carlson felt a lump in his throat. If only it was always like this, he thought. If only we could bring all the kids home. If only we could rid the world of all the predators. But this time at least, we got a happy ending.

The twins were wearing blue-flowered pajamas. Two little girls in blue, he thought. Two little girls in blue . . .